I0676000

CANAL STREET

BED & BREAKFAST

A CAMRYN ALEXANDER MYSTERY

KERI SMITH

ISBN: 979-8-9921402-0-0

Copyright © 2024 by Keri Smith

Cover design © 2024 by Keri Smith

All rights reserved. No part of this book may be reproduced in any form or by any electronic or mechanical means including information storage and retrieval systems—except in the case of brief quotations embodied in critical articles or reviews—without permission in writing from the author.

The characters and events portrayed in this book are fictitious or are used fictitiously. Apart from well-known historical figures, any similarity to real persons, dead or living, is purely coincidental and not intended by the author.

All brand names and product names used in this book are trademarks, registered trademarks, or trade names of their respective holders.

This book is dedicated to my family. Your unwavering love and support is invaluable.

To my wonderful husband, Aaron. Thank you for providing me with a life that has allowed me to explore creative endeavors.

To my favorite true crime podcasters, Ellyn and Joey. Thank you for bringing me my weekly true crime with a smile!

Camryn's Playlist

Summertime
Louis Armstrong

Let's Call the Whole Thing Off
Louis Armstrong & Ella Fitzgerald

When the Saints Go Marching In
Louis Armstrong

Do You Know What It Means to Miss New Orleans?
Louis Armstrong

The Nearness of You
Louis Armstrong & Ella Fitzgerald

A Kiss to Build a Dream On
Louis Armstrong

La Vie en Rose

Louis Armstrong

Love Is Here to Stay

Louis Armstrong & Ella Fitzgerald

C'est Si Bon

Louis Armstrong

Dream a Little Dream of Me

Louis Armstrong & Ella Fitzgerald

Lazy River

Louis Armstrong

I'm Thru With Love

Ella Fitzgerald

The Man I Love

Billie Holiday

Author's Note

The mystery in this book was inspired by the real-life unsolved disappearance of Brian Shaffer, who was last seen in Columbus, Ohio on April 1, 2006. After reading this book, I encourage you to research Brian Shaffer's story and to contact the proper authorities if you have any pertinent information.

PROLOGUE

"Why are you still following me? I told you to leave me alone when I caught you at the coffee shop."

"You didn't tell anyone about that, did you?"

"No, they'd think I'm crazy. No one has ever known about us, and no one ever will. Plus, I barely even know most of them. Why are you still here?"

"I don't know what else to do. I just need to talk to you, and you won't answer my calls."

"There's nothing to talk about. We're done."

"No, we're not! Please, I made a mistake, and it will never happen again. I promise. I love you, Liv!"

"Don't touch me!"

"I'm sorry. I just—"

"It was all a mistake to begin with. I was insane to think someone like you could ever take someone like me seriously and believe any of the promises you made."

"Come on. You know I love you, Liv. If I didn't, I wouldn't have come all this way to apologize to you."

"I don't believe you. And this whole *creepy stalker* act isn't a good look. Just go away! I need to get back out there."

"I can't lose you, Liv. Come on, you're drunk, and you're not thinking clearly. Let's go somewhere so we can talk and work this out."

"And what about *her*, huh? Are you going to leave her? Of course, you aren't."

"You know that it's not that simple. Come on, let's get out of here."

"No."

"Come here. Let me hold you."

"I said don't touch me! *You* lost that right when you hit me."

"I promise that will never happen again."

"You're right, because we're done! Now, if you'll excuse me, I need to get back out there before they notice I'm gone."

"What? You think you'll ever meet someone like me again?"

"God, I hope not!"

"No one will ever love you or take care of you the way that I do."

"I'll take my chances."

"Liv..."

"Move out of my way!"

"Come on, Livvie! Give me another chance."

"No! I said move!"

"Liv, stop! Okay, hear me out. Can we at least be friends? We're too important to each other, and we have to work together, anyway."

"No, I think we're past the point of being friends. You followed me all the way to New Orleans, like some psycho! And don't worry. I already plan to request a reassignment as soon as I get back."

"I can't let that happen."

"*Let that happen?* You don't have a choice. Now move out of my way!"

"Liv..."

"No! Move!"

"Why? So you can go back out there and dance like a little slut?"

"I said *move!*"

"I'm not letting you go, Liv!"

"Get your hands off me! No! Let go of my arm! *You're hurting me!*"

KERI SMITH

Chapter 1

"If you know anything about the brutal slaying of Michelle Slater, or the whereabouts of Joseph Bryant, you can contact the San Diego County Sherriff's Office. And remember, all calls can remain anonymous. Tune in next week when I'll have another shocking tale of when love goes wrong. Until then, I'm Stephanie Tolentino, and this is, 'The One You Love.' Take care of each other!"

As if on cue, after the last note of the theme song for the podcast that started my true crime obsession, I hear a familiar *bing* overhead. I look up to see the glow of the fasten seatbelt sign. There's a quick rustling sound on the intercom, and the captain makes the announcement we've all been waiting for.

"Attention passengers." His voice is deep with a slight southern drawl I hadn't noticed earlier in the flight. I only detect it now because the *-ers* in *"passengers"* sounds more like *-uhs.* "Looks like we are, uh, twenty minutes out from arrival and are about to make our final descent into New Orleans." Once again, the accent comes through and makes it sound more like *Nawlins.* I giggle, thinking that he has probably spent his life trying to fight off the southern drawl, just as I have. But I'd like to think I've been a bit more successful.

I check my smartwatch and notice that we're arriving fifteen minutes early, as the captain predicted prior to takeoff.

"It's a beautiful Friday afternoon in the Big Easy with very few clouds and temps hovering around ninety degrees. We hope you've enjoyed this flight from Charlotte *(Shawlut)*. We thank you for choosing American Airlines, and we hope that you'll fly with us again soon." There's a slight pause in the airy static coming through the speakers, but it quickly returns. "Flight attendants, please prepare the cabin for *landin'*."

I feel a rumble in my stomach as it begs for some sustenance. The Biscoff cookies provided by the airline are all I've eaten since I grabbed a pre-packaged smoothie from the fridge early this morning. I had raced out of my apartment to make the hour drive to Richmond and catch a nine A.M. flight, which then required a forty-minute layover in Charlotte—not nearly enough time to grab a snack before boarding my next flight to New Orleans.

It occurs to me that I've changed time zones, so I look at my smartwatch again. It's a little after one P.M. central time. I make a plan to grab a quick bite before heading to the gate where my mom and sister's plane will arrive from Dallas, even if it's just a snack from an airport store. We chose their flight so it would arrive thirty minutes after my flight was scheduled to arrive. If their flight is on time, that now gives me nearly forty-five minutes to eat and relax.

Neither my sister nor my mom have visited New Orleans before, but this will be my sixth trip, if you don't include a work conference I attended eight years ago. I don't count that trip, since we only left the hotel once to have a group dinner and drinks at Pat O'Briens. At the age of twenty-six, and as the upscale multi-residential management company's youngest property manager, I was too timid to wander the streets of the French Quarter by myself. So, I went along with everyone else and came straight back to the hotel. Two years later, I won a two-hundred-dollar gift certificate for a bed and breakfast locator website at another company event, and I immediately knew how I'd want to use it.

Despite my age, I'm a big fan of old school jazz. I prefer listening to it over today's music. Ella Fitzgerald, Billie Holiday, and Duke Ellington. But my all-time favorite is Louis Armstrong, who is affectionately referred to as "Satchmo." I convinced my friend, Tasha, to join me for the Satchmo Summerfest—the annual festival that occurs on the first weekend of August to celebrate the late coronet-blowing and raspy-voiced New Orleans-native's birthday. It takes a true friend to tag along for that particular festival because the late-summer weather tends to be extremely hot and humid. But to me, it's worth spending a day's salary on bottled water to stay cool and hydrated—a small investment to spend the weekend enjoying jazz music and dancing in second line parades with my fellow Louis lovers.

I spent an entire Saturday scouring the locator website to find the perfect bed and breakfast and quickly learned that two hundred dollars was the equivalent of one night's stay at most of the nicer options. Time after time, I found that I kept coming back to one listing, and Tasha agreed that it was the right choice. It only took that one trip for New Orleans to become my favorite city, and I've been back every year since and stayed at the same bed and breakfast every time.

The flight attendant instructs us over the intercom to lift our trays and return our seats to the upright position. Neither applies to me, since I lifted my tray after I gave her my empty can of ginger ale and plastic cookie wrapper earlier in the flight. And I never recline my seat on flights, in fear of disturbing the passenger behind me.

I glance past the passengers next to me in the middle and window seats and peer through the window. The pilot was right. There are just a few clouds, which was forecasted for our entire four-day, three-night stay. It's typical late-June weather for New Orleans, although with the gulf coast's notorious summer heat and humidity, I always welcome a random cloudy day.

My eyes shift to the left of the window at the passenger in the window seat. He is a young Hispanic boy, likely around eight years old, sleeping soundly with his head leaning against the wall. There's a colorful granny square crocheted blanket draped over his legs. The woman in the middle seat turns her head towards me and catches me looking at the boy. She gives me a slight, crooked smile.

"Miguel talks so much," she says with a strong Spanish accent, looking at me apologetically with saggy brown eyes. She is a heavy-set woman with salt and pepper hair pulled into a tight bun directly on top of her head. The colorful Otomi print around the neckline of her white top is likely a nod to her Mexican heritage. By the looks, I figure she's the young boy's grandmother. But who am I to assume? Reality is that, at my rate, I may be mistaken for my future child's grandmother one day.

I smile to put the sweet lady at ease. "Is this his first flight?" It was a safe assumption, considering his earlier round of animated, rapid-fire questions in a mix of English and Spanish about every little thing he saw inside and outside the plane. As soon as the woman answered one question, even with an exhausted, *"I don't know, Mijo,"* he had the next question locked and loaded. It took him about thirty minutes to wear himself out and finally fall asleep.

"Sí. My daughter and his baby sister are at the back of the plane. We couldn't find seats together. He was so excited to be on an airplane. Sorry if he was too loud."

I nod, then shake my head. "No worries, I was listening to music the whole time and didn't hear a thing." I say, pointing to my wireless earbuds, still in my ears. I have convinced myself that the double white lie was warranted. She already feels bad about her grandson's understandable, yet annoying, excitement, and I can't bring myself to explain to this stranger that the person next to her has been enjoying a podcast about a man who decapitated his mother-in-law. I try to end both the conversation and my self-induced guilt for lying to this sweet woman. "I'm Camryn, by the way."

"I'm Juanita. So nice to meet you." Her broad smile makes her eyes squint so much that they almost close. I take pleasure in knowing that I was able to relieve her anxiety over any disturbances her grandson had caused and will likely cause before we all disembark.

I return her friendly smile, this time showing teeth, and she turns to gently wake her grandson. I pick up my phone to find something to listen to, in case the next round of airplane *Jeopardy* starts again. There isn't enough time for me to sneak in another full podcast episode, so I settle for a playlist of my favorite Louis Armstrong and Ella Fitzgerald duets. I hit shuffle, hoping my phone will choose to play my favorite, *Summertime*. I smile at the sound of Satchmo's distinctive horn, as if he knows I'm returning to his home and wants to welcome me back by granting my request.

Only fifteen minutes left until everything becomes real. Am I really going on my last mother-daughter trip with my sister as an Alexander girl? I mean, the name Camille Henderson doesn't even sound right—to my biased ear, anyway. It doesn't roll off the tongue like *Camille Alexander.*

Dad let Mom choose both of our names. She named me after her grandfather, Cameron Johnson. Her super-spiritual friends convinced her I was going to be a boy. But when I came out, proving them wrong—which would become a lifelong trait of mine—she kept the name, but changed the spelling.

Then, with the surprise of another baby girl ten years later, Mom decided this namesake would be for her best friend from her school days in Albuquerque—Camille. So, we are Camryn and Camille. Cam and Cam, as we became affectionately known to our extended family.

And how? How in the world is my baby sister *getting married?* And before I've ever even come close—something I've said to myself countless times but never dared to share out loud. I try hard to let my thoughts remain positive when I think about it. I *am* happy for Camille, but the fact that my twenty-four-year-old sister is getting married, and I don't have a single prospect at thirty-four... it stings a little.

I want to be married and live happily ever after. Attracting men isn't the problem. I just attract the wrong men. Either they are emotionally unavailable or physically unavailable, like that guy I dated for three weeks before I discovered that he was actually married. And it can't be *me*. I think I'm a great girlfriend and will make a great wife. I'm loyal and affectionate, and I'm not clingy because I love having time to myself. I have a successful career in property management, and I don't expect a man to take care of me. So, what is it? Why hasn't it happened for me yet?

Camille met her fiancé, Alan, on a blind date set up by one of her sorority sisters a year after she graduated from TCU and got her teacher's certificate. It was the same year she started teaching kindergarten at a public school in our old school district. Alan was four years her senior and did not impress her at all. She found him arrogant and lazy, like most of the good-looking jocks she'd dated in the past. But Alan was smitten, and her sorority sister was so convinced that this handsome former-college athlete turned engineer was the perfect match for Camille that she convinced her to give him a second chance a couple of weeks later.

Alan must have gotten tips the second time around because he took Camille to her favorite hole-in-the-wall Italian restaurant and brought her favorite flowers, pink tulips. One year later to the day, Alan proposed by renting out the same restaurant and had a bouquet of pink tulips on each table. As soon as they had entered the empty, candlelit restaurant, he figured she knew what was happening. However, he waited until after the meal to get down on one knee and propose with a one and a half carat solitaire diamond ring. Neither of them can remember exactly what he said, but from the photos I saw taken by a photographer hidden behind the bar, Camille had a tear rolling down her left cheek when she said yes.

I guess I shouldn't be too surprised that it happened so quickly for her. Camille has always been a hopeless romantic. She was obsessed with Disney princesses as a child, and it has continued into adulthood. She dressed up as a princess for Halloween every year in elementary school and even a couple of times in college. In fact, she and Alan will honeymoon at Disney World!

As for me, I am a cautious romantic. It's hard for me to fall into a whirlwind of a romance, like Camille did. I've spent my entire adulthood dating and always waiting for the other shoe to drop.

My teenage heart was certain that my high school sweetheart would be the guy I'd marry. My parents absolutely adored Derrick, and his father once told me he'd love to have me as a daughter-in-law. Derrick was two years older than me and was a senior on the varsity basketball team when we started dating. He was tall, with toffee-colored skin, hair in tidy cornrows and an adorable, crooked smile. We were inseparable and spent nearly every day together. But he enlisted in the Navy soon after graduating from high school, following in his father's footsteps. After basic training, he was stationed in San Juan, Puerto Rico, and I kept in touch the only way a seventeen-year-old could back then—through email.

My senior year, Derrick requested leave and booked a flight to come back to Dallas and take me to my senior prom. To my surprise, I received an email a week before prom from a woman whose name I didn't recognize. She claimed to be Derrick's girlfriend and said she read one of my emails when he left his computer on during a party being held in his barracks. She mentioned that she knew he was coming back to Dallas for a "family funeral" and that I shouldn't expect to see him while he was in town. I noticed she copied Derrick on the email, so I waited for him to reply and convince me the woman was some psycho stalker, or at least a jealous friend. But the reply never came, and neither did he. I was furious—but mostly heartbroken, and entirely too embarrassed to show up to prom by myself. So, I didn't go. And honestly, I don't think I've completely opened my heart to another man since.

Well, except that one time I did. During my late-twenties, I wasted three years of my life on Marcus, who was an uber-narcissist. That was the end of old me—the woman who gave men the benefit of the doubt and saw the good in everyone. The new me isn't nearly as patient or forgiving. For the past six years, I have either been single or slowly starting relationships, only to back out when the guy displays even the slightest Marcus-like behavior or when I realize he doesn't fit into my ideal life—an image that I admit is constantly changing. I've gone from my outlook on love being Billie Holiday's *The Man I Love* to Ella Fitzgerald's *I'm Thru with Love.*

The thought of Marcus, now referred to as *"my horrible ex"* in my relationship stories, prompts me to let out a loud sigh, clearly audible to those in the surrounding rows. I stare at my phone to avoid eye contact with anyone, especially the flight attendant passing by, making her final checks.

I never thought I'd still be single at thirty-four. I'm supposed to be married with a couple of kids by now. I've tried to remain optimistic, and I guess I still am. But I decided years ago that I can't let anyone else know that. It's better that everyone thinks I'm happily single, especially so I don't have to face the pitiful looks of family members at Camille's wedding next weekend. I just have to keep silently believing that Mr. Right is out there somewhere.

I swipe through the photos on my phone until I get to the engagement picture of Camille and Alan. I can't help but to smile and tear up a bit when I see the glowing and gitty expressions on their faces. Their premarital bliss is palpable. They took their engagement photos early last fall at the park across from our childhood home. The trees are orange, gold, and red, which was all photoshopped, since North Texas doesn't see trees fully change colors until mid-November. I always think this photo makes them look like a couple from a Hallmark movie cover.

Both Camille and Alan are conservative dressers. In the picture, Alan wears a brown blazer over a light blue and tan checkered shirt with dark washed blue jeans. He looks handsome with his ebony skin, shaved and perfectly tapered fade, and straight white teeth shining in the middle of his neatly trimmed beard. Camille looks perfectly coiffed, as usual. She and I share the same caramel skin color, courtesy of our white mother and black father, and we are both considered very attractive, according to American beauty standards. But that's where our physical similarities end.

Camille's hair is wavy and cut short in a side-swept, dark brown bob that covers one ear and displays the other with a pearl stud—her signature look. She rarely ever wears makeup because she has flawless skin with microscopic pores, and she was blessed with perfectly arched, full eyebrows. Meanwhile, my hair is very curly and stops just past my shoulders with bangs to cover my larger than average forehead. I've struggled with acne since adolescence and use makeup to cover my blemishes and even out my skin tone. And a few years ago, I started having my sparse eyebrows microbladed to avoid having to use an eyebrow pencil to shade them in every morning.

Then there are our clothing styles, which reflect our differing personalities perfectly. In the photo, Camille wears a cream sweater with a tan and brown plaid scarf wrapped around her shoulders with dark washed jeans that appear to match Alan's. My style tends to be a bit more fluid, as I try to keep up with modern trends. I occasionally wear bold colors and mismatched patterns. Sometimes my style is casual-chic, while other times it can be more boho. But never conservative.

How Camille and I differ the most is height. Although we both have petite frames, Camille is a modest five feet, five inches, while I stand at five feet, ten inches. This height advantage benefited me greatly during my high school volleyball days and my short-lived modeling career the summer after my freshman year of college.

The photo perfectly captures the love and joy shared between my sister and her Prince Charming. Alan is lifting her up, leaning slightly back, with his arms wrapped around her waist. Despite their height difference of eleven inches, they are chest-to-chest. Camille seems to be almost flying, with her arms spread out and her left hand displaying the sparkly rock on her ring finger. The image depicts the love we all dream of having someday. I truly believe Alan and Camille have this kind of love, and he will make my sister happy forever.

"He better," I say under my breath.

I slip my phone into my light brown Kate Spade crossbody. After shoving it under the seat in front of me, I glance out the window again, just in time to watch us speed past trees and hangar tops seconds before we make an appropriately bumpy landing.

I'm thrilled about this weekend with Mom and Camille, and I can't wait to introduce them to *my* city! A new song has started from the playlist, and I quietly hum along as Louis and Ella banter about tomatoes versus to-*mah*-toes and suggest that they call the whole thing off.

Chapter 2

I struggle just as much getting my carry-on luggage out of the restroom stall at Louis Armstrong International Airport as I did getting it in. I wash my hands and analyze my reflection in the mirror. Yep, I look as tired as I feel. Not having the option for a direct flight from Richmond to New Orleans is not ideal for a wannabe jetsetter like me.

I tussle my curly bangs and fluff out my hair, which flattened while I was seated for three and a half hours. I attempt to smooth out the wrinkles in my black linen short jumpsuit, but to no avail. It takes forever to find my lip gloss in my purse to reapply and make myself appear as refreshed as possible. It's been over six months since I last saw my mom and sister in person. I don't want them to see a tired and overworked version of the "new life, new me" Camryn they saw on Christmas.

The best I can find in the way of food at the airport mini-mart is their version of a protein snack, consisting of grapes, cheese cubes, almonds and crackers. I snatch the largest bottle of overpriced water I can find and make my way to the register. While waiting in line next to rows of fashion and tabloid magazines, I use the preview feature in my text messages to check the status of my family's flight. Thankfully, it's arriving on time.

Once I make it to their gate, I sit and place my luggage in front of the seat next to me and people-watch. It's the same thing every time. People running to catch a flight. Parents trying to keep their impatient children entertained, mostly with apps on their phones or tablets. Businesspeople sitting with their laptops at charging stations, finishing up some last-minute work before heading to their next destinations. I'm excited to greet them at the gate, like people did before airports restricted access to passengers only after the World Trade Center attacks.

I've finished my snack and half of my water when I observe a Southwest Airlines plane pull up to the gate. Within a few minutes, an airline employee opens the gate door to allow passengers into the terminal. Around thirty people have come through the doors when I see the unmistakable style of Mrs. Ann Marie Alexander—my mother. She was a child of hippies and has always embraced their lifestyle and fashion. Today she's wearing a muted aqua print kaftan, wide leg gray pants, and the same beige crocheted hobo bag she's carried for the past three years. Her long brown hair is in her signature braid, tossed over her right shoulder. I notice streaks of silver hair that remind me of the tinsel we'd strewn all over the Christmas tree when I was a little girl.

Mom and I are the same height—five-feet, ten inches—and she's a naturally beautiful woman. At fifty-eight years old, she doesn't look a day over forty-five. Her olive skin is smooth with minimal lines, thanks to her healthy lifestyle. She recently changed her diet from vegetarian to pescatarian, which will make it much easier to find restaurants to suit all three of us this weekend.

Steps behind my mother is the bride-to-be. My baby sister also looks exactly as I expected. Camille's hair is styled just as it was in the engagement photo I was admiring less than an hour ago. She is wearing a dusty rose sleeveless knit top accented with a short pearl necklace, cropped khaki slacks and beige loafers. As soon as our eyes meet, it's time for us to do our traditional greeting.

"*Diva!*" we both yell, grabbing the attention of everyone at the gate. We've been doing this ever since we saw an old rerun of *The Fresh Prince of Bel-Air,* where Will's mom and her sisters greeted each other the same way. Camille trots over, using her hand to keep her purse strap from falling off her shoulder. We hug and rock from side to side as Mom approaches us with that proud mother smile.

I release Camille and give Mom a peck on the cheek, melting into her warm embrace. With my eyes closed, I absorb the loving energy I always feel when I'm in the arms of the woman who gave me life. I'm consumed by the familiar fragrance of vanilla and amber that always seems to exude from her pores.

"Miss Camille Alexander," I say, returning my focus to the betrothed. Even after all these years, I still see her only as my baby sister, and not yet as an accomplished adult.

"Only for nine more days!" She shows me the back of her hand and the massive diamond ring.

I roll my eyes dramatically. "I know, but you can't blame me for trying to hold on to you being one of *us* as long as I can." I make a sad face.

"Leave your sister alone," Mom says. "She'll always be one of us!" She gives Camille an air kiss.

"Thank you, Mommy!" Camille returns the kiss and then sticks out her tongue in my direction.

"Whatever." I reach for my phone. "Okay, I'll book the ride share to take us to the bed and breakfast. I can't wait for you to—"

Mom abruptly cuts me off. "We have to go to baggage claim first."

I glance down next to her and notice that she has her carry-on suitcase, but Camille doesn't. I stare at my sister in disbelief. "You checked a bag for a three-night stay? Really?"

"I needed to pack some things that I couldn't carry on," she says defensively.

I give her a stern look. "Such as?"

"A can of disinfectant, for starters. You never know who or what has been in that room before us or what they did on that bed."

"They have stores in New Orleans, Camille." I shove my phone back in my purse and grab my luggage to head towards baggage claim.

Camille links her arm in mine. "Yeah, but I didn't want to waste any time in *your* city." She obviously wants to get back on my good side. "I assumed you'd be checking a bag too, since you're coming back to Dallas with us for the next week."

"Nope. I've learned how and what to pack to avoid checking bags." I tap my overstuffed weekender bag, balancing on top of my carry-on suitcase. "And since I had my maid of honor dress and shoes shipped directly to Mom and Dad's house, I just plan to wash my clothes and re-wear."

Mom links her arm into Camille's other arm, and we make our way out to baggage claim—something I haven't done in years. "I'm so glad we made this trip happen!" She looks around the airport. "Camille, promise me we'll keep this tradition going, even after you become Mrs. Alan Henderson."

Mom began taking the two of us on a private getaway every summer, beginning with the year that I graduated from high school. She figured my friends would likely take up most of my time when I came home from college to visit, so she started our annual trips to ensure that eight-year-old Camille and I would remain close as I entered adulthood. Little did Mom know that I'd be back home permanently by the next summer after deciding college wasn't for me.

We've traveled all over Texas and visited the surrounding states, including Oklahoma, Arkansas, and, of course, New Mexico to visit her side of the family in Albuquerque. We also took family trips with Dad, but there was always one annual trip for just us Alexander girls.

"Of course, Mother!" Camille leans her head against Mom's arm, just below her shoulder. "I wouldn't miss this for the world! Maybe I'll have daughters that can join us one day, too."

I know this is music to my mother's ears, but I can't help but question if that would be in my future as well.

Before we make it to baggage claim, we stop and take a group selfie in front of a massive Louis Armstrong statue. He is situated perfectly to welcome incoming passengers to his home city. He's holding his trumpet to his mouth and pointing it up at the ceiling, as if he's ready to play a rendition of *When the Saints Go Marching In* and start an impromptu second line.

***

Camille grabs her suitcase from the baggage claim carousel, and we go outside to find the designated area to wait for our ride share. While we're waiting, I remember the special surprises I have in my weekender bag. I quietly pull out a tiara with white tulle sticking straight up and silver rhinestone letters that spell out *"BRIDE TO BE."* I place it on Camille's head and reach into my tote for the second surprise—a white satin sash with *"Bride"* written in silver cursive font and engagement rings on both sides. I slip it over her head and drape it on her shoulder.

"What's this all about?" Camille asks excitedly.

I straighten the sash. "Just because I didn't want to run around the Las Vegas strip with your friends for your bachelorette party doesn't mean that I don't want to celebrate with you!"

"Oh, I love this!" Mom says. "A family bachelorette party! What a great idea! Now I really feel like one of the girls!" We give a group hug.

"You're always one of the girls, Mom." Camille says, using a finger to wipe a tear away from the corner of her eye. "And thanks, sis! But remember, this weekend may be for me, but I still want to experience *your* city *your* way."

I glance over and notice a car that matches the black four-door Toyota Camry the app told me to expect. I check the license plate number, and it's a match.

"Here we go!" I usher them over to the trunk door that pops open automatically. We shove our luggage into the trunk and make our way to the passenger side of the car. Mom slides into the back seat, followed by me, and Camille jumps into the front passenger seat. There's barely audible hip hop music coming from the speakers.

"Camryn?" the driver asks, looking at Camille, who points back at me.

"I'm Camryn." I inspect the driver to confirm she's the same woman pictured on the app. She matches the woman in the photo—cocoa brown-skin, probably around my age, bright red lips, a septum piercing, and feathered fake eyelashes. She has very short, platinum blond hair and is wearing huge gold hoop earrings. "You're LaShay, right?"

"That's me!" She gives me a wink and looks back at Camille. "Y'all here for a bachelorette party?"

Camille flashes her ring and a ridiculous grin. "Yes, mine!"

"Ooh, girl! Let me see that ring!" LaShay grabs Camille's hand to admire it up close. "Now *that's* what I call a ring! Congratulations!"

"Thank you!" Camille gushes, bringing her hand back in and grinning at the massive token of Alan's affection.

LaShay pulls the car away from the curb, and we start the twenty-minute drive towards the French Quarter. I grab Mom's hand and give it a squeeze as she looks at everything we pass on our way out of the airport. She turns and gives me a wink and mouths, *Thank you.* I smile and squeeze her hand again.

I quietly sniff the air. "It smells amazing in here." I can't identify exactly what fragrance it is, but I can detect a bit of citrus and perhaps some spices. Whatever it is, it isn't a typical air freshener.

LaShay looks back at me through the rearview mirror. "Thanks, love. It's a mix of a bunch of oils. I don't even know which ones." She giggles.

I lean forward and discover that Camille is scrolling through Instagram on her phone. Most people are surprised to learn that my conservative and reserved baby sister loves the ratchetness of reality TV. It started with *The Bachelor* and grew to be an obsession with the entire genre. She knows every housewife's life story from every city.

Meanwhile, I have never watched a single episode.

"Oh, my God! Things are about to get crazy in Atlanta!" Camille shouts from the front seat. I assume she is referring to the *Housewives* show.

LaShay slaps the steering wheel. "*Guuurl*, I know! Did you hear the news about the divorce today?" Camille has obviously met her reality show soul mate in our driver.

I attempt to drown out the chatter by catching up with Mom. "How's Dad doing?"

She smiles. "Oh, he's as busy as ever! Taking one day at a time until he can take early retirement from the accounting firm and sell his share to his partner."

"I haven't talked to him in a couple of weeks. I need to do better," I say, feeling ashamed that it's been that long.

Mom gently slaps my leg. "Aw, don't talk like that. He's fine. You're fine. And you know us... every day is pretty much the same. Dad works, and I paint during the week, and we both relax by gardening on the weekends. How's work going for you?"

"Fine, I guess." I shrug my shoulders and turn my head to glance out the window. There's a sign stating that we're entering the town of Metairie, so I know we're getting close.

"That maintenance manager still giving you a hard time?" she asks, looking at me harder to detect what's bothering her first born.

I turn back and face her. "No. I think we've finally worked out our personality differences."

"Well, *something* is bothering you."

I shrug again. "I don't know." I try to find the right words to tell her I'm unhappy in Virginia, but not quite enough to pack up and come back to Dallas. "It's just not what I was expecting."

She looks concerned. "What were you expecting?"

I hesitate as I think back to a year ago when I first accepted the student housing property manager position and moved from Texas to Virginia. "I just didn't think it would be this hard. It took me months to gain the trust of the staff and convince them I wasn't a *big city girl* coming to change the way they did everything. And even now, I still don't have the respect that I had from my teams in Dallas."

Mom frowns.

"I'm also tired because we finally finished inspecting all the vacant units, now that most of the college students have gone home for the summer. I didn't realize how exhausting it would be to inspect large, century-old houses that have been converted into student housing. They are spread out along several blocks. And since most students move out at the same time, I'm bombarded with a ton of work over a few weeks. It's nothing like when I was a property manager of mid-rise buildings in Dallas, where people moved out sporadically throughout the year. I think I've averaged around fifteen thousand steps a day for the past two weeks, and I've worked a minimum of ten hours a day to get them all knocked out before I left for this trip."

"What about Nicole? Have you been able to visit her in New York?" Mom asks, referring to my best friend.

"No. She's busy with her job, and we haven't been able to synchronize our schedules."

"I'm so sorry, sweetie." Mom strokes my knee.

"Plus—" I stop and reconsider telling her what I want to say. I gaze into the loving brown eyes of the woman who has always been my trusted confidant and decide to tell her. "I'm so lonely out there.

24

There's no one my age to hang out with, except maybe the wife of the new soccer coach who just moved into one of our units."

I remember feeling relieved when the tall blonde walked into the leasing office with their seven-year-old daughter. The rental options in a town that small are extremely limited, so they couldn't find a house. They weren't thrilled about having to live between two sorority houses, but I was happy to finally have hope for a social life.

"It's a good thing that I've given up on dating," I lie. "There are no prospects out there. Nothing but students or men who have lived in that tiny town their whole lives and have no intentions of leaving." That is the God-honest truth.

"A professor, maybe?" Mom suggests.

"Maybe," I say, but only to appease her. She still looks concerned. I force a smile on my face and change the subject. "I'll be fine. Have you sold any pieces lately?"

Mom is a full-time artist and is well known in the Dallas art scene. She specializes in abstract expressionism, and her pieces resemble those of Jackson Pollock. I have one hanging over my sofa that matches the dark blue color scheme of my apartment. The promise of visiting art galleries is one of the main reasons she is so excited about coming to New Orleans.

She thinks for a moment. "No, I don't think I've sold any since the one that was purchased by that Dallas Cowboy last month."

"But you still have the upcoming exhibition in September, right?"

"Yes, and there's talk of some other pieces being a part of an exhibition in Houston this December."

I shake my head. "You're amazing, Mom! It's incredible that you've been an artist for so many years, and you're still going strong."

"Thank you, darling!" She caresses my cheek with the back of her hand. I can tell she's still concerned about me.

We continue the ride, discussing extended family and announcements I may have missed. I've been taking a break from social media since spring, so I am clueless about what the aunts, uncles and cousins have been up to lately.

By the time we exit the freeway and make our way closer to the French Quarter, LaShay and Camille are still cackling over *Housewives* gossip. I see the familiar sight of the famous aboveground cemeteries as we turn right onto Canal Street and find ourselves sandwiched between cemeteries on both sides of the street. Mom and Camille look like tennis spectators with their heads going back and forth to snap photos on their phones.

"Now, why are they aboveground?" Mom asks.

LaShay opens her mouth to answer, but I cut her off. "You'll learn all about it when we go on the cemetery tour."

"*Cemetery* tour?" Camille slowly turns back to face me.

I lean forward and get closer to her face. "Yes, a cemetery tour! You said you wanted to see *my* city, *my* way, right?"

"Yeah, but I didn't know we'd be doing *that!*" She looks at Mom for support.

"Oh, I can't wait!" Mom says, to Camille's dismay.

I give Camille a smug look and sit back in my seat. She turns back around and remains silent for the final five minutes of the ride.

The car slows down as we reach our destination. LaShay parks alongside the curb under the shade of an enormous tree. The four of us peer out the right side of the car at the magnificent sight. We have arrived at my favorite place to stay in New Orleans—well, in the world—Canal Street Bed and Breakfast.

Chapter 3

How could I have known that a gift certificate I won at a company holiday party would change my life? I had never stayed in a bed and breakfast before and didn't travel often, but I knew how I'd put it to use after I learned about the Satchmo Summerfest while researching Louis Armstrong. My friend Tasha was excited about coming with me, and I was thrilled when I found the perfect place to stay.

The listing for Canal Street Bed and Breakfast caught my attention because of its striking exterior photo. Built in 1911, the house is an ideal example of Neo-Classical architecture, characterized by white columns and a mosaic wall made of large natural stones. The front yard boasts of beautiful landscaping with traditional southern plants, like azalea and camellia bushes, as well as a large oak tree that's over a hundred years old.

Even after all these years, I am still in awe. It's an impressive sight with no other property that compares—none that I've seen, anyway. I can tell that Mom and Camille—and even LaShay—would agree.

"Camryn, I loved it when you showed me the pictures, but it's even better in person!" Camille gushes, her eyes sweeping the exterior as she steps onto the curb. She grabs her phone out of her purse and takes a few pictures and then a selfie with the house as the picture-perfect background.

I step out of the car and flash a loving smile at the house, as if I've been greeted by an old friend. "I know."

Mom exits the car after me and gazes up at the branches of the old oak tree hovering overhead, as if it's enveloping us in our own oasis. "Oh, Camryn, this place is stunning!"

I smile. "Wait until we get inside. It's even better."

We retrieve our luggage from the trunk and wave goodbye to our lively driver. LaShay and Camille now follow each other on Instagram, so I'm sure there will be many over-the-top DMs and meme exchanges in their future.

I proudly lead my companions up the grand marble staircase in front of the center of the house. We approach a covered porch that extends across the entire front of the property. There's cozy-looking patio furniture on both sides of the porch, perfect for relaxing outside and also for watching people and the infamous red streetcars go by.

That is another big selling feature that made me choose this place six years ago—the streetcars stop in the median of Canal Street, directly in front of the house. This convenience is perfect for people like me who don't want to stay in the middle of the hustle and bustle of the French Quarter.

We reach the mahogany double doors and enter a small vestibule with another set of locked double doors. The space has a rack of pamphlets for tours and other sites for visitors to pick through for information on the many things to do during their stay. I ring the doorbell, and within a few seconds, I see Maggie walking towards the door to greet us.

"Camryn, you're back!" She opens the door and gives me an aggressive hug. "So good to see you again, *bay-beh*," she says with a thick New Orleans accent. Maggie is a short, mocha-skinned Creole woman in her mid-sixties, with short gray hair. In all of my visits, I have never seen her without her hair perfectly in place—something in which she obviously takes much pride. Even without knowing Maggie, you can sense her sweet disposition by just one look into her hazel eyes. Her narrow nose is littered with freckles, and her wide, friendly smile seems to go from ear to ear.

I step back and hold both of her hands. "Maggie, it's so good to be back at my home away from home." I usher Mom and Camille to step forward. "This is my mom, Ann Marie, and my sister, Camille."

"Ah, welcome to *Nawlins*!" She greets Camille with the same warm hug that I just received. "I'm Marguerite Gelineau, but please call me Maggie." She takes a step back and looks at the glittery accessories Camille is wearing. "It looks like y'all are celebrating something special this weekend, huh?"

Camille looks up and touches her tiara, as if she forgot it was there. "Oh, yes ma'am! I'm getting married next Sunday."

"Well, congratulations, *bay-beh*!" she says, giving Camille another exuberant hug. She turns to Mom, and they embrace.

"Thank you so much," Mom says. "I've been wanting to visit the place that Camryn's been raving about for the past several years." She looks around the foyer. "I have to say, she didn't do it justice!"

"Aw, thank you, *bay-beh*." Maggie closes and locks the door. She walks back through the foyer, which is decorated with vintage paintings and photos. The aesthetic fits perfectly with the ambiance of the turn-of-the-century home. The house smells fresh, with a slight scent of the original wood floors. She stops at a black antique console table adorned with a stack of old books and other small antiques and retrieves a set of keys from a drawer. "Here are the keys to your room. There's one for your door and one that works for all the exit doors, which we keep locked at all times."

I take the keys. "Yes, ma'am. I remember."

Maggie chuckles. "I know you do. I'm just so used to saying that to everyone when they arrive. Let me show your mama and sister around before I take you to your room."

We follow Maggie to an open dining room to the left of the foyer. It's located at the front of the house, looking out at the porch. The walls are painted a deep red, and the room features a black, ornate fireplace and a stunning crystal chandelier. There are several small tables with chairs to accommodate guests for breakfast.

She guides us further into the house and into the next room. We pass a long table with seating for six and a cabinet holding coffee and tea supplies, along with wine glasses and bottled water. The space also has a fireplace identical to the one in the dining room and a smaller crystal chandelier. Both rooms feature ornamental crown molding, vintage art and a touch of Mardi Gras-themed decorations.

The last room is a sitting area furnished with a blue suede sofa and three matching chairs. I gaze upward and admire the beams stretching across the ceiling. As my eyes follow them, I see a grand fireplace reaching all the way to the ceiling. The entire exterior wall is windows over a wall-to-wall window bench.

"How many suites are in this house?" Mom asks.

Maggie counts on her fingers. "Eleven total. Four downstairs, four here on this level, and three upstairs."

"From what I remember, our room is upstairs on the third floor, right?" I ask.

"Yes," Maggie says. "Room number nine. It's the first door at the top of the stairs." She starts to turn away but stops. "I almost forgot to tell you about breakfast. We usually give you a choice between seven A.M. and nine A.M. But we have a full house and other guests have already reserved the earlier breakfast. So, your breakfast is at nine."

"Yes, ma'am," I say with a smile. "Thanks, Maggie! See you in the morning."

***

The Fleur-de-lis Suite looks exactly as it did six years ago. Tasha and I chose this room back then because it was one of the few rooms that has two beds—a king-size bed and a full-size bed on opposite walls. Tasha was gracious enough to let me have the king, since it was my gift certificate that slashed the out-of-pocket expense for our stay. All other suites have only a king- or queen-size bed.

Camille and Mom survey the room. There's a desk with a chair, a small glass table with a coffee maker and bottles of water, and a small refrigerator with a bottle of wine and two wine glasses.

Mom points up at the ceiling. "Ooh, I love those wood beams!"

"And I see why it's called the Fleur-de-lis Suite," Camille says, looking at the big brown fleur-de-lis painting on the wall over the king bed.

Mom walks over to the smaller bed and places her luggage beside it. "I'll take this one, and you girls can share the king. That way, if you two decide to go have some fun in the evenings, I won't be disturbed."

Camille opens her suitcase on the opposite side of the king bed, having already determined it would be hers. "Works for me!"

I open the closet and pull out the small luggage rack so I can find clothes to change into after a quick shower. I glance up and notice Camille holding a bundle of what looks like sticks and leaves in a large Ziploc bag.

"What on earth is that?" I ask.

Mom peers over to see what I'm referring to and immediately recognizes it. "Why did you bring my sage?"

Camille looks at me skeptically. "Knowing Camryn, she brought us to a haunted house, and I don't want to wake up in the middle of the night and find some old man rattling chains at the foot of the bed."

I lean over the bed and snatch the bag from her hand. "This place is not haunted." I toss it to Mom for her to keep.

Without missing a beat, Camille pulls out a can of disinfectant spray and removes the pillows and bedding.

"What are you doing now?" I ask, getting increasingly annoyed.

Camille shifts her weight and puts her hand on her hip. "Bedbugs, hello? After what went down in Paris before the Olympics, I'm not taking any chances." Apparently, she thinks I'm an idiot for even asking.

I roll my eyes and grab Mom's hand. "Let's go downstairs, and I'll show you around the garden. We don't want to be in here while Camille fumigates."

"Great idea," Mom says, just as Camille is pulling off the fitted sheet.

"We'll be right back, honey."

As soon as the door latches shut, Camille lifts a corner of the mattress to inspect underneath it and the box spring. Once that area is to her satisfaction, she gives it a hearty spray with the disinfectant and returns it to the original position. She follows the same routine on all four corners; but on the last one, the mattress slips from her hand and slams down onto the box spring. Almost immediately, she hears a light thud under the bed. Worried that she broke the footboard, Camille crouches down and peers under the bed. When her eyes adjust to the darkness, she spots a small, blue spiral notebook. She stretches to reach it and drags it along the floor with her fingertips until she can get a good grip on the notebook. Standing up, she inspects the front and back for any identifying marks. Finding none, she opens it.

The first few pages are nothing but diagrams and math formulas. Camille goes through several more pages and sees a bunch of acronyms, abbreviations, and more diagrams. As she fans through the rest of the pages with the intention of going downstairs and turn it in to Maggie, something catches her eye—a page doodled with hearts. Camille briefly reads the writing on that page. After a few lines, she skims through the next couple of pages and realizes that it's a journal chronicling a budding relationship.

Now Camille, she thinks to herself. *This is none of your business. Go downstairs and turn this in right now.* But her curiosity outweighs her morals, and she stuffs the notebook in her suitcase pocket with the book she brought from home.

If curiosity killed the cat, then my sister had to be on her ninth life.

***

After leaving Camille in the room, Mom and I make our way down the stairs and take a left towards the rear of the house. We pass a small business office and see a light brown-skinned, middle-aged woman with a short, loose-curled afro sitting at the desk. She's focused on the computer screen.

"Knock, knock," I say in a loud whisper as I tap on the door.

The woman looks up and recognizes me. "Hey, stranger!" Her face lights up a bit, but she doesn't actually crack a smile. "Mama told me you were here. Welcome back!"

"Thank you! Mom, this is Pat, Maggie's daughter. They both run this place." I usher Mom into the office. "Pat, meet my mom, Ann Marie. My sister is upstairs getting settled in."

"Nice to meet you, ma'am." Pat stands to shake Mom's hand, doing one of those closed-mouth smiles where the corners of her mouth go down. She's dressed a bit more casually than Maggie, wearing jeans and a maroon v-neck sleeveless top. She's much taller than her mother and very slender.

"So nice to meet you, too," Mom says. "This place is so nice!"

Pat bows her head slightly. "Thank you, ma'am! We're happy to have you."

"I was just about to show Mom the garden, so we'll see you around." We wave goodbye and head down the hall to the back door. As soon as we exit the house, we step onto a large screened-in patio littered with potted and hanging plants and cushioned wicker patio furniture.

Mom gasps. "Oh, I'm definitely going to spend time out here, especially in the morning with my cup of tea."

I open the screen door and guide her down the steps to the lush garden. It spans the rear of the house and wraps around to the side. We pass an outdoor kitchen and observe a large white pergola and an open grassy area, where I once watched a wedding take place from the window in the sitting room. I remember thinking that this would be the perfect place for my wedding—if that day ever comes. There are small benches, tables, and chairs scattered across the garden to provide private seating.

Mom stops and looks around, taking it all in.

I glance at my smartwatch and notice it's getting close to four. "Let's head back upstairs. We can freshen up and relax a bit before I take you and Camille out to the French Quarter for dinner and our first excursion."

"That sounds great!" Mom takes another look at the grounds as we make our way back into the house.

I guide her back to our room, determined to do everything I can to make this my most unforgettable trip to New Orleans yet.

Chapter 4

For our first night, I plan to take Mom and Camille to dinner at one of the most well-known restaurants in the French Quarter. I chose Muriel's because of its location and the large balcony on the second floor that overlooks Jackson Square, which is where I hope to be seated. Then, we're going on a true crime walking tour afterwards. I had planned to tell them before now, but after seeing Camille's reaction to the cemetery tour, I didn't want to give her the chance to object.

The three of us take turns freshening up and changing into clean clothes. Prior to the trip, I made recommendations on what to pack—mainly attire appropriate for spending a lot of time outside and walking in the heat. I've made reservations at the Criollo Restaurant for our last evening's dinner, which is located inside the ritzy Hotel Monteleone, so I also suggested bringing something dressy for that occasion.

Camille changes into a pink belted linen dress that stops mid-thigh and camel-colored Tory Burch sandals. She spent most of her down time propped up against the pillows on the bed, talking to Alan—mostly fishing for him to cosign on her anxiety about tomorrow's cemetery tour.

Mom calls Dad to inform him of her fascination with the bed and breakfast and makes him promise to bring her back for their anniversary next spring. Once the bathroom is vacant, she freshens up and changes into a red and gold paisley print maxi dress and strappy flat espadrilles.

Since we have the tour immediately afterwards, I'm wearing tan high-waisted shorts with a black sleeveless crop top and the pair of sandals I wear most days during my trips to New Orleans. I've found these sandals to be the most comfortable shoes to wear when I'm going to be on my feet all day. They have interchangeable ribbon straps that I wrap and tie just above my ankles, and I can swap out colors to coordinate with my outfits. I choose the black ribbons today.

I sit on the bed and use the remote to turn on the TV. After flipping through several channels, I stop on an old episode of *Dateline* that I don't recall seeing before about an all-American teenage boy suspected of murdering his parents while they slept. I can't help but to overhear Camille's conversation, and I start to feel guilty about springing another tour on her at the last minute. I knew she'd protest if I told her in advance, but I've been excited about doing this true crime tour since I learned about it at the end of my visit last year. But if she insists on not doing either tour, I'll have to cancel the reservation. It's only fair, and I don't want it to ruin our trip.

Once Camille has successfully received the validation she desires, she and Alan say their goodbyes. She turns over on her side to face me with her head propped up on her hand. "So, what exactly are we doing tonight?"

"Well, first we're going to have dinner on the balcony of a famous restaurant in the French Quarter, and then we're going on a true crime walking tour." I avoid eye contact with her on that last part.

Camille sits up abruptly. "A *what?* I thought you said this weekend was for *me?*"

"And I thought you said you wanted to see *my* city, *my* way?"

She crosses her arms and sits back against her pillow. "Murderers and ghosts. What a bachelorette party," she says facetiously.

I stand up beside the bed. "Okay, listen. These tours aren't what you think. The guides are only teaching French Quarter history with stories and myths that are associated with the area. Yes, the tours might have a bit of creepiness to them; but they're supposed to teach you, not scare you." I look at each of them to see if they believe me. Mom seems to, but Camille looks like she'll take more convincing. "Plus, I already bought the tickets."

Camille still has her arms folded. "If I don't like the tour tonight, then I'm not doing the cemetery tour tomorrow."

"Fair enough." I sit back down, grateful that I don't have to cancel tonight's tour.

Mom joins us on the bed. "I'll do the tour tonight, but I'm not young like you girls. I can't do much in the evenings. So, I'll plan to stay here after dinner the next couple of nights, and you two can go and have fun."

"Okay," Camille and I say in unison, exchanging mischievous looks.

I check my smartwatch and jump back to my feet when I see the time. "It's five-thirty. We should probably head down to the Quarter now to eat dinner. The tour starts at eight."

"How are we getting there?" Mom asks.

I look at her with a smug Cheshire Cat grin. "We're taking the streetcar, of course!"

"Yes!" Camille pumps her arm like Kevin McCallister in her favorite Christmas movie, *Home Alone*. "Is it free?"

I freeze. "Oh, I forgot. You'll both have to download an app on your phones to buy a pass that will last you for the entire stay."

I help each of them navigate the app to purchase their passes, and we leave the room for our first adventure of the weekend. Just as we reach the stairs, Camille remembers something she left in the room and asks for the keys. She goes into the room and quickly returns wearing the tiara and sash.

"I want to get as many freebies as I can this weekend!" she says, straightening the sash. "I got every drink for free in Vegas!"

***

The streetcar arrives about five minutes after we walk across the street to the median, where the stop is located. The iconic New Orleans streetcars that run up and down Canal Street are red with bright yellow trim, doors, and windows with wood seating. We sit side-by-side on a bench that runs along the side of the car, with a window behind us. Camille has us take a selfie, just as the streetcar starts to move.

The ride takes about ten minutes, making several stops along the way to allow people to board and disembark. The excitement is palpable once we reach the French Quarter, which is likely a result of the surge in energy we collectively feel from the thousands of people walking around the area. It's an early Friday evening, so there's a mix of locals and tourists celebrating the end of another long work week.

Camille alternates between taking photos from the window behind us and the one in front of us, looking like a typical tourist. She puts her phone down and does a double take. "Why do the streets on one side have one name, but a different name on the other side?"

I sit up proudly and prepare to share my New Orleans prowess. "Back in the day, English Protestants inhabited the north side of Canal Street, and the south side was French Catholics. Each had their own names for the same street that was divided by Canal Street." I notice a couple of other passengers looking back and forth as I explain, likely learning this information for the first time as well.

"That's fascinating, honey!" Mom pats my knee. "I have a feeling we're going to learn a lot on this trip, whether it's on the tours or from our own private tour guide," she says with a wink.

I smile proudly. "I hope so! That's why I love bringing people here for the first time. The French Quarter is so much more than just partying."

The streetcar stops between Royal Street and Chartres Street. "This is where we get off!" I grab a pole to pull myself up. We step off the streetcar and quickly cross Canal Street.

"Are we going down Bourbon Street?" Camille asks excitedly.

I shake my head. "Let's save that for tomorrow night after we take Mom back to the bed and breakfast."

"Good idea," Mom says. Bourbon Street has a reputation for being a rowdy party scene, especially in the evenings, because of the all-day bars, restaurants, and strip clubs. I usually take my travel companions to experience it, even if it's just walking down the street to people-watch.

We turn left onto Chartres Street and walk a few blocks, passing multiple restaurants and businesses. Mom makes note of several places she wants to visit during the trip, and I assure her that we will have time to do so over the next couple of days. Most of the buildings in the French Quarter have maintained their original aesthetic, letting visitors know they are somewhere with a unique history. From the iron railings to the classic architecture, there's always something to stop and admire.

I hear a chorus of *"Congratulations"* as we pass a group of young women. All six of them are wearing form-fitting minidresses and stilettos.

"Thank you!" Camille exclaims, basking in the attention. She points to the one wearing a white mini-veil. "Congrats to you too, girl!" The group cheers as they walk away, squawking like a colony of seagulls.

I gesture ahead to Muriel's as it comes into view, as well as the iconic sites just in front of it. This area is one of the most well-known tourist spots in the French Quarter.

To the left is the Saint Louis Cathedral—an impressive, majestic building that has mixed French, Spanish and Caribbean architecture styles. We stop and face the perfectly symmetrical front, admiring the all-white exterior with three slate-colored steeples soaring into the sky. I tell Mom and Camille the little information I can recall about it, and the sign posted by the entry doors informs us that the church still conducts services to this day.

Behind us, across the cobblestone road from the cathedral, is Jackson Square—a large courtyard that was built in the 1700s as the town square. It served as a gathering place for the locals and a spot for markets and other special occasions. Today, it's a small park filled with grass, trees, pathways, and benches. A statue of Andrew Jackson, mounted on a horse standing on its rear legs, is one of the most popular and iconic sites in New Orleans. Tourists make it a point to stop here to take a souvenir photo, since the cathedral is perfectly centered in the background behind the statue.

"There's so much history and energy here," Mom says in awe.

As we pass between the two landmarks, we walk through a maze of fortune tellers who have set up small tables and chairs on the cobblestone path—most of them occupied by customers hoping to hear that their dreams of love and success will one day come true. We see several street artists with their paintings and sketches hanging on the railings of Jackson Square, giving visitors one last chance to purchase their art before they pack up for the day. One is actively sketching a jazz band using nothing but paper and charcoal. We stop to let Mom observe her technique and admire the work of the other talented artists. After a couple of minutes, I take Mom's hand to pull her away from her fellow aesthetes.

"We can come back tomorrow to see even more street artists and take pictures in the Square in front of the statue." I'm anxious to get to the restaurant and don't want to rush through dinner before the tour.

Muriel's is everything you'd expect from a historic French Quarter restaurant. It sits proudly on the corner of Chartres Street and St. Ann Street, as if it's monitoring all the activity in the heavily trafficked area. The structure served as a residence when it was originally built in the mid-1800s and underwent remodeling in the early 2000s to transform it into a restaurant. It still maintains the original nineteenth century aesthetic, including the red brick exterior, tall windows with transom glass and black iron railing for the second-story balcony, which sprawls along the restaurant's entirety. The late afternoon sunset gives it an electric-looking glow, as it beckons us to experience the piece of New Orleans history that only it can provide.

We answer its call and approach a smiling hostess waiting for us as we cross the threshold. "Welcome to Muriel's," she greets us. "Do you have a reservation?"

"Not today," I reply. "We were hoping to get a table on the balcony."

Her smile falls, and I brace myself for her to dash my hopes. "I'm so sorry, but the balcony has been reserved for a party this evening."

"That's okay," I say, disappointed.

The hostess checks the seating chart on her podium, her smile returning. "But I do have a table here on this level that's in the corner, next to a window with a view of Jackson Square." She collects three menus. "It's the closest you'll get to the view you would have from the balcony."

I smile gratefully. "That's perfect. Thank you—" I glance at her name tag—"Isabel!"

"Of course!" she says, guiding us to our table.

We continue our excursion back in time, as Muriel's transports us from the twenty-first century to the nineteenth century. As we follow Isabel, we survey the room. The walls are a rich burgundy, clad with large oil paintings, and the windows feature elegant burgundy drapery. The round tables are draped in white linen tablecloths, and the Victorian seating is covered in burgundy leather.

Isabel guides us to our table, which is situated perfectly to give us the exact view she promised of Jackson Square. She places menus on each of our place settings and informs us that our server will be with us shortly.

Mom and Camille look around to take it all in. The large, elegant crystal chandeliers seem to be their primary focus.

"I thought I knew what to expect before we walked in, but nothing like this." Mom shakes her head in awe.

I glance out the window to see an artist at the corner of Jackson Square packing up his art into large wood crates. He's posted in that same spot every year. I inquired about his work last year, and he shared that he started painting when he was in his forties. He uses his skills as a woodworker to make his own frames using repurposed wood from buildings that were destroyed during Hurricane Katrina. I promised him last year that I would purchase a painting one day.

Camille is examining the drink menu when our server approaches the table. He's a scrawny gentleman who looks to be in his fifties. His hairline is receding, and he is proudly sporting an impressive brown handlebar mustache. He pulls a small pad and pencil from his apron pocket and introduces himself.

"Good evening, ladies," he says with the familiar New Orleans accent, making eye contact with each of us. "I'm Glen, and I'll be your server this evening. May I take your drink orders?"

I request my usual evening beverage, an Old Fashioned, while Mom orders water with lemon. I don't think Mom has ever drunk an alcoholic beverage in her life, which is likely why she appears to age at half the rate as most of her peers.

Camille asks Glen for recommendations and, after hearing her options, chooses the Louisiana Rum Runner—the sweetest drink on the menu. He nods and fills us in on their daily special entrées and assures us he will return with our drinks promptly.

I pick up my menu and review the appetizers. "So, what do you think of the place?"

Camille scans the room again. "I can see why you love this city. It's definitely not like any place I've ever been."

I chuckle to myself, because aside from the trips with our mom, Camille hasn't been anywhere. She's not as adventurous as I am. And, true to the stereotype of the baby of the family, she clings to our parents and has never had the desire to venture out too far away from them. This is the reason she attended TCU, since Fort Worth is only about a forty-five-minute drive from our parents' house.

"What about you, Mom?" I ask, although I'm sure I already know what she's going to say.

"I just love it, Camryn! It's so *me!* I can't believe I've never made it a point to come out here before."

Honestly, I'm surprised as well. New Orleans is a very spiritual town. At one point, it was the only port in the United States where goods and people could come through, which resulted in people of all cultures and beliefs congregating in one place. With that kind of eclectic history, plus the spiritual practices of the Africans who were shipped in and enslaved on the mineral-rich plantations, what remains is a metaphysical energy that can't be explained. All of this, along with the tremendous art scene, is why Mom fits right in here.

I look over at my baby sister as she studies the menu and evaluates her options. "I still can't believe you're actually getting married," I say. "Like, you're really going to be a *wife!*"

"I know." Camille places her menu down on the table. She takes a deep breath and looks down at her lap. "Honestly, I'm starting to get a little scared." She looks up at me and then Mom to see our reactions to this revelation, expecting to see judgment. "I'm being silly, aren't I?"

I find myself a bit stunned hearing this. Camille has always seemed to me like she was born to be a wife. When she was little, she'd beg me to play house with her in the child-size kitchen set she got from Santa Claus one Christmas. She was always the wife, and I was always the husband. She would cook dinner, iron the clothes, and take care of the babies.

Sometimes I would stand outside her room and watch her play with her dolls. Never once did I see her playing with multiple girl dolls, making them be friends, resolving conflict, or just having a good time together—which, now that I think of it, probably has something to do with how she isn't turned off by the bickering between friends on the reality shows. No, it was always a boy doll and a girl doll with a family. To hear Camille now questioning her ability to be in that role in real life is perplexing to me.

If anyone should doubt themselves, it's me. Sure, I played house when I was little. But I outgrew that once I was introduced to sports and started prioritizing my friends over everything else. I've only had one roommate, and that was for my one year of college. Plus, I've never lived with a boyfriend, so I have no idea what it's like to share my space, money, or food with someone else. I've never had to prioritize anyone but myself when making day-to-day decisions. Maybe I'm too selfish to make a relationship last. It only makes me wonder why I have been so confident that I will make such a good wife.

Mom reaches over and touches Camille's hand. "Oh, honey, that's totally normal. Getting married is life-changing. And when reality sets in, there's always going to be nerves and questions about the unknown."

I piggy-back on Mom's encouragement. "Seriously, Camille. If there's anyone that I'm confident will be a great wife, it's you. You and Alan love each other so much. You've both taken your time in getting to this point in your relationship." I look at her intently. "You know how critical I am. The fact that Alan has met my approval to be *my* brother-in-law and responsible for *my* baby sister's heart and life says a lot." I smile genuinely. "You're going to be a wonderful wife for him, and he's going to be a wonderful husband for you. There's no doubt in my mind."

Camille takes a cleansing breath and exhales slowly, allowing a tear to fall down the same cheek as I saw in the proposal photos. "Thank you," she says with a shaky voice and her lips quivering. "I really needed to hear all of that." She sighs again. "I've never mentioned anything about this before. Everyone always thinks that I have it all together, and I don't want Alan to think that I'm doubting him or us." She uses the napkin on her lap to dab her cheek and the corner of her eye.

Mom is still holding her hand. "I understand, sweetie. You can always tell us anything."

"Yeah. And who cares what anyone else thinks? You have to be true to yourself." I reach over and put my hand on top of theirs. "We love you, and we will always have your back."

We spend the next ninety minutes discussing the ins and outs of wedding planning, as Mom and Camille reminisce on the times they spent together throughout the process. Since I live over twelve hundred miles away, I could only participate in the gown shopping via

FaceTime, and the two of them handled all other in-person planning. It's fun listening to their stories about finding a florist and the perfect table settings, but it also makes me realize all that I've missed out on by living so far away.

When each course arrives, I enjoy watching them experience their first taste of New Orleans delicacies, which include Boudin egg rolls, seafood gumbo, sautéed snapper, roasted duck and a wood-grilled filet mignon. Camille chooses vanilla bean crème brûlée, which we all split for dessert.

Once we're done, I lean towards Camille. "Are you ready for the tour?" I ask in a dramatic tone, wiggling my eyebrows up and down.

She rolls her eyes and sighs. "No, but whatever." Mom and I chuckle.

We place our napkins on the table and stand up to leave. I wrap my arm around Camille's shoulder and pull her in tight to my side, causing her petite shoulder to dig into my rib cage.

"You'll be fine! I promise."

Chapter 5

We make the ten-minute walk to the meeting spot for the true crime tour, which is at an outdoor bar on Decatur Street at the edge of the Mississippi River. The sun is setting, and the temperature has dropped about five degrees, thanks to the courteous breeze from the river; however, the thick humidity still has me in a choke hold.

The tour starts at eight, but the confirmation email suggests that we arrive early, since the admission price includes a free adult beverage at the bar. When we arrive, there are already numerous people seated at the bar and in the uncovered seating area.

I look around and find a short young man with glasses and straight brown hair, with the top half pulled up in a mini-man bun. He's wearing jeans and a black t-shirt that reads *GHOST TOURS*. I recognize the shirt as the same one worn by all the tour guides from previous tours I've attended with this same company.

"Excuse me," I say as we approach the man who is likely in his late-twenties. I determine he's about four inches shorter than me, and I'm always surprised at how I tend to slouch a little—especially around men—in an attempt to ease any intimidation about my stature. "We're here for the true crime tour."

He smiles and speaks in an unexpected British accent. "Ah, welcome! Can I get your name?"

"Camryn Alexander."

He scrolls through his phone until he finds my name. "Ah, yes! I see you here with two guests." He reaches into his back pocket and pulls out a stack of black and white stickers with the tour company name. He counts out three and hands them to me. "Please wear these so I can keep track of everyone in our group and ensure we don't have random people tagging along."

I take the stickers and hand two of them to Camille and Mom, each of us placing one on our chests near our left shoulders.

"My name is Geoff." He shakes each of our hands as Mom and Camille introduce themselves. "Follow me, and we can get your drink orders. One drink is included with each of your tickets."

We follow our guide to the bar where the drink menu is written in colorful chalk on a blackboard overhead. Geoff whistles to get the bartender's attention and points to the three of us, advising him that we are with the group and are not responsible for payment. There are no available barstools, so we stand and review the drink options.

The bartender walks over to us and swipes his corkscrew blond hair away from his sweat-soaked face. "Do you know what you want?"

I review the menu again and turn to Camille. "I think it's time for you to have your first Hurricane. It's the signature drink of New Orleans."

"Sounds good to me!" She spots a large and loud bachelorette party wearing the same black and white stickers as us, confirming that they are a part of our tour group.

I order two frozen Hurricanes and an ice water, which the bartender prepares and hands to us promptly. All three drinks are in clear plastic cups with hot pink straws. Camille takes a sip of the frozen, dark pink beverage and smiles without removing her lips from the straw.

"Mmm, this is good!" she says with her teeth clenching the straw.

I take a sip of mine and give her a thumbs up. The sweet, icy sensation going down my throat is exactly what I need to take the edge off this heat. I make a mental note to wear my hair up the rest of the trip, since my thick curls are already suffocating the back of my neck like a coconut-scented wet blanket.

Mom spots a group of people leaving. "Let's grab that table before someone else does." There are no chairs, so the tall, white bistro table is for us to use solely as a place to rest our drinks.

I leave a small tip for the bartender, and we hustle over to the table. We watch the rowdy bachelorette party Camille spotted earlier. It's obvious that this isn't their first stop for drinks this evening, since they are ridiculously loud and currently taking lemon drops shots—all but confirming that I made the right choice by passing on Camille's party in Vegas.

I count twelve of them in total, and they all speak with unmistakable Long Island accents. The bride-to-be is wearing a white t-shirt with black lettering that reads *Bridin' Dirty.* Her party consists of all women and one tall, flamboyant man with a stack of colorful Mardi Gras beads around his neck. They are all wearing hot pink t-shirts that read *They See Us Rollin', We Celebratin'*—a play on the Chamillionaire song that I likely won't be able to get out of my head for the remainder of the night.

A few minutes later, Geoff reappears and speaks in a booming voice. "Everyone here for the crime tour, please follow me!" He guides our group of thirty or so to the sidewalk along Decatur Street. "First and foremost, thank you so much for being here tonight. Our tour will last for two hours. We will make a stop halfway to take a quick break. At that time, you can grab a drink at your own expense and use the restroom."

I look at Mom and Camille to make sure they are still on board, and they both shoot me identical smiles. I think the Hurricane is doing its job and giving Camille a bit of liquid courage, or at least helping her forget how much she's been dreading this tour.

Geoff continues his instructions. "Please be sure to stay behind me and out of the streets. Whenever we stop, make a tight circle around me on the sidewalk so we can ensure everyone safely hears the fascinating tales of true crime. Any questions before we begin?"

After getting a slurred, *"Let's get this party started!"* from one of the bachelorettes, resulting in cheers from the others, he turns and walks towards a crosswalk to begin the tour.

***

The tour is as expected—long, hot and fascinating! We learn about murders, suicides, serial killers, mysterious deaths, and arsons. I was sure that Geoff's story about the gruesome murder-suicide of Zack and Addie would put Camille over the edge; but by that time, she had already embedded herself in the larger bachelorette party and had spent most of the tour discussing reality show gossip with one of the women.

Mom remains quiet and listens intently to the stories. I occasionally glance her way, and she either smiles or winks at me. I feel guilty, as I know this is totally out of her element. She is all about peace and love, not violence and murder.

It's dark outside, with only streetlights and headlights from cars driving by to illuminate our path as we navigate our way through the streets of the French Quarter. As promised, we stop halfway through the tour at a bar I recognize from a haunted history tour I attended on my first trip to New Orleans.

Lafitte's Blacksmith Shop Bar is said to be haunted by the infamous pirate, Jean Lafitte. His crimes of looting and pillaging in the 1700s are what qualify the bar to be a part of this true crime tour. The dismal bar looks like a rundown shack on the corner of Bourbon Street and St. Philip Street and matches the aesthetic you'd expect of an eighteenth-century pirate hang out. It has a mostly brick exterior on one side and grungy plaster on the other, with hints of exposed brick in the worn-down areas. The roof has seen better days and has dormer windows with broken shutters overlooking both streets. Although it's not much to look at and appears to be just another old building, it's definitely hard to miss with the hard rock music blasting onto the streets.

After sharing Lafitte's story, Geoff moves closer to the bar's entrance. "We're going to take a quick break here for about twenty minutes. There are restrooms at the back of the bar. You can order drinks, but remember, these are at your own expense." People are already making their way into the bar, so he has to yell. "Please meet me at this exact spot in twenty minutes!"

"I'm going to the restroom," Mom says as she scurries inside to avoid any lines.

Camille follows her. "Me, too."

I walk behind them and yell over the music. "Do you want me to order any drinks?"

"No, I've had enough!" Camille has never been much of a drinker. With her tiny frame, that one Hurricane was enough to get her a little more than buzzed, but not sloppy drunk.

The place is dark and dank, with almost no lights aside from the ones at the bar and votive candles lined up along the bar itself. Any other illumination is courtesy of the streetlight at the corner outside. There's a slight smell of mildew, which I assume is an attempt to keep with the rustic ambiance while avoiding the expense of locating the source of the odor. No matter what, I love everything about it! The entire scene reminds me of The Snuggly Duckling from the Rapunzel movie *Tangled* I watched with my six-year-old cousin on our last visit to Albuquerque.

I ask the bartender for a beer and two waters, but before he has the chance to leave, a sweaty Geoff steps up to the bar and requests a water, too. He turns around and rests his elbows on the bar, displaying his scrawny arms. "Enjoying the tour?"

"Every second of it!" I say enthusiastically. "I dragged my mom and sister to come along with me, even though we're supposed to be celebrating my sister getting married next weekend."

Geoff laughs. "I take it this isn't their *thing*."

"Not at all. And I promised my sister that if she doesn't enjoy this tour, we wouldn't do the cemetery tour I booked for tomorrow morning." I lean closer to him. "So, you better make it good, or your company will be short three participants tomorrow."

He gives me a dramatic wink and turns his head to evaluate if the line to the restrooms is short enough to adhere to the twenty-minute time limit he gave everyone.

"How long have you lived in New Orleans?" I ask. I'd already determined that Geoff's thick British accent is too strong for him to have lived here for very long.

"About four years. I moved here when my wife got a job working on the set of an independent film that was shot here. She's a makeup artist."

"I see."

"Her sister moved here a couple of years prior, and we stayed with her. More TV shows and movies are being filmed here now. So, she got more assignments, and we ended up making this home."

"Is this what you do full time? Giving tours?"

"No." He laughs. "I'm a cook at a restaurant downtown. I do this on my nights off to make some extra money."

"Gotcha," I say as the bartender places all four drinks in front of us.

Geoff grabs his cup. "Well, I better go and remind the blokes in line how much time we have left. And I promise not to let you down." He straightens his glasses, gives me a smile, and walks away.

As if there was a revolving door, the moment he leaves, the tall guy from the bachelorette party slides into his place with one long stride and leans against the bar.

"He's so cute," he says with his eyes glued to Geoff, tangling his fingers in the glimmering Mardi Gras beads displayed on his chest. "Do you know if he's single?"

I frown. "Sorry. Not only is he married, but I think he's straight."

He stands up and gives Geoff another once over. "Damn, the accent always throws me off!"

I laugh at the unexpected *Sex and the City* quote. "Sorry, Mr. Blatch," I say, acknowledging the reference to the iconic show that teaches thirty-something singles what *not* to do when dating.

He dances his way back to his party just as Mom and Camille approach the bar. I hand Mom her water.

"Thank you, honey!" She drinks the water out of the plastic cup.

I hand the other to Camille. "You look like you could use some, too. I'm glad you're having fun!"

She gulps down the entire cup and hands it back to me. "As long as I don't have to hear what he's talking about, I'm fine!" She makes her way back to the other bachelorette party and remains with them for the rest of the evening.

"That's totally fine with me," I say to Mom. "If she doesn't walk away from this evening terrorized, we're more likely to go on tomorrow's tour."

Mom gives me a wink and takes another sip of her water.

The tour continues, and we make several more stops over the next forty-five minutes. Just when my feet are starting to scream for me to call it a night, we make it to our final destination at the far end of the activity on Bourbon Street.

Geoff stops in front of a gray building. "This, my friends, will be our last stop." He takes the four steps up to a black door so everyone can see and hear him clearly. I notice a blue piece of paper taped to the door, but Geoff is blocking my view, and I can't see what it says. I glance over and see a matching door about twenty feet down, closer to the end of the building. There's a black iron balcony surrounding the entire upper level, with a sign hanging down directly above me, preventing me from seeing what it says.

He looks back at the door. "This bar is the scene of one of our most recent mysteries." He turns back around and looks at us. "A college student named Olivia Peterson came here with her friends for a *bachelorette party*." He emphasizes the last part in hopes of getting the attention of the two brides-to-be and several of the party-goers who are chattering and not listening. It works.

"Her friends reported her missing after losing track of her in this bar. Police saw video of everyone in the bar that night going in at some point and then coming out. Everyone—except Olivia. No one ever saw her leave the bar, and she has been missing ever since. There were no witnesses and no clues." He scans the entire group, watching for reactions.

I hear mumbles from the crowd, and surprisingly, Camille is the one that asks a question.

"How can someone just disappear in a bar? I mean, where could she go without someone seeing her?"

Geoff shrugs. "No one knows."

I'm baffled. Out of all the true crime podcasts I've listened to daily over the past four years, I've never heard of Olivia Peterson or any disappearance case like this—especially in New Orleans.

"Police checked the entire building, including the space next door, which the owner had recently purchased and was having remodeled to be a room with a stage for live music." Geoff shrugs again. "No one's ever found her." He pauses, attempting to create more suspense.

I open my mouth to inquire about theories, but Geoff beats me to the punch.

"Police have theories and even questioned a suspect, but there's no real evidence that can prove that he did anything. And that's where her case has remained ever since. In fact, there is going to be a vigil right here outside of the bar on Monday evening to commemorate the ten-year anniversary of her disappearance."

"Who was the suspect?" asks a deep voice from the crowd.

"A man she danced with and got a drink with at the bar," Geoff replies. "Apparently, he was someone she knew. Police questioned him, but like I said before, they had no evidence to prove he left with her or caused her any harm."

After a few seconds of mumbling and no new questions, Geoff concludes the tour. "Thank you so much for coming along on this tour! Please keep us in mind for any other tours you want to experience during your stay in New Orleans. We have haunted history tours, cemetery tours, voodoo tours and more!" He steps back down to the sidewalk with us. "I'll be around for another few minutes if you have any questions about this tour or any of the other tours we offer."

Before anyone has a chance to bombard him with their questions and theories, I rush to Geoff with a ten-dollar tip and thank him for the informative tour. I find Mom and Camille and usher them down Dauphine Street, avoiding the action on Bourbon Street. We walk towards Canal Street to wait for a streetcar.

After about ten minutes of waiting, we board, and I sit between the two of them in the same seat as earlier. Mom looks tired, of course, and I feel bad for dragging her around the French Quarter into all hours of the night.

Camille is quiet, scrolling through the many photos and selfies she took with her new bachelorette friends. She occasionally smiles and giggles, which helps ease some of the guilt I've been feeling.

I reach over and place a hand on each of their laps. "Thanks for staying up and going on the tour for me tonight. I know neither of you was very thrilled about it."

"Are you kidding?" Mom says. "I enjoyed every minute of it! If it wasn't so late, I could have gone another two hours listening to stories and seeing all these old buildings."

Mom's enthusiasm catches me completely off-guard, since her expression throughout the tour seemed so somber. I had assumed she was counting the minutes until it was over, so I'm surprised and relieved to know that she wasn't bored, but listening intently.

"Your father definitely needs to bring me back here. I'm sure there's so much more to learn in a city with as much history as this one."

"Wow, Mom! I'm so glad to hear that!" I turn to my other side and look at Camille, whose eyes are still glued to her phone. "What about you? It wasn't too bad, was it?"

Camille turns off her phone and takes her time sliding it into her purse. She turns her head slowly and looks at me with one eyebrow raised. "Well, as much as I didn't appreciate having to go on the tour in the first place—" She crosses her arms over her chest. "I had a *blast!* I felt like I was back in Vegas with my friends!"

Mom and I laugh.

"Great! I'm glad they didn't mind you crashing their bachelorette party." I scoot closer to Camille and grab her hand, lacing my fingers into hers. "Does this mean you'll go on the cemetery tour tomorrow?" I squeeze her hand a little harder and give her my best puppy dog eyes.

Camille turns her head forward, but keeps her eyes on me, giving me a side-eye. "Yes, but only because I know Mom wants to do it, too."

I applaud quietly, using only my fingers. "Yay! I promise you'll like it. I've been on the tour several times, and I learn something new every time."

"If you say so." Camille rolls her eyes.

"Well, I can't wait," Mom says, looking through the streetcar windshield. "I think our stop is coming up."

I pull the overhead cord to alert the conductor that we will get off at the next stop, directly in front of Canal Street Bed and Breakfast. Once we arrive, we step off the streetcar and cross the street arm-in-arm. We quickly make our way up the stairs to the front door.

"I'm going to take the first shower, if you don't mind," Mom says. "I'm exhausted."

I locate the keys in my purse and unlock the door. "That's fine with me. And I'll go last. I'm sure both of you are ready to get to bed."

I'm tired, too, but I won't fall asleep for a while tonight. Once I've showered, I plan to get in bed, grab my phone and earbuds, and start a deep dive into the disappearance of Olivia Peterson.

Chapter 6

Mom falls asleep almost immediately after her head hits the pillow, lulled by the soft sound of Camille's shower water running. I can hear her lightly snoring as I'm responding to text messages from my maintenance manager about a late night roof leak in one of our units. Once I handle that crisis, I'm ready to begin my search for details about the missing college student that have been consuming my thoughts for the past hour. I'm about to google the name *Olivia Peterson* on my phone when I hear a sharp squeak of the vintage crystal handle turning on the bathroom door.

Camille steps out of the bathroom after completing her twenty-minute nighttime skin and hair routine. She's wearing a gray ribbed tank top with matching shorts, a pink and green plaid satin scarf wrapped around her head, and clear-rimmed oversized glasses. I can smell the fragrance of lavender and vanilla wafting from the still-steamy bathroom, courtesy of her body wash and lotion.

"I can't wait to get in that bed," Camille says, placing her toiletry bag in her suitcase. "My feet are *done!*"

I grab a graphic t-shirt and cut-off cotton shorts and make my way to the bathroom with plans to scrub my favorite city off my body. "Well, good night." I say, assuming she will be asleep by the time I'm finished.

"I'm going to read a little of my book before I go to sleep, so I'll probably still be up." Camille reaches into the pocket of her suitcase just as I'm closing the door. She rummages through the pocket and finds the book and something else—the notebook she hid earlier in the day, which she had forgotten about until now. She peers over to ensure Mom is still asleep and scurries to the bed with both the book and notebook in-hand. Positioned quietly on the bed with her back against the pillows and headboard, she raises her knees up towards her chest and places the hardcover book on her thighs, hiding the small notebook in front of it.

The notebook begins exactly as Camille remembers, with drawings, diagrams, measurements and words she doesn't recognize. She flips through more pages of what looks to her like hieroglyphics until she finds what she's looking for—the page with doodles of small hearts in the top corners. This is the first page that has writing and not drawings and acronyms. Camille is eager to discover what it's about.

***

I must be crazy. I have to be. There's no way what I think happened today really happened. And I can't tell anyone because I know they'll say I'm crazy, too. But I need to get all of this out of my head, so I guess there's no better place than here... although I've never had a diary or journal before. I just need a way to sort out my thoughts and get a reality check about this, because I just know I must be wrong.

It started a few of weeks ago when I applied for the summer internship at my dream architecture firm, James and Sullivan. At the end of the summer, they will choose one intern to join them permanently at an entry-level position. I was hesitant to apply, as I figured it would be a long shot for me to get the position, since so many graduates from colleges in the Austin area had applied. I talked to one of my professors about my chances, and he encouraged me to apply. He told me that I have plenty of talent and would be a great candidate for the program. So, I completed the application and waited.

It only took a week, and I received an email informing me of my acceptance! The email stated that there would be three teams of five interns, with each group assisting with the design of new buildings in the Austin area. I was excited and relieved to see that my professor was our project lead, and a guy named Noah from my class (who I've been secretly crushing on all year) was in my group!

Our first meeting was tonight in our lecture hall, where I met the other interns in my group. I was surprised to learn that I'm one of only two women. We learned that our assignment is to work on a project for a new children's hospital, which will begin construction early next year. We discussed the firm's expectations of our roles in the project, our summer schedule of Tuesday through Friday, and agreed to meet as a group for thirty minutes every Tuesday and Thursday immediately after work.

But here's the deal... I could have sworn that I caught him looking at me a few times. At first, I assumed he was in deep thought about something. But then I saw him looking at me again while we were supposed to be reading our contracts... and he smiled at me! And it didn't look like a quick, friendly smile, either. It looked like a flirty smile that wanted a smile back in return. I didn't know what to do, so I just looked back down at my contract and tried to avoid eye contact the rest of the meeting.

It's possible I was just seeing what I wanted to see. He has never paid any attention to me like this before. And there's no way that someone like him would actually flirt with a someone like me. Now I'm even more nervous about our first day at the firm next Tuesday!

***

Camille is definitely intrigued. Is this woman's crush going to become something more? The shower is still running, so she determines she has enough time to read a bit more. She turns a few pages of more diagrams and notes until she finds another entry, now noticing that nothing has been dated. Camille begins to wonder how old this notebook is.

***

If I thought I was crazy before, then I must be delusional now. I felt my heart race when I first saw him again yesterday morning. But he didn't really smile at me like he did before, which, if I'm honest, made me feel a bit disappointed. So, I went on with the day, convinced that it was all in my head.

It was exciting to be at the firm and get started on our project. If I work hard, I could be the one with a job at the end of the summer. And today turned out to be a great day! Everyone loved my ideas, and even asked me to present our daily recap to the partners at the end of the day. For the first time, I actually believed that I could have a great career as an architect!

And then it happened. I was getting on the elevator to leave for the day after our team meeting, and just as the doors were closing, he stepped inside. I gave him a quick smile, and he smiled back. There was an awkward silence, but then he told me that he really liked my ideas and was glad that we were working together. I thanked him, and although I was still unsure if he was flirting or not, I felt butterflies in my stomach standing next to him alone in that elevator. When the doors opened on the first floor, he leaned over to kiss me on my cheek. He told me that he thought I was really special, and then he stepped off the elevator. I watched him walk across the lobby as the elevator doors closed, forgetting that I needed to get off, too.

I mean... what was that? We've never even shaken hands before, and now he puts his lips on my face? That means something, right? I mean, we're not French. Kissing on the cheek isn't a part of our social etiquette. So, what was that all about? Am I crazy???

***

Now Camille is hooked! She listens again and notices that the shower has stopped and hears the clamor of my toiletries on the bathroom counter. She decides to try her luck and read one more journal entry, in hopes she can finish before I come out. This time, there are only two pages of diagrams before she finds it.

***

Well, there's nothing to question anymore. Yesterday, I caught him looking at me and smiling the same smile I saw before! Only this time, I smiled back. The whole day was like this, and I tried desperately to not let it distract me. Our group went to lunch together, and he sat next to me. When our food was ready, we both reached for the same rolled up silverware, and our hands touched. We just looked at each other and smiled, but we didn't move our hands right away. Wow! It felt like magic! I've never felt anything like that before!

But then there's what happened today. I stayed a little late to finish some sketches, and when I approached the elevator, I was surprised to find him standing there. Had he waited for me, or did he just happen to stay late, too? I guess I had been so focused on my work that I didn't notice if anyone else was still working.

Anyway, we both got on the elevator and talked about the day. That tension that I felt the last time we were alone together was gone this time. Everything felt more natural between us. He walked me to my car in the parking garage, and just when I was about to open my car door, he actually grabbed my hand! I turned around and looked at him, but he didn't say anything. He just looked at me and smiled. I thought he was going to kiss me, so I started to stand up on my toes. But he just kissed the back of my hand and then walked away.

I can't believe this is happening to me! I wish I could tell someone. Anyone! But I can't. I've never told anyone about any guy I've dated until I knew it was serious, because I don't want to jinx it. And I definitely don't want to jinx this. I hope this is real. It feels real.

This is going to be a long three days, waiting for the next time I get to see him. I can't wait until Tuesday!

Chapter 7

By the time I finish my shower, I'm relaxed thanks to my sister's lavender aromatherapy body wash—so relaxed that I question if I even have the energy to begin my investigation after all. I step out of the bathroom while adjusting the black satin bonnet I wear every night when I'm not sleeping at home. It extends past my shoulders, which is perfect for my long hair. Typically, I sleep on a satin pillowcase to keep my hair from drying and my face from breaking out—which is what happens with cotton pillowcases, like the ones at hotels and here at the bed and breakfast.

Mom is still sound asleep, but I'm surprised to find Camille wide awake, reading her book. She looks so tiny, sitting curled up on the massive king-size bed with the book propped up on her legs, reminiscent of how she looked as a child doing the same thing every night before she fell asleep. Being ten years older than Camille makes it easy for me to have maternal-like memories of her childhood, feeling more nostalgia for hers than I do for my own.

"What are you reading?" I ask.

She brings her legs closer to her chest. "Oh. Um. Just this book a friend recommended about a girl that goes on an annual summer trip with friends and has to share a room with her ex-fiancé, because they haven't told anyone they broke up."

"Yuck, what a nightmare," I say with a shudder.

"I know. But I have a feeling they might end up together, because this author is known for her great love stories."

I lie down on the bed and pull up the covers, adjusting the pillow to have my head slightly elevated. "We'll need to turn off the light soon so we don't disturb Mom."

"That's fine." Camille leans over and discreetly slides the book and notebook into the nightstand drawer and removes her glasses. "Go ahead and turn it off. I can't keep my eyes open for another second."

I reach over to the lamp and pull the chain to turn off the light. The room is dark except for slits of light peeking through the window blinds. I stick the earbuds in my ears and wiggle myself further under the covers into a comfortable position. I begin my web sleuthing by typing OLIVIA PETERSON MISSING into my phone.

The search results in over two hundred links and previews of several videos. With so many results, I'm surprised that I've heard nothing about this case in all the shows, movies and podcasts I've obsessed over for the past few years. I tap on the first video, which opens my TikTok app, and I see a handsome twenty-something man with dark hair and bewitching green eyes. He tells a one-minute version of the story in a monotone voice with sinister music playing in the background, giving young Rod Serling vibes. I tap on #oliviapeterson in the caption and watch a handful of other videos, most with content creators re-telling the story and some sharing their theories on what happened to Olivia. One ridiculous theory is that she was vaporized by an alien disguised as a human.

I need to find solid information, so I close TikTok and go back to the search results. Camille has fallen asleep, so I dim the light on my phone's screen and continue scrolling through video links. After expanding the results, I see a forty-two-minute video from the true crime network show, *Disappearances*. I've watched several episodes of this series before, and I'm certain that it will show videos and interviews that will provide a more detailed portrayal of the story. I tap the link and sink deeper into my pillow.

The episode begins with a black and white video of young women dancing in slow motion as a deep, raspy voiceover explains that bachelorette parties are supposed to be fun and celebrate the end of one chapter in a woman's life and the beginning of another. The narrator then reports that the violent crime and murder rates in New Orleans during 2014 were the lowest they had been in over forty years, but were still high compared to the average city of similar size in the United States.

Then I see her.

A photo slideshow of Olivia Peterson appears on my screen. She is a Chinese-American woman with shoulder-length, straight black hair. She has a big, beautiful smile in every photo.

I learn that Olivia's parents adopted her in Arlington, Texas when she was only ten days old. Her biological parents died in a car accident three years after they immigrated to the United States from China. Her biological mother was eight months pregnant with Olivia at the time and arrived at the hospital in critical condition; but she died shortly after Olivia was delivered by an emergency c-section.

Family photos and home videos show her as a baby and toddler with her adoptive family. Olivia's father is a stocky white man with dirty blonde hair, who is wearing a sweater vest over a collared shirt in almost every photo. Her mother is a slender white woman who wears large round glasses and has red hair. Some of the photos show Olivia with her older brother, who was seven years old when she was adopted.

According to the narrator, Olivia fit the ideal image of the perfect child. She was a national scholar, played the flute in her high school band, and was involved in Girl Scouts throughout high school—all depicted in another slideshow of photos. She received multiple academic scholarships, including a full-ride scholarship from the School of Architecture at Hoskins University, a small private college just outside of Austin, TX.

The next photo is of Olivia and her roommate, Erin, in their college dorm. They are both sitting on their bunks on opposite sides of the room, with wood desks and rolling chairs underneath the beds. The narrator shares that Olivia and Erin would become close friends and remain roommates every year they attended Hoskins University together—first in the dorms and then in an off-campus apartment during their junior and senior years.

Olivia's parents are interviewed by someone off-screen. Kirk Peterson, Olivia's father, shares that she chose to attend Hoskins University despite being accepted to larger schools, like the University of Texas. She maintained a 4.0 GPA while working part-time at the college bookstore, and she graduated summa cum laude.

Her mother, Sheila, informs the interviewer that Olivia was selected to be a part of an exclusive summer internship at a major architecture firm in Austin, beating out candidates from much larger schools. It's obvious that they were very proud of their daughter.

The narrator ominously shares that Kirk and Sheila couldn't have

71

known that Olivia's visit over spring break during her senior year would be the last time they would ever see her in person.

The slow-motion video of young women dancing appears again, and I learn that Olivia's roommate, Erin, was getting married in early July, a little over a month after they graduated from college. Two weeks before the wedding, Erin and her bridal party had planned a three-day bachelorette weekend in New Orleans.

I see four women sitting in the corner of a gray sectional in a living room in front of a large window. They are identified as the bridal party, minus Olivia. All four of them are wearing white t-shirts screen-printed with a copy of Olivia's missing poster.

On the far left is Erin—the bride, and Olivia's roommate. She's a petite woman with chin-length, sandy brown hair. Next to her is her younger sister, Amanda, who is almost identical to Erin, but with a fuller figure and long, wavy hair. To Amanda's right is Jennifer, a Hispanic woman with dark hair pulled back in a ponytail and bold red lips. And at the end is Anaya, an Indian-American woman with large brown eyes and thick black hair cut into a short bob. I learn that Jennifer and Anaya are Erin's childhood friends. They all take turns telling stories about the weekend Olivia went missing.

Erin says they checked into their rooms on Friday afternoon after flying into New Orleans from Austin. She shared a room with Olivia and Amanda, while Jennifer and Anaya shared the room next door. Erin recalls that everyone was excited about the trip, but she noticed that Olivia—or Liv, as she referred to her—seemed distracted.

Anaya remembers trying hard to befriend Olivia, since Erin was the only one that had a relationship with her. She assumed Olivia was just uncomfortable being around three other women she didn't know, because she never seemed to be fully relaxed.

Amanda recalls hearing Olivia's phone vibrate on the nightstand while Olivia was in the bathroom shortly before they planned to walk around the French Quarter. She noticed the person's name for the incoming call was only the letter "N", which she found odd. Amanda told Olivia about the call, but Olivia brushed it off, saying she'd return the call later.

The group spent Friday evening eating, drinking, and checking off dares from a bachelorette party scavenger hunt list. I see photos taken that night, showing Anaya kissing a bald man's head, Erin hugging another bride-to-be, Jennifer and a random young man holding a wrapped condom, and both Olivia and Jennifer posed next to a cute police officer.

Erin shares that Olivia seemed to loosen up once they got to a bar on Bourbon Street. They were there for about thirty minutes when Olivia's demeanor changed again, and she seemed agitated and jumpy again. When Erin asked her about it, Olivia said she thought she saw someone she knew, but was likely just tipsy and seeing things.

According to Amanda, they went to a coffee shop that Saturday morning before meeting up for a tour of the Saint Louis Cemetery. While they were in line, she noticed Olivia's phone light up and audibly vibrate in her back pocket. But Olivia just ignored it.

Next, a new woman appears on the screen. She's identified as Janet Nedbalek, the owner of NOLA Coffee Bistro, and is being interviewed outside of the coffee shop. I estimate that she's in her forties, and her dirty blonde hair with dark roots appears to be wet and pulled back in a low ponytail. Her white t-shirt shows the black company logo of a steaming coffee mug with a gold fleur-de-lis on its front. She tells the off-camera interviewer that she remembers that particular morning because when she tried to hand Olivia the cup of coffee she ordered, Olivia suddenly looked over her shoulder and missed the cup. The coffee spilled all over the counter and onto the floor. Janet offered to make another cup, but Olivia stormed outside after telling her friends she wasn't feeling well and needed to get some fresh air.

I see the bridal party again. Erin adds to the story by saying she felt bad for Liv, but she knew her well enough to know that giving her introverted friend some time to herself would probably be beneficial. So, Erin had gone back to socializing with the others.

Janet, the coffee shop owner, continues her interview by saying that she went outside to find Olivia and give her a new cup of coffee. She observed Olivia standing about thirty feet away on the corner of the street, talking to a tall man with brown hair and a navy blue baseball cap. They appeared to be arguing, so Janet went back inside the shop and placed the cup on the party's table. She advised them to check on their friend, but didn't specify what she saw.

There's a close-up of Erin saying that when she went outside, Olivia was walking back to the coffee shop, still looking frazzled. Erin asked her if she was okay, but Olivia just apologized for being a party pooper and promised to have more fun the rest of the trip.

The last time I see Janet, she says that people came by the shop a couple of days later asking if they could tape a poster of a missing woman on the shop window. She remembers that she immediately recognized the photo and called the phone number on the poster to report what she had witnessed. The police came by and asked a bunch of questions, but she couldn't tell them much since she hadn't seen the man's face. Janet could only recall that he was much taller than Olivia and provided his hair and hat color. She said that he just looked like an average white guy to her.

The next clip shows a slow pan of above-ground crypts in one of New Orleans' famous cemeteries. Erin remembers thinking that Olivia was trying hard to enjoy herself on the cemetery tour, but it was obvious that she was upset. In the photo showing the five of them inside the cemetery with their tour guide, everyone has a huge smile on their face except Olivia. Hers seems a bit forced.

Amanda explains that once they left the cemetery, Olivia seemed to suddenly cheer up. They all had a great time the rest of the day, finishing their scavenger hunt and doing some sightseeing. After dressing up and having a fancy dinner that night at Antoine's, they went back to their rooms to change into party clothes with plans to return to Bourbon Street.

A photo shows of all five of them standing in the middle of Bourbon Street at night, with neon lights glowing from businesses on both sides of the street. They are all wearing short black outfits consisting of tank tops, shorts, minidresses, crop tops, and miniskirts. This is the first picture of Olivia from the trip with the same carefree smile I saw in the photos at the very beginning of the episode.

I see the slow motion video of women dancing again, and the show's background music changes to something more ominous and sinister. The narrator states that after stopping at a few other bars, the group ended the night at the Sinful Spirits Bar on Bourbon Street. I see a video of people walking into the actual bar at night, and I immediately recognize the gray building from the tour.

Jennifer shares that by the time they got to the last bar, they were all drunk, and it was the most fun time of the entire trip. They all danced with each other and random guys, took tons of pictures on their phones and drank a variety of cocktails and shots. After some time, Jennifer noticed Olivia wasn't with the group but quickly located her dancing with a tall, cute guy.

Oh boy, I think to myself, knowing that I'm about to get into the meat of the story. But all the beverages I've consumed today have caught up with me. I press pause and tiptoe to the restroom.

Chapter 8

I make the controversial decision to not risk waking Mom or Camille by flushing the toilet and wash my hands with a light drizzle of water. I sit down slowly on the bed and gently insert each leg under the covers, remembering that my sister has always been a very light sleeper. Once I'm settled, I proceed with the episode of *Disappearances*, noticing there's only about twenty minutes remaining. I reach over and tap my smartwatch charging on the nightstand. It's just after midnight, so I have time to get plenty of sleep before waking for breakfast at nine.

When the episode resumes, I see a photo of a very handsome young man with thick eyebrows and hazel eyes. His mouth forms more of a smirk than a smile, reminding me of a guy from high school that every girl had a crush on, but only the most popular girls had any chance of claiming as their boyfriend. His thick brown hair is cut low on the sides, and the top is gelled and brushed back, giving Justin Bieber vibes—a very common hairstyle in the mid-2010s. He's wearing a light pink Polo shirt, and the picture appears to be cropped and taken outdoors somewhere with water and boats in the background.

The narrator introduces the man with the model-good looks as Noah Andrews, who had recently graduated from Hoskins University with a degree in architecture—just like Olivia. The photo changes to one of a smiling Noah embracing a woman with long blond hair, whose face has been pixilated to hide her identity. She has her left hand resting on Noah's bicep, flaunting a solitaire diamond ring. I quickly learn that she was Noah's fiancé, to whom he proposed in the spring of the same year.

Anaya then tells the off-screen interviewer she remembers being excited for Olivia and took a picture of her dancing with Noah on her phone. I see a photo showing the back of Olivia with her legs slightly bent, her hip tilted, and both arms straight in the air with a plastic cup in her hand. Noah is facing her, towering over the petite woman. He's looking down at her with the same smirk on his face as I saw in the original photo. It's not obvious that he's dancing, but it appears to me that he's having a good time.

Erin continues the story by saying she recognized Noah from their university but didn't know much about him—only his first name. She says she found it odd that he happened to be in New Orleans the same weekend. But before she had time to process that, Noah and Olivia walked towards the bar, presumably to get more drinks. Erin admits that she wanted to follow them but didn't want to ruin the night for Olivia, since she was finally enjoying herself. Erin looks down at her clasped hands in her lap and says in a shaky voice that it was the last time she had ever seen Olivia.

I feel a tinge of sympathy for Erin, remembering how my friends and I made a pact to never accept drinks from strangers when we go out and to never leave our drinks unattended. You don't have to be a crime junkie to know a story or two about someone being drugged and unspeakable things happening to them while they are unconscious.

Amanda adds that once Erin told her the guy's name was Noah, she thought he may have been the "N" whose calls Olivia had been avoiding. She also wondered if Olivia knew he was in New Orleans and was the reason she was acting so jumpy.

An older, round-faced man with tan skin appears on the screen with a full head of salt and pepper hair and Tom Selleck mustache. He's sitting in an empty, dimly lit room. His eyes are a dark, almost-black shade of brown, and he's wearing a light blue collared shirt with the top button unbuttoned. The show identifies him as retired NOPD Detective Donald Wiley, who informs us in a deep and raspy smoker's voice that upon receiving the missing persons report, he requested all CCTV footage from the bar.

The screen changes to a low-quality, black and white video taken from over the left side of the bar, angled down. At the top of the screen is the date and a running time of the recording. There is no audio, but I can see the bartender making drinks and patrons either waiting for him or simply standing against the bar. The voice of Detective Wiley guides us through the video, pointing out when Olivia and Noah approach the bar.

I follow the video as Olivia unsuccessfully attempts to get the bartender's attention twice from the left side of the bar, with Noah standing behind her. They move to the right side of the bar, where the view is partially cut off. I can see Olivia's hands and forearms resting on the bar and the top of her head as she leans forward to get the bartender's attention. Once she talks to the bartender and leans back, only her hands and forearms are visible.

After about ten seconds of seeing only Olivia's forearms, a hand suddenly comes out of nowhere from her right side and snatches both of her wrists off the bar. It happens in the blink of an eye, and I let out an audible gasp when I see it—mostly because of the sound of screeching violins added by the show for effect. I see a replay of the video and then two more replays in slow motion.

The show returns to Detective Wiley, and he matter-of-factly states that this is the last visual evidence they have of Olivia being in the Sinful Spirits Bar and the last time she was ever seen.

I press pause as I try to collect my thoughts about what I just watched. My mind spins as it attempts to come up with different scenarios that could explain what happened at that moment.

Did Noah grab Olivia and have an intimate moment with her out of the view of the camera, and then they left together? Maybe.

Did one of her friends grab her to stop her from getting another drink? No, that doesn't make sense.

Or is there a chance that it was a complete stranger? Possibly.

The room feels warmer as my anxiety level rises, and I remove both of my legs from under the comforter to help me cool down. I eagerly tap play again, desperate for more information.

There's another CCTV video taken above the entry to the bar. Detective Wiley explains that they reviewed video of the entire evening to determine the exact time each person who entered the bar arrived and confirm the time they left. He explains that they have footage of the front entry and the rear service entry, both with date and time stamps. I watch the black and white video showing Olivia and the rest of the bridal party arriving shortly after eleven-thirty. All five of them are laughing and stumbling a bit as they hand the bouncer their IDs. The video speeds through the next twenty minutes, then slows back down to regular speed. Detective Wiley points out Noah and two friends entering the bar.

Next, there is a video taken at twelve-forty-five showing Noah and his friends casually leaving the bar, followed by time-lapsed video. It slows back down to regular speed and shows Anaya, Jennifer, Amanda, and Erin leaving a little after one-thirty. Erin hesitates and looks back into the bar, but Amanda takes her hand and pulls her away. It appears to me that Erin doesn't want to go, presumably not wanting to leave the last place she saw her friend.

A solemn Erin explains that they looked everywhere in the bar once they realized they couldn't find Olivia. She says that Amanda suggested calling Olivia's phone, which Erin knew wouldn't do any good, since Olivia left her phone in Austin. But that's when Amanda told her about the phone she saw and the mysterious "N" caller.

After checking the restrooms, they searched for Noah and his friends and couldn't find them either. Erin says she started to panic, worried that the guys took advantage of Olivia's small size and impaired state. She asked the bouncer at the door if he saw Olivia leave with anyone. He said he didn't remember seeing her leave, but instructed another bouncer to take them to the back of the bar to see if she was out back near the service entrance. After making their way through the crowd of dancing people, they all exited the back door and stepped into the moonlit alleyway. But they found nothing but a large dumpster and some construction debris.

Jennifer remembers seeing a door near the restrooms with a yellow and black sign that warned it was a construction zone. She asked the bouncer if Olivia could have gone through that door. He said they always kept all doors to that area locked, but to put their minds at ease, he took them over to verify. To his surprise, the door was unlocked. He opened the door, and they all peered inside the room.

Detective Wiley shares that the owner of the Sinful Souls Bar had recently purchased the space next door and was converting it to become a room with a stage and seating, with plans to offer live entertainment. I see a slideshow of three photos depicting the different stages of demolition it had undergone by that time.

Anaya says the room was completely dark, but they could make out the construction by the light from the bar shining through the open door. She asked if they could go inside, but the bouncer insisted they couldn't because he could get fired and suggested they call the police.

Amanda called 9-1-1 and requested help to find their friend who disappeared from a bar. About five minutes later, a police officer arrived, and they explained the situation. He asked to see a recent photo of Olivia, and Anaya showed him photos from her phone. The four worried women followed him back inside, where he asked them to stay near the entrance while he searched for any sign of Olivia.

They watched the officer slowly make his way through the crowd, scanning the faces of people on the dance floor and at the bar. He disappeared to the back, presumably to check the service entrance, and reappeared shortly thereafter. After inspecting both the women's and men's restrooms, he had the same bouncer take him to the construction site door. The officer entered the room using his flashlight. Light suddenly filled the doorway, indicating that he located a light switch, and he briefly searched the area. He eventually returned to the bar entrance and told them that it didn't appear that Olivia was there. He predicted that she would probably show up in the morning, since it was most likely that she left with the guy she was last seen with.

The camera returns to Erin, who dabs her tear-stained cheeks with a balled-up tissue. She says that she didn't want to leave the bar, but they all agreed it would be best to go back to their rooms and wait for Olivia to show up. She thought about calling Olivia's parents, but she didn't want to worry them or embarrass Olivia if she truly *had* left to hook up with Noah. But when she didn't show up the next morning, Erin made the call.

I see Kirk and Sheila Peterson again, and they both look more somber than when I saw them earlier in the episode. Kirk recounts calling the New Orleans Police Department to report Olivia missing immediately after hearing from Erin. I'm annoyed, but not surprised, to learn that Olivia's parents were told they had to wait twenty-four hours before reporting an adult missing. I've heard many stories about authorities shrugging off loved ones who call in about a missing family member. Police usually say that an adult has every right to disappear if they want, and they can only be reported missing after an allotted amount of time. So, they got on the next flight to New Orleans to search for Olivia themselves.

Olivia's family scoured the area around the bar. When they checked the alleyway, all they saw was construction debris and the dumpster. Kirk says he peeked into the dumpster, but he only saw a bunch of wood and trash. They walked around the French Quarter that entire Sunday showing everyone they passed a photo of Olivia, asking if the person had seen her.

That night, Kirk and Sheila went to the Sinful Spirits Bar and questioned patrons and employees until a bouncer told them they needed to leave. They filed the missing persons report first thing Monday morning and continued searching throughout the day.

Detective Wiley returns to the screen and says that he received notification about the missing persons report around nine o'clock Monday morning. He immediately got to work locating the contact information for the owner of the Sinful Spirits Bar. He explains that he and his partner met with the owner at the bar around ten-thirty. They gathered as much information as they could about the bar employees who were working Saturday night and information on the companies doing construction in the space next door. While the owner worked on getting them copies of the CCTV footage from that evening, the detectives did a thorough search of the bar and the construction site next door.

During the inspection, they found no evidence of a violent altercation or that Olivia was being held anywhere in the bar. The construction area took more time to inspect, since there were tools, wood, and debris strewn everywhere; but they didn't find blood or anything else to indicate that it was the scene of a crime. They also checked the small alleyway behind the bar and found it empty, despite the reports of seeing construction debris and a dumpster the night Olivia disappeared. When asked, the bar owner explained that the construction dumpster was removed every Monday morning at eight and a new one was returned by noon.

Detective Wiley felt confident that Olivia had disappeared by choice, since there was no evidence of any crime taking place on the premises. While his partner began gathering surveillance videos and scheduling potential witness interviews, Detective Wiley met with Erin, Amanda, Anaya, and Jennifer individually to get audio recordings of their statements.

Within a couple of hours, the detectives had reviewed the video footage from the bar showing Noah and Olivia together and determined that they needed to find Noah to get a statement. Detective Wiley did a Google search for the keywords *Hoskins University*, *Noah*, and *Class of 2014*. He found the name Noah Andrews on the school's baseball roster. Another quick search resulted in a Facebook page with a profile photo and bio that positively identified Noah. As Detective Wiley scrolled down the Facebook profile, he saw a photo of Noah and two other young men smiling and holding up shot glasses. Someone had tagged him in the photo at the Maison Creole Hotel the day before.

After getting confirmation that Noah was still a guest at that hotel, Detective Wiley and his partner knocked on a hotel room door and were greeted by a groggy Noah. They identified themselves as detectives and asked if he could answer a few questions about a missing woman. Noah looked perplexed, but invited them in without requesting further details.

He asked Noah if he knew Olivia Peterson, and Noah responded by saying that he knew her from school, and they were working on a project together for a summer internship. When asked if he had any other relationship with Olivia, Noah denied he had ever seen her outside of those two scenarios. But just when the detectives thought they caught him in a lie, he suddenly remembered seeing her Saturday night at a bar in the French Quarter.

Detective Wiley informed Noah that Olivia's family reported her missing, and he was the last person she was seen with, which visibly shook Noah. They asked him if he would come with them to the precinct to answer some questions about that night and make a formal statement, which he agreed to do.

I see a surveillance video looking down into in a small, brightly lit room furnished with only three chairs. Noah is sitting in a chair in the corner of the room, crouched over, with his forearms resting on his knees. His hair appears disheveled, and he's wearing a light-colored hoodie, shorts and casual flip flops, depicting someone who arrived shortly after waking up. Detective Wiley and his partner join Noah in the room and sit down in chairs opposite him. Detective Wiley moves his chair in closer to Noah and asks him to recount his movements on Saturday evening.

In the video, Noah says he and his friends, Dave and Charlie, had been out barhopping on Bourbon Street that evening, starting around nine P.M., and they stopped at the Sinful Spirits Bar because Charlie saw a girl walk in that he wanted to meet. They had only been there for a few minutes when Olivia approached him with a drink in her hand and started dancing. He says he could tell she was drunk, which surprised him because he only knew her as a quiet, nerdy girl from school and the intern program. He recalls seeing her friends watching them and feeling very awkward; but he didn't want to embarrass Olivia, so he danced with her. He remembers noticing her eyes looking glazed and suggesting they go get some water to help sober her up. It took a while to get the bartender's attention, but she eventually ordered herself some water. The restrooms were right behind them, so he used that as an excuse to get out of the awkward situation. He found Dave and Charlie, and they all left immediately after that.

Detective Wiley leans forward to get himself closer to Noah—an intimidation technique I've seen many detectives use in interrogation videos. He asks Noah why he and his friends were in New Orleans that weekend, and Noah responds by saying they went at the last minute to celebrate Dave's birthday. They flew in on Saturday morning and were supposed to leave early Monday evening.

After a slight pause, unmoving, Detective Wiley asks Noah if he knew Olivia was going to be in New Orleans that weekend. Noah says he had no clue and that he knew nothing about Olivia, aside from basic things he learned during icebreaker events for the internship. When asked what he thought about Olivia, he responds by saying she was a cute girl who was really smart and admits that he saw her as his biggest competition for a chance at landing a job at the architecture firm they were interning for.

This makes Detective Wiley recline back in his chair and take another dramatic pause. I can tell that Noah is getting very uncomfortable at this point, because he sits up straight. Detective Wiley inquires about any potential romantic interest in Olivia. Noah replies emphatically that he has no interest in her and says that he's engaged to get married next spring.

When asked if he left the bar at any time with Olivia, Noah responds with a simple, "*No, sir.*" Then Detective Wiley asks him if he caused any harm to Olivia, and Noah is silent. He looks at both detectives and sits back in his chair, seeming to realize the gravity of the situation. He crosses his arms over his chest and says that he won't answer any further questions without a lawyer.

I don't know what to think. If Noah did anything to Olivia and took her from the bar, one of the CCTV videos would have shown that. But at the same time, if *anyone* took her from the bar, the videos would have shown that, too. I can't help but to conclude that the only person who could have possibly done something to Olivia would have been Noah. But when? Why? And how?

After taking much more time than the forty minutes I've spent investigating the case, the detectives appear to have come to the same conclusion. The rest of the episode shows Detective Wiley explaining that, after a thorough search of the bar and construction area next door, there were no signs of Olivia. They interviewed bar employees, construction workers and some of the patrons they were able to track down from their credit card transactions. They were all excluded as suspects or witnesses who knew anything about Olivia's disappearance. No one recalled seeing anything suspicious happen that night. The detectives accounted for every face that entered the bar throughout that day and confirmed that they saw them exiting at some point that evening or the early morning after. Every face—except Olivia's.

Detective Wiley reports that, after reviewing cell phone records and emails, they uncovered no communication between Noah and Olivia prior to her disappearance outside of group emails regarding the architecture project. He interviewed Noah's friends, Dave and Charlie, and they both said that the trip was Dave's idea, insisting that Noah had no intentions of seeing anyone in New Orleans, let alone Olivia. Their hotel key card records show that they each entered their individual hotel rooms at approximately the same time, around one-thirty A.M., and they didn't use their key cards again until late the next morning.

The detectives continued to keep track of Olivia's bank records, and there had been no transactions on her debit card since her disappearance. After examining her cell phone records going back six months, detectives concluded that most of her calls and texts were to and from her close friends and family. But without the phone Amanda saw in their room, there was no way to identify the mysterious "N" caller.

The last thing Detective Wiley recounts is flying to Austin to interview more of Olivia's friends. No one could recall anything suspicious about her behavior prior to the trip. She didn't appear to have any problems with anyone, and there was no reason for someone to want to cause her harm. When he questioned Olivia's professor and intern colleagues about her interactions with Noah Andrews, everyone said Olivia and Noah appeared to have a standard working relationship and were surprised to hear that he was a person of interest. They also knew nothing about an extra phone she would have used to communicate with them, leading investigators to believe Olivia was keeping secrets from her friends and loved ones.

The episode concludes, alternating between Olivia's friends tearfully expressing their *shoulda, coulda, woulda's* about that last evening with her. Erin recounts how hard it was to go through with the wedding without Olivia, while a photo appears on the screen showing a place set at the reception table for her. There is one lit votive candle set in front of her bridesmaid bouquet.

Olivia's parents try to remain stoic. They share what they miss about their daughter and the bright future that was taken away from her. The off-camera interviewer asks what they think happened to her. Kirk looks at Sheila, whose head drops to hide her emerging tears. He says they believe Olivia is no longer with them, as there is no way that she would leave her family like this. Then he asks the interviewer why

Olivia would leave with so much of life ahead of her. It's a rhetorical question that would never have an answer. Kirk puts his arm around his wife, who looks up with bloodshot, tear-soaked eyes behind her glasses and sobs that they just miss their baby.

Detective Wiley appears back on the screen. He's asked the same question, and he responds by saying that there's always a chance that Olivia left on her own volition; but since she was last seen very intoxicated, he doesn't believe she was in a state of mind to pull off a Houdini-type disappearance. He states that her bank account has remained untouched, and her social security number has never been used. The only person of interest they've had in this case was Noah Andrews, but there has been little to no evidence to convince a judge to issue a warrant of any kind. He doesn't believe that Noah could keep this big of a secret all this time without help, so someone out there has to know what happened. He's just waiting for that person to relieve themselves of the burden of that secret and come forward.

The final scene of the show is a photo of Olivia in her navy blue college cap and gown, smiling, with a bouquet of colorful flowers in her arms. A message fades in across the screen with a plea for anyone with information to contact the New Orleans Police Department, along with their tip hotline number. It then adds that Noah Andrews never responded to requests to be a part of the episode and has refused further interviews with the police and media, upon the advice of his attorney.

I turn off my phone and plug it into the charger on the nightstand. I spend the rest of the evening thinking about what I've learned about a bright young woman named Olivia Peterson. Questions stack up in my mind with no definitive answers:

Who could have done this?

It had to have been Noah, right? But why?

How did he get her out of that bar? And when?

Why won't Noah talk to the police to clear his name?

What about his friends? Could they have helped him cover something up?

Was it just a coincidence Olivia and Noah were in New Orleans on the same weekend?

Was Noah is the mysterious "N" caller?

Were they planning to meet up?

Did Noah commit the perfect crime?

Why was that door to the construction area unlocked?

Was a killer lurking there, waiting for a victim?

Could Olivia have planned to disappear?

Her friends all said she was acting weird. Was she depressed?

Suicidal?

Or was Olivia just stressed?

How could there be no trace of her whatsoever and no witnesses or evidence to explain what happened to her?

How does someone vanish off the face of the earth?

The questions are never-ending. But at some point, my mind settles and allows me to doze off into a world where there is no concern about a man named Noah Andrews.

Chapter 9

It's seven-thirty when Camille wakes up and notices that Mom and I are still asleep. She reaches over to her nightstand, intending to doom scroll Instagram reels, but she suddenly remembers the secret notebook in the nightstand drawer. Quietly, she opens the drawer and retrieves the books. The slits of daylight shining through the closed blinds don't provide enough light to see the pages, so she unplugs her phone and turns the flashlight on to the dimmest setting. Camille settles back into her reading position and places her phone on her chest so the light shines onto the pages.

***

I feel so stupid. I've had the weekend to think about everything, and I've decided that I need to let go of this dumb fantasy. I know that he's not single, so why would I even entertain this? I checked his Facebook page, and my heart dropped when I saw that his profile pic is with HER! So, I immediately closed it, already feeling a bit heartbroken. I need to get a grip. If he tries to flirt again, I'm going to ignore him. We have a long summer ahead of us, and the last thing I need is this kind of drama. No more distractions.

***

"*Boo!*" Camille whispers. She is already invested in this budding romance and is disappointed that it might already be coming to an end. After flipping through several more pages of sketches and diagrams, hoping to see more journal entries, she muffles her squeal of excitement when she finds one.

***

Why am I like this? I tried to ignore him. I wouldn't even look at him, which was hard because we work so close together. And I limited any conversation I had with him to professional topics. It worked for a couple of days, but now it seems like that only made him try even harder. Somehow, the two of us were the last to leave the boardroom after our Thursday meeting. He grabbed my hand as I was walking out and pulled me back into the room. He asked me why I was ignoring him, but I wasn't sure what to tell him. I decided honesty would be best. So, I told him that I was really starting to like him, but I knew he wasn't single, and I didn't want to get hurt. He told me that things aren't what they seem and asked me to meet him for coffee after work so he could explain. For some reason, looking into his pleading eyes made me lose my head again... and I said yes.

He was already sitting on one of the small sofas when I got there. He didn't have a cup of coffee, so I didn't order one either. I sat next to him,

94

and he grabbed my hand. At first, he didn't say anything, but then he explained that he wasn't really in love with her. They had been together since their sophomore year of high school, and everyone always expected them to get married after college. Since he didn't want to disappoint everyone, he just went along with it. He told me that she doesn't treat him well, and he recently started thinking about ending things.

But then he said what I secretly hoped he would. He told me that I have made him realize what he does want. He likes that I'm so down to earth and smart and that he can talk to me about architecture. And then he said it... He said he could see himself falling in love with me!

We sat and talked for a couple of hours, still with no coffee, getting to know each other better. It was like no one else existed. He walked me out—

***

"Good morning!" Mom whispers, startling Camille. She quietly shuffles into the bathroom without another word while Camille continues reading.

***

He walked me out to my car, holding my hand. And this time... he kissed me! It was everything I'd hoped it would be. I've spent the past hour at home trying to focus on anything other than him, but that's proving to be impossible. This is real. I can't believe it! I just wish I could tell someone.

***

Camille is torn. On one hand, she's excited to get a peek into a new romance, remembering how magical everything feels in the beginning. But on the other hand, rom-coms and reality shows have taught her that love triangles like this typically end in disappointment and heartbreak for *someone*. She hears the toilet flush and closes the notebook and decoy book, returning them to the nightstand drawer. Breakfast is at nine, so she will need to get ready soon.

Chapter 10

I feel a gentle nudge on my arm, and a few seconds later, a more aggressive shake. I slowly open my eyes. When the room comes into focus, I see Camille sitting next to me on the edge of the bed with her face only a few feet away from mine.

"Finally!" Camille sighs as she stands up. "We've been trying to wake you for almost an hour now." She reaches down to my ear and pulls out an earbud. "I found the other one on the floor."

I take the earbud from her and look around the room after briefly forgetting that I'm not in Virginia. Camille is fully dressed, wearing khaki shorts and a white and gold striped tank top.

Mom steps out of the bathroom, completing the long braid swept over her shoulder. She's also already dressed in an eggshell linen, loose-fitting tank and matching capris. "Good morning, sleepyhead!" she says cheerfully. "Breakfast is in fifteen minutes, so you might want to get dressed."

I pick up my phone to confirm the time. "Wow! I can't believe I slept in this late."

"It's no surprise, considering how busy you've been at work and all the walking we did yesterday." Mom steps into her sandals. "You deserve to get some good rest."

I sit up and gently rub my eyes to remove bits of crust.

Camille stands next to the bed, looking at me. "So, are you going to get up and do something with yourself?"

I remove the bedding and slowly swing my legs over the side of the bed. "I'll just wash my face and brush my teeth real quick. No one will care what I look like at breakfast."

"So much for taking cute breakfast pics," Camille mumbles under her breath.

I glare at her and then roll my eyes as I lift myself off the bed and shuffle into the bathroom.

When I splash the water on my face, Olivia's sweet smile suddenly flashes before me. I'm jolted into the memory of her mysterious disappearance I learned about last night. I want to share all the details with my mom and sister but decide not to press my luck with Camille, since we still have the cemetery tour today. I brush my teeth and step back into the room and search for my flip-flops.

Camille looks at me in disgust. "Please do us all a favor and take that *thing* off your head, too."

I slip off the bonnet and toss it to Camille, causing her to jerk her shoulder back and dodge it like it's a moldy sponge. I shake out my hair. "Okay, I'm ready."

We can smell breakfast cooking halfway down the stairs. As we enter the dining room, I notice that each table already has full place settings, with a few guests at their tables talking quietly. I locate a table in the front corner of the room with my name on a place card.

The first several times I stayed here, the dining room contained one long table, and all guests ate together. In fact, my friend Ashley and

I once reenacted the Easter dinner scene from *The Color Purple* one morning before the other guests arrived, giving Maggie and Pat a good laugh. But in 2020, they changed the furnishings to several smaller tables to accommodate Covid-19 social distancing requirements.

I sit down across from Mom and Camille at our assigned table, facing the other tables in the room. "So, did y'all sleep well?"

"I certainly did," Mom says. "Probably the best night's sleep I've had since I started menopause!"

Camille and I look at each other and then at Mom. "TMI," we say in unison, which makes Mom chuckle.

"How about you?" she asks.

I open my mouth to respond, but I'm interrupted by a singsong greeting from Maggie. "Good morning, everyone!" She walks toward us carrying a tray of glasses filled with parfaits and a pitcher of water.

"Good morning," we say in unison.

Maggie places a parfait in front of each of us and fills our glasses with water. "We have your favorite this morning, Camryn. Andouille sausage and potatoes!"

I wiggle in my seat and shimmy my shoulders. "Oh, y'all are going to love this! All the breakfasts are amazing, but this one is the best! I think I had three servings the first time I stayed here."

"Um," Mom raises her hand slightly. "I can't eat sausage."

"No worries at all, Mrs. Alexander." Maggie places her hand on Mom's shoulder. "I've prepared some with no sausage and no eggs just for you. But I promise you'll still enjoy the potatoes, onions and peppers and all the creole spices!"

Mom puts her hand on top of Maggie's and looks up at her sweetly. "Please call me Ann Marie. And thank you so much!"

"Of course, I'll take good care of you," Maggie assures her. "What can I get for you to drink?"

Camille abruptly answers for all of us. "A hot tea for Mom and two orange juices for us." In all our years of traveling together, we've always had the same drink order for every breakfast, every time.

"Sure, *bay-beh*." Maggie turns to give the other guests their parfaits and water. A few minutes later, she disappears into the hallway, and I hear her voice again in the distance. *"Good morning! I'll be right in there."*

I glance up and feel my breath escape me.

A man enters the room and stops to look for his table. He's tall with auburn red hair and a well-groomed beard. I give him a brief scan and appreciate his casual style—a white v-neck tee and khaki shorts with white Nikes. I follow his blue eyes as he locates his table directly in front of ours. He pulls his phone out of his pocket and sits down at the table, facing me. I have the perfect view of the beautiful man when I peer between Mom and Camille, and I quickly determine that he's an even more handsome version of Prince Harry, whom I've had a huge intercontinental crush on for years.

"Earth to Camryn!" Camille taps her water glass with a fork. I'm jolted out of my stupor and realize that I'm blushing. She turns around in her seat to see what has me so flustered, then slowly turns back around and sits back. "Mm, hmm."

Mom glances back and then nudges Camille. "Oh, stop. Leave her alone." She looks at me and winks.

"Seriously," I whisper. "His wife will probably be here any minute."

"I didn't see a wedding band," Camille says, a little too loudly.

I shush her and whisper a bit more aggressively. "How do you know? You only looked for a second."

She shrugs. "I'm just that good."

I roll my eyes. "Whatever. Then I'm sure his *girlfriend* is coming."

"We'll see." She raises one eyebrow and smirks.

I glance at him again. He's still focused on his phone, completely oblivious to us gawking at him—or at least pretending to be. I search desperately for something to change the subject.

"So, I did a little research on that missing woman from last night."

"I figured that's what you were doing," Mom says just before she takes a sip of water. "I woke up for a second and saw you on your phone."

I smile sympathetically, remembering her telling me about the night sweats she's been experiencing over the past several years.

Maggie should return with our food soon, so I give them a brief summary of the story. "Her name is Olivia Peterson. She went to that bar from the end of our tour with her friends on their last night in New Orleans. They were all really drunk. She ran into a guy she knew from school and was last seen with him at the bar getting another drink. Her friends soon noticed that both of them were gone. But Olivia didn't bring her cell phone, so they had no way of getting in touch with her. They searched all over the bar and the place next door that was under construction, and there was still no sign of her. They went back to their hotel, hoping Olivia left to hook up with that guy—I think his name was Noah—and would show up by the next morning. But as we know, she never did. The police got involved and talked to Noah, but he swore that he left the bar with his friends right after Olivia ordered herself some water."

Camille looks skeptical. "I still don't understand how someone can just disappear. She had to have left with someone."

I shake my head. "There was video footage from both entries at the front and the back of the bar. They saw when every person there that night arrived and when they left, including Noah and his friends. The only person they didn't see leaving was Olivia."

"Maybe something happened to her there, and someone snuck her out after everyone left," Mom suggests.

"I don't think so. The police scoured both videos that went into the next day, and they searched the bar and the space next door that same night. If she were there, I think they would have seen her."

Maggie and Pat enter the room with trays full of food and drinks. Maggie places our steaming dishes on our table and then walks over to place a parfait down in front of the beautiful stranger. I notice she didn't bring anything for a second person, which makes me smirk.

Mom and Camille take their first bites of food, followed by a round of boisterous noises showing their satisfaction. I decide to redirect my energy to enjoying my meal as well.

After a couple of minutes, Camille chimes back in. "I don't think she just disappeared. She left with *somebody*."

"Or maybe she left on her own and ran into some trouble out on the streets," Mom adds.

I shrug. "Honestly, we could come up with a million scenarios. But the fact of the matter is, if Olivia left at any point, it would have shown up on one of the videos."

Camille places her fork on the plate and looks away in deep thought, resting her chin on her fist. "I've heard about people who make elaborate plans to run away and change their identities to start whole new lives. Maybe she had someone there that helped her do that, and she's alive and well in Mexico." She squints her eyes. "Or maybe someone killed her, and she's buried under the floors or in the walls."

I take another bite of potatoes as Maggie returns with a plate of food for the gorgeous man. I'm about to swallow when he suddenly stands, scraping his chair on the wood floor. He snatches his phone from the table and glares at us.

"You know," he says in a booming voice, with his crystal blue eyes piercing daggers into mine. "You really shouldn't talk about things you don't understand." He storms past Maggie and disappears into the hallway.

I still haven't swallowed my food, and I feel my body temperature rising. I'm equal parts confused and embarrassed, as everyone in the room stares at us.

After watching him leave, Maggie walks over to our table and sits in the empty chair next to me. "I couldn't help but overhear your conversation. And that," she points to the hallway, "is that poor girl's brother."

I put my face in my hands in total disbelief. Then I remember the old family photos showing an older brother with red hair, just like their mother's.

"Why is he here?" Camille asks.

Maggie settles into the chair and leans her elbows onto the table, speaking quietly. "That girl and her friends were staying here when that happened. In fact, she stayed in your room. That was the year before Pat and I took over. It was part of the reason the last owner wanted to wash her hands of the business. The police were always in and out, and the business suffered."

We look at her intently with curiosity, so she continues. "His name is Eric, and he stays here every year on the anniversary of when she went missing."

Mom nods. "I remember the guide last night mentioning a vigil for her on Monday. It's been ten years, right?"

"Oh, that's right," I recollect. "God, I feel awful. I had no idea."

"How could you know?" Maggie says, comforting me with a light tap on my arm. She stands and picks up the tray from Eric's table. "He'll be fine. Don't let it ruin your day."

At this point, we've all lost our appetites and place our napkins on our plates.

"Well, I guess we should get our day started," Mom says, attempting to salvage the fun spirit of our trip.

We make the trek back upstairs to our room. I sit down on the bed, still trying to wrap my brain around the fact that we are staying in the same bed and breakfast that a missing woman was staying in before she disappeared. *And* I had just pissed off her grieving brother—her sexy grieving brother, at that.

I look up and see Camille and Mom sitting on her bed, staring at me. "What?"

"We're just waiting for you." Camille's eyes scan me up and down.

I look down at my vintage Wonder Woman shirt and faded red cutoff shorts and realize that I just made a total fool of myself in front of everyone in the house, including the most handsome man I've seen in years, while wearing my pajamas! I drag myself into the bathroom and turn on the shower to the hottest temperature my skin can tolerate, hoping I can steam away the humiliating events of the past ten minutes.

***

I spend more time getting ready than usual, now painfully aware that presenting myself as anything less than a seven for the rest of the trip is no longer an option. I opt for a cute navy mini-sundress with a sunflower print and my go-to strappy sandals—this time with gold straps. I pull my hair up into a bun with only my bangs hanging loose. After second-guessing myself, I choose to accent my outfit with some gold polymer clay hoop earrings I purchased from a woman I found on Instagram who makes handmade jewelry.

Once my look is complete, I step out of the bathroom to find Mom and Camille taking a selfie with the large fleur-de-lis on the wall in the background. Camille is wearing her tiara and sash, still hoping for the special treatment she received in Vegas during her bachelorette party. She looks over at me and gives a wolf whistle.

"Well, don't you look cute?" she teases.

I walk by them without making eye contact and reply with a quick, "Thanks." I locate my phone and keys on the nightstand and slip them into my crossbody purse. "Y'all ready?"

"More than ready," Mom says before Camille has a chance to respond with a sarcastic remark.

"You might want to bring a hat or something," I suggest. "There is no shade in the cemetery, and the heat can get pretty intense with the sun reflecting off the white crypts."

Camille searches her suitcase for a small pink and green umbrella and hangs it by the strap on her arm. "We can all fit under this."

With sunglasses in-hand, we quickly make our way downstairs and across the street, just as the streetcar is pulling up. I hope that it's a sign that the rest of the day is going to be better than how it began. Camille stops us to take a group selfie as we're stepping onto the streetcar, much to the annoyance of the streetcar conductor. It's Saturday morning, and there is only one small bench available in the back of the packed streetcar. Camille slides in first and then Mom. I stand next to them, holding onto the overhead rail.

After numerous stops and a slight delay when a car making a U-turn stopped on the track, we get off at the stop between Bourbon Street and Royal Street. We cross Canal Street, and I give Mom and Camille a minute to peer down Bourbon Street. There are plenty of people roaming around, some already enjoying a morning alcoholic beverage.

We are supposed to meet our tour guide at eleven A.M. on the steps of the Louisiana Supreme Court building on Royal Street. I check my smartwatch, and it's ten thirty-five, leaving time for us to potentially make a couple of stops along the way that I know Camille and Mom will enjoy.

As we stroll down Royal Street, we make our first stop at the Magnolia Sugar and Spice Praline Kitchen and Hot Sauce Bar. Upon entering, we watch a man actively folding a brown, taffy-looking substance. There's a tray in front of the sneeze guard with samples of their famous pecan pralines. We each take one and let it melt in our mouths. They are the best pralines I've ever tasted, and I usually leave New Orleans with a box to take home and savor for several days.

I guide Camille and Mom through the rest of the store, where we see hundreds of bottles of hot sauces and other seasonings. There is an island in the center of the room with hot sauce samples. We choose not to try any but enjoy reading the clever, yet disgusting names, like Devil's Discharge and Anal Angst. I laugh so hard that I cry every time Mom or Camille yells out the name of another one.

After we exit the store, we walk further down Royal Street, and just before we reach our destination, I see one of my favorite places to stop for a treat—Café Beignet. Most people make a big deal about Café DuMonde and their beignets, since it's so famous. But I've only eaten there twice because the line is always so long. Café Beignet occasionally has a long line, but it's never *too* long. I cross my fingers, hoping we'll have time to stop and treat ourselves. As we approach the small cafe, I notice the tables outside are all occupied, dashing my hopes; but then I'm pleasantly surprised to find that there are only a handful of people in line.

"Do you want to try a beignet?" I ask with an expectant grin.

"Yes!" Mom and Camille say in unison.

In less than five minutes, we are back outside with a bag of warm beignets and three cold bottles of water. We make the short walk to the Supreme Court building and set up a small picnic on a shaded area of the steps, spreading napkins across our laps to catch the powdered sugar that will inevitably fall off. After the first couple of bites, we take turns snapping photos of each other taking ridiculously large bites, leaving bits of powdered sugar around our mouths and on the tips of our noses.

Before we're finished, we hear a loud voice yelling over the street noise. "If you're here for the cemetery tour, please see me to check in!"

I glance over and see a short woman with weathered skin and obviously dyed burgundy hair under a black top hat covered with plastic skulls and spiderwebs. She's wearing the familiar black t-shirt with *GHOST TOURS* in white writing. I immediately recognize her as the guide for one of the cemetery tours I attended before. I approach her and give her my name.

"Camryn Alexander? Ah, I have you down here with two guests."

"Yes, ma'am." The pin on her shirt reminds me that her name is Maureen. "I remember you from a tour I did a few years back. You're still out here giving tours in this heat?"

Maureen shuffles through a pack of black and white stickers and hands me three. "Honey, I'm too broke to quit, too young to retire, and too old to strip!" She doesn't smile but squints her eyes in a friendly gesture. I believe Tyra Banks called it *smeyes-ing*—smiling with your eyes.

Her response gives me a good laugh, and I go back to Mom and Camille, who are shoving their napkins into the empty paper bag and wiping powdered sugar off their clothes. "I've had this tour guide before. She's a hoot!" I glance back at Maureen, and it occurs to me that she seems familiar for some other reason that I can't quite put my finger on.

Camille takes a long drink of her water, emptying the bottle. She wipes her mouth with a fingertip and opens her umbrella. "Let's get this over with."

Chapter 11

The tour begins just as I remember, with Maureen giving us a quick lesson on the history of shotgun houses and the Romeo spikes on poles underneath balconies as we walk down St. Louis Street. Mom points out signs hanging from the balconies of condos for sale or rent that say *Haunted* or *Not Haunted,* resulting in a quick *"Nope!"* from Camille each time.

We cross an intersection, and I notice a window with a familiar name—NOLA Coffee Bistro. It occurs to me that it is the same coffee shop where they interviewed the owner about Olivia on the episode of *Disappearances!* I peer through the window as we walk by, and I'm surprised to recognize the owner behind the counter. I make a mental note of where we are, determined to return to the coffee shop at some point during our trip.

Our group of less than twenty makes its way across Rampart Street and approaches the entry to St. Louis Cemetery Number One. A white concrete wall surrounds the cemetery and takes up the entire block. Maureen stops at a black iron gate and informs us about the rules of etiquette when touring this ancient cemetery, explaining that access has been tightly restricted in recent years because of an increase in vandalism. These days, only tour companies and families who own tombs have access. After completing her spiel, Maureen unlocks the gate and holds it open as we all enter, closing and locking it behind us.

Camille hands her umbrella to Mom to hold over the both of them, and they link arms. I can't see her eyes behind her oversized Michael Kors tortoise shell sunglasses, but it's obvious that she's very nervous—as if a disembodied spirit is going to jump out from behind a tomb at any moment.

Maureen begins by sharing the history of the cemetery, dating back to 1789. She explains that it is currently owned by the Roman Catholic Archdiocese of New Orleans, and only those approved by them can be laid to rest there. At times, she quizzes us on our knowledge of New Orleans interment traditions. I remain quiet, since I've attended this tour several times in the past and know most of the answers. Maureen informs us about how dozens of bodies can fit in tombs that look like they could hold only a few. As I'd hoped, every once in a while, she throws in something that I hadn't heard on previous tours.

We've been inside the cemetery for only fifteen minutes when the heat begins to take its toll, and I'm glad that I didn't finish my bottle of water while we were enjoying our beignets. I take a long, refreshing swig as we turn the corner and see a familiar tomb—a large white pyramid-shaped mausoleum with the words *OMNIA AB UNO* printed on the front. Maureen translates it from Latin to *Everything From One* and shares that the tomb is currently empty, but will one day hold the remains of its famous owner—actor Nicolas Cage.

I glance over to check on Mom and Camille, and they are still arm-in-arm, huddled underneath Camille's pink and green umbrella. Camille looks miserable, fanning herself with Mom's empty water bottle.

On the other hand, Mom looks excited! She has always been a big Nicolas Cage fan. She made me watch *Peggy Sue Got Married* more times than I can count. I walk next to her and share other stories about him and his connection to New Orleans that I learned on the haunted history tour.

We've been walking for about forty-five minutes, and I can tell that we're near the end of our time in the cemetery when we reach one of the highlights of the tour. It's a tall, white tomb with colorful triple-x's scribbled all over it. The only area where I don't observe an *XXX* is up high, where people cannot reach. The ground is littered with cosmetic items—lipstick, eyeshadow, and mascara—as well as Mardi Gras beads, flowers, and a few voodoo dolls. I recognize this as the tomb of the infamous voodoo priestess, Marie Laveau.

Maureen shares reported stories about how Marie Laveau used her trade as a beautician to access wealthy New Orleanians and achieve fame and notoriety for her voodoo practices in the 1800s. She became a religious leader and community activist, and her legacy has lived on in New Orleans for centuries.

As we leave the cemetery, Maureen continues to educate us about myths and truths of voodoo, including the fact that it is an actual practicing religion, and not the wicked magic it's been portrayed to be. She explains the beliefs and practices as she leads us over to Congo Square a couple of blocks away from the cemetery.

Once we reach the center of the park, we stop in front of a sculpture of enslaved Africans dancing and playing drums. Our tour group huddles under a canopy of trees, appreciative of the shade that has been eluding us for the past hour. I join Mom and Camille on a bench as Maureen shares stories of enslaved and freed Africans congregating in this park on Sundays to socialize, trade, and celebrate their African cultures and religious practices.

I look over at Camille and can tell that she is very intrigued by this part of the tour. We have both been interested in learning more about black history in the United States ever since we took part in an online book club during the Covid-19 pandemic. We read and discussed *Caste* by Isabel Wilkerson, which left us eager to learn more about the untold truths of our country.

The tour ends, and Maureen addresses the group. "I want to thank all of you for braving the heat today and joining me on this tour." She removes her top hat and places it over her heart as she takes a bow. "I hope you learned a lot, and if you have any questions about this tour or want information about the other tours we provide, please let me know."

A few people in the group give a light applause, and she turns to gestures behind herself. "If you have time, be sure to visit Louis Armstrong Park, just behind us. You'll find statues honoring Satchmo, plus beautiful gardens and ponds. Thank you, again!"

Some of the group has already departed, likely in search of anything cold and wet to help rehydrate. We remain on the bench and enjoy a few moments of relaxation and shade. Once the rest of the participants have finished talking to Maureen, I grab Mom's hand and gesture for us to talk to her.

"Thank you so much, Maureen!" I say, as I hand her a tip. "I'm always surprised that I still learn new things after taking this tour so many times."

Maureen *smeyes*-es again. "Oh, thank you! That's so good to hear!"

"Can we get a picture with you?" Camille holds up her phone, as if Maureen needs a visual aid to understand what she's requesting.

"Of course!" Maureen ushers us to huddle together in front of the sculpture.

Camille hands me the phone to take the selfie, since I have the longest arms and will have an easier time getting four people in the frame. I count to three and snap several pictures. When I'm done, I swipe through the photos to make sure I got everyone in, while Mom thanks Maureen for the educational experience.

I notice Maureen is smiling in the photo, displaying a missing canine tooth, and I instantly remember where else I've seen her. She's the same tour guide in the photo of Olivia and her friends! I didn't put it together until I saw her smile.

Camille opens her umbrella and begins walking with Mom towards Louis Armstrong Park.

"Y'all go ahead. I'll catch up in a second." As they walk away, I turn to Maureen and speak in a quiet voice. "This is going to sound weird, but I saw a picture of you last night on a show I was watching."

She looks perplexed. "You did? Are you sure it was me?"

I nod. "Yes. In fact, I didn't realize it until I looked at *our* photo. But you took a picture with a group of women that were visiting for a bachelorette party. One of the women ended up missing."

Maureen's eyes widen as she realizes what I'm referring to. "Oh yeah, I remember that. It was a big deal for a while. What was that... maybe ten years ago?"

"Yes, I believe they are having a vigil for her on Monday because it's the ten-year anniversary."

She nods. "Right. One of our guides, Geoff, told me about that earlier this week, since the story is a part of our true crime tour."

"That's how I first heard about it."

Maureen tilts her head, as if she's remembering something. "You know, it's funny. The same day that I did that tour with them, the guide from another company that did the twelve o'clock tour after mine stopped by our office. He handed me a phone he found that might have been left in the cemetery by someone in my group." She gestures with her fingers to make the shape of a small rectangle. "It looked like one of those cheap throwaway phones."

"A burner phone?" My true crime curiosity is piqued.

"Yeah, I think that's what they're called. Anyway, I tried to turn it on and see if I could call some contacts in the phone, but it was dead. So, I called all the phone numbers I had noted on the reservations from that tour and asked if anyone was missing a phone. But no one claimed it."

"That's weird." I look into the distance and see Camille and Mom gazing at another sculpture.

"A couple of days later, I saw something on the morning news about that woman being missing, and I recognized her from the tour. I remembered the phone and figured it wouldn't hurt to tell the police about it, in case it was hers."

My eyes widen. "What did they say?"

Maureen sighs. "By the time I got back to the office to get the phone, it was gone."

I let out a disappointed grunt.

"Turns out, the guy who used to do our voodoo tours found it on the counter and gave it to some teenager who claimed it was her phone. I don't know if it was or not, but that was the end of that." She squints her eyes and looks at me intently. "But deep down, I've always thought it had something to do with that missing woman."

I nod my head while my mind spins like a kaleidoscope with potential connections between Olivia and the phone. "Well, at least you can rest assured knowing that you did your part to find the owner, whether or not it was her."

Maureen *smeyes-es* again and pats my arm. "Right. Thanks again for coming on the tour. I need to get some water in this old body before I shrivel up like a raisin."

"Yes, ma'am. Thank you again, Maureen." I walk over to Camille and Mom, who slowly make their way back toward the French Quarter when they see me heading their way.

"What was that all about?" Camille asks.

I'm dying to fill them in on the probable clue and connection to Olivia Peterson I've just learned about, but I decide to not let on that I'm still secretly obsessed with her story. "Oh, I was just asking a few more questions about Marie Laveau. Let's go get something cold to drink."

"Yes, please!" Camille walks ahead of us. "There was a cute little coffee shop on our way to the tour. I'd kill for an iced latte right now."

My face lights up.

"Do you remember which street it was on?" Mom asks.

I quickly respond. "I do!"

***

I hear a mechanical doorbell chime as we enter the coffee shop. The entire front of the shop is floor to ceiling windows, and the interior is all-white with black accents. The aesthetic is very modern and the opposite of the dim, cozy vibe of most coffee shops. There's a large black NOLA Coffee Bistro logo on the wall behind the counter, matching the one I remember seeing on the owner's shirt in the *Disappearances* episode. Four black barstools surround tall black bistro tables, and only two tables are vacant. But since there's no one in line, I'm not concerned about having somewhere to sit and recharge.

We gasp in relief as we feel the welcoming embrace of the air conditioner. I search for the woman from the *Disappearances* episode, but I'm disappointed to only find a young barista restocking cups and lids.

Mom spots the sign for the restrooms. "Order an iced green tea for me. I'm going to visit the ladies' room."

"Sure thing," I say, scanning the menu on the monitor in the upper corner of the room, just above the cash register.

I'm startled by a boisterous voice coming from a door behind the other end of the counter. "Welcome to NOLA Coffee Bistro! What can I get you today?"

I instantly recognize the face as the one I spotted through the window this morning and a slightly older version of the one I saw on my phone last night. Her hair is dark now with gray streaks, but it's still slicked back in a low ponytail, and she's wearing glasses. I notice her name embroidered on her apron.

"Hi, Janet!" I flash a friendly smile. "We'd like a medium iced mocha, a medium iced green tea, and—" I look over at Camille to add

116

her order.

"I'll take a medium iced latte, please."

Janet nods and smiles. "Coming right up!"

I point out the empty tables to Camille. "Grab a table, and I'll get the drinks when they're ready."

As soon as Camille reaches a table, I lean over, resting my arms on the counter. "Can I ask you a question, Janet?"

She looks up from one of the many machines with a cup in her hand. "Sure, what'cha got for me?"

"Were you on an episode of a show called *Disappearances* about a woman named Olivia that went missing ten years ago?"

Janet grins and goes back to preparing our drinks. "Yes, that was me back in my younger days!"

"I thought so," I say, pretending that I wasn't already certain. "I just learned about the story last night on a true crime tour, and I watched that episode once we got back to our room."

She gives me a sly look with her head still down, peering over the top of her glasses. "And you just happened to show up at my shop today?"

Busted!

"I didn't plan to, but we walked by earlier on our way to a cemetery tour."

She nods.

"So, nothing ever came of her case?" I ask.

Janet shrugs as she places lids on each of our cups. "Not that I know of. But to be honest, I haven't really kept up with it." She slides all three icy drinks across the counter in front of me. "In fact, I was surprised when producers from the show reached out to me. They must have found my name in the police report."

"Makes sense," I say. "And you remembered nothing else about that guy you saw Olivia talking to?"

"Nope." Janet shifts her weight onto one leg, putting one hand on her hip and the other on the counter. "There really wasn't much to remember. It didn't occur to me to pay any attention to him at the time. We were busy, and I needed to get back inside to my customers."

I nod.

"I wish I could have told them more. It's a shame that they never found her."

"Did you see pictures of that guy Noah, the person she was last seen with?"

"I did." Janet looks up in thought. "But I couldn't say whether or not it was him."

I reach into my purse for my wallet. "Gotcha. How much do we owe you?"

"It's on the house." She looks over at Camille with a wink. "Congrats to the bride-to-be!"

"Thank you!" Camille shouts from the table, touching the tiara she had forgotten she was wearing.

"Well, thank you, and thanks for entertaining my nosiness." I pick up all three cups with both hands.

"No problem, doll!" Janet turns to help her barista restock cups.

By the time I reach the table, Mom has already joined Camille. They both look at me curiously, so I decide that it's time to tell them about Maureen and Janet. I briefly explain that I recognized them from the *Disappearances* episode, but I don't go into detail about what we discussed.

Mom's eyes are wide with wonder. "Wow, what a coincidence that we'd see two people from that show today!"

"I know!" I stare down at my iced mocha to avoid making eye contact with Camille. But she calls me out, anyway.

"Are you done playing detective now, and can we please get back to acting like this is a bachelorette party?"

"Yes," I say with a forced smile as I peer out the window to the street corner that must have been where Janet saw Olivia talking to *someone*. And I can't help but wonder... was it Noah Andrews?

Chapter 12

We choose Oceana Grill for lunch, another one of the French Quarter's famous restaurants. It's tucked away on Conti Street, but it stands out with a bright blue sign hanging from the second-floor balcony with a red crawfish sporting a chef's cap, a bib and huge grin. Typically, there's a long line of people standing along the sidewalk outside, especially on weekends; but since we're eating a late lunch, we're able to walk right in.

We follow our hostess upstairs, and we're seated at a table next to a window facing the courtyard. Camille and Mom survey the room. The walls of the restaurant are a mix of exposed brick, wood, and colorful murals. Televisions are mounted in different areas of the room, showing a number of sports channels, and the walls are clad with photos of the many celebrities that have dined here over the years.

Oceana Grill is very casual, which is reflected in the menu. The restaurant offers an enormous variety of dishes—traditional Louisiana options, pasta, po'boys, blackened seafood, fried platters, and oysters. I always order the fried seafood platter, so I know that there's more than enough fried oysters, shrimp, and catfish to satisfy two lightweight eaters, like my sister and me. Camille and I decide to share the platter, and Mom selects the blackened fish. We all agree that we need to properly rehydrate with water only, since we've consumed nothing but sugar over the past few hours.

Over the next hour, Camille tells us of her and Alan's plans for their honeymoon in Orlando and entertains us with tales from her bachelorette party escapades in Las Vegas. Mom nearly shoots water out of her nose when Camille regales us with a story about one of her bridesmaids being mistaken for a sex worker after she approached a car identical to the ride share they were waiting for.

After eating more than enough food, we discuss how we'd like to spend the rest of the afternoon.

"Why don't we check out Royal Street?" I suggest. "There are a bunch of art galleries and nice souvenir shops. It's my favorite street in the Quarter."

As expected, Mom's face lights up at the mention of art galleries. "Sounds good to me!"

"Okay, and I can pick up some souvenirs for Alan and my soon-to-be in-laws," Camille says as we walk back downstairs.

We visit an array of galleries, including one of my favorites—Galerie Rue Royale. I stare in awe at the stunning paintings of glamorous mid-century women by French artist, Marc Clauzade, and colorful celebrity pop art by the artist DeVon.

Just a few doors down is Sutton Galleries—a two-level gallery featuring many talented artists. The bright space invites us in, enticed by hundreds of colorful pieces by artists who use all types of techniques and mediums. There's so much to see that we spend a good thirty minutes in this gallery alone.

"Incredible," Camille repeatedly whispers as we walk through the

Kezic Gallery. Diego Lukezic creates colorful, textured floral and landscape paintings. Each petal or leaf is prominently defined and coated with a glossy finish, making them appear three-dimensional. I take a photo of Mom and Camille from behind, mesmerized by a massive piece showing a field of white petals flying into an ombré turquoise sky.

I also bring them to smaller galleries, like Lejardin. The walls are littered with art pieces from artists who are less-known than those featured in the fancier galleries, but just as talented. These galleries are usually small rooms or alleyways and offer many smaller pieces, resulting in a large variety of reasonably priced art and souvenirs—some that can be carried on the flight back home.

We reach an intersection and find a jazz quartet set up near the curb. Two men are sitting, playing a guitar and a banjo, and two are standing, playing a bass and a washboard. They play an upbeat song, and I can't help but to dance along as we approach them. We stop for a few minutes to listen, and Camille squeezes through the crowd of spectators to drop a couple of dollars into the guitar case before we move on.

After some shopping at Forever New Orleans, a store selling high-quality souvenirs, I keep my promise to Mom, and we walk a block over to find the local street artists around Jackson Square. The artists have their art posted along the iron gate that surrounds all four sides of the park. We take our time viewing an incredible variety of art, complimenting each artist on their work. Occasionally, Mom stops and talks to an artist while Camille and I visit the retail stores across the cobblestone walkway.

When we reach the side of Jackson Square facing Decatur Street,

I point across the street, past the horse-drawn carriages, to the green and white striped awnings of Café DuMonde. As expected, the line waiting to experience their famous beignets is wrapped around the building, confirming that I made the right choice to stop at Café Beignet earlier in the day.

We stroll into Jackson Square, where groups of tourists are taking pictures and selfies in front of the Andrew Jackson statue. I notice a young couple with twin toddlers struggling to take a selfie, and I hurry over to offer my assistance.

"Would you like for me to take a few pictures for you?" I ask the young mom, presumptively reaching for the phone.

"Oh, thank you so much!" She taps her screen to change to the rear-facing camera. "These two make it next to impossible."

She hands me the phone, and I take a few steps back, waiting for the overwhelmed parents to each put a twin on their hip, begging them to smile.

"Say cheese!" I say, showing the kids my most dramatic smile in hopes they will reciprocate. I take several pictures and say a silent prayer that at least one image captured everyone smiling and looking at the camera at the same time.

"Thank you so much!" She places her twin down in front of her husband. "Can I take a photo of you three, too?"

Camille already has her phone ready, anticipating the offer. "Yes, please!"

The three of us stand in front of the statue, with Camille in the middle. She has the back of her left hand stretched out in front of her, showing the ring, while Mom and I point at it.

"I took a bunch of pics so you'll have options," the young mom tells us, handing the phone back to Camille and glancing at her sash. "And congratulations!"

"Thank you!" we all say in unison.

We complete our lap around Jackson Square, ending at the corner facing Muriel's. I make it a point to stop and visit the artist I told Mom about last night at dinner. His name is Wade Griffin, and I always find him in this same spot every weekend when I come to New Orleans. He paints colorful acrylic paintings showing iconic scenes from New Orleans, such as streetcars, Canal Street, shotgun houses, swamps and jazz bands. Since he makes his own frames, I'm sure collectors appreciate that his pieces are ready to ship and hang as soon as they arrive at their homes.

Wade remembers me from my previous visits, and I introduce him to my mother, the artist. But Camille is busy examining one of his paintings of a blue-toned swamp. The tall trees stretch towards the azure sky, and the entire scene is reflected in the swampy land below.

"Wade," I say with a smirk, "I think I'm finally ready to purchase one of your pieces." I nod my head towards Camille. "That one."

Camille turns and looks at me. "Which one?"

I grin. "It's your wedding present and a souvenir, so you'll always remember your first trip to New Orleans."

She gives me a tight hug. "Thank you, Camryn! Not just for the painting, but for everything. And I could *never* forget this trip."

I pay Wade for the painting, and Camille gives him her address to have the painting shipped after she and Alan return from their honeymoon.

"There's one more artist I want you to see before we head back to the bed and breakfast." I link arms with both of them and guide them past Muriel's. "Follow me."

Camille closes her umbrella, relieved to be on the shaded side of Chartres Street. "Please make this our last stop. I really need to chill for a bit. This heat has been a lot today."

I keep looking ahead with a smirk. "You're really going to like this one."

We enter a small studio, and I turn to watch their reactions—which don't disappoint. Lyla Clayre is a watercolor artist who creates stunning paintings of New Orleans architecture, landscapes, and wildlife.

I follow Mom and Camille as they take their time admiring each piece, *ooh*-ing and *ahh*-ing over the fine details of every shotgun house, pelican and French Quarter street. We're near the back of the store, and we all stop in our tracks when we see a large painting of a pink alligator. He appears to be looking at us with a wide grin, as if he's saying, *I'm amazing, aren't I?*

Mom's eyes scan the entire piece, attempting to identify the technique used to make each individual scale on the gator's back. "In all my years, I've never been able to master watercolors."

"Are you the artist?" Camille asks, looking over her shoulder at the woman sitting on a stool behind the counter, pulling her hair back into a messy bun.

The young brunette smiles. "I wish! No, I just work here."

Mom is still admiring the alligator. "Well, this is spectacular!" She pulls Camille closer to point out the details of the claws.

The salesclerk clears her throat. "Almost all the pieces are also available as prints."

I step behind Camille to glance over her head at the gorgeous gator when I hear the clerk greet a new patron. "Welcome to the Lyla Clayre Studio!"

When I see who enters, I gasp as everything around me disappears, and the only thing that I can see is *him*. Eric doesn't notice us at first. He's focused on a painting near the door that likely drew him in.

I feel a tingling sensation in my toes, and just as the entire studio seems to turn into a big, pink watercolor painting, I'm jerked back into reality when Camille elbows me in the gut.

"You see him, too?" I whisper, trying to determine if he's real or a mirage.

Mom and Camille giggle and inch their way further back into the studio, leaving me glued to my spot.

Eric's eyes follow the paintings on the wall until they meet mine. I give him a reluctant wave and a smile. He looks at me for a second and then back at the art.

Is he annoyed that I'm here? Or does he not even recognize me now that I look presentable?

I nervously tussle my bangs and look at Mom and Camille, who both shoo me in his direction.

Camille mouths, *Say something.*

Eric looks at me again, so I decide to stop acting like a pathetic idiot and approach him.

He's still wearing the same white v-neck and khaki shorts that I saw him in this morning. His auburn hair looks a bit lighter with the natural light shining into the studio behind him. He's taller than I thought—which says a lot coming from a woman with my height—and somehow, he's even more handsome than I remember.

"Hi!" I try to give the illusion of confidence by maintaining eye contact. "I'm Camryn."

He forces a smile. "I'm Eric." He glances over my shoulder at Mom and Camille, who are watching us from the corner like a couple of giggling schoolgirls.

I give them a stern look and turn back to Eric. "That's my mom and my sister."

He gives them a nod.

I nervously play with my purse zipper. "I'm really sorry about this morning. I had no idea you were Olivia's brother. In fact, I didn't even know about Olivia until last night. You see, we went on a true crime tour, and Geoff, the tour guide, told us about Olivia going missing from that bar. So, I looked her up on my phone and watched a show that told me more about it." My mouth has become a speeding locomotive that shows no signs of slowing. "My sister brought it up at breakfast, and I just started talking about it, and—"

Eric lifts his hands, putting a merciful end to my rant. "It's okay. I understand. There's no way you could have known."

I feel my anxiety decrease with every second his eyes look into mine.

"I'm actually embarrassed that I erupted the way that I did." He looks at me apologetically. "It just caught me off-guard. Honestly, it seems like everyone has forgotten about Olivia. So, hearing *anyone* saying *anything* about her is just... surprising."

"I get it." I search for something else to say as Eric redirects his focus to the paintings. "Are you a fan of this artist?"

He looks back at me. "Yeah, I've been trying to convince myself for years to actually buy a piece, and I think today is the day for me to pull the trigger."

I look at the piece he is gazing at—a pink shotgun house with a balcony, surrounded by greenery. "I don't take you for a watercolor kinda guy." *Okay, Camryn! I see you trying to flirt!*

Eric chuckles. "I like it because it reminds me of Olivia. Her favorite color was pink."

"Oh." I feel about three inches tall. "Well, I think it's a good one." *How articulate, Camryn.*

He looks at me and smiles, making my heart race. "Me, too."

Eric's smile transports me back into the watercolor world where only he and I exist, just as the eavesdropping salesclerk scurries over to secure the sale.

"Well, maybe we'll see you around," I say hopefully, taking a step back to join my awaiting audience of two.

"Yeah. Maybe." Eric gives us one last wave and directs his attention to the small brunette, who is salivating over her potential commission... or the dreamy patron.

Camille and Mom come up behind me and usher me out of the store. When I step onto the sidewalk, I feel like I've emerged from one of the watercolor paintings and returned to reality. My pulse returns to its regular rhythm, and my body temperature normalizes.

"I have never seen you like that before," Mom says with a smirk.

I give her a confused look. "Like what?"

"Like a sad, pathetic puppy pining for scraps from the dinner table," Camille says.

I shove her. "Well, it certainly didn't help to have y'all back there watching us like we were one of your little reality show couples." I glance back at the studio as we make our way down Chartres Street and think back to the expression on Eric's face. "I think he's still mad at me. Well—at us."

"I'm sure he's not mad." Mom wraps her arm around my shoulder. "He misses his sister. Remember, he's here to attend the vigil in a couple of days. That would have anyone on edge."

Camille smirks and nods. "Yeah, Camryn. I'm sure it has nothing to do with you suggesting that his sister's dead body is decaying under the floors of that bar."

"Excuse me?" I twist around to face her behind us. "*You* said that!" She shrugs. "But does *he* know that?"

I take a few more steps, then stop and put my face in my hands. "I'm so embarrassed."

"Oh, honey," Mom says, rubbing my back. "Everything will be fine."

My hands still cover my eyes when Camille takes one last sisterly jab. "Mom, I don't blame her. I'd be devastated if someone *that* hot thought I was a heartless monster."

I turn and give her a dirty look. "Oh, really, *Mrs. Henderson*? He's hot, and I'm heartless?"

"Just yesterday I was still *Miss* Camille Alexander, and now I'm suddenly *Mrs.* Henderson?" I notice she's avoided answering the question.

"Now, girls." Mom inserts herself in between her bickering daughters. "We have so much more of the trip ahead of us. Let's not let something like this spoil even one second of it."

We continue walking.

"Sorry," Camille says, nudging me with her elbow. "Just giving you a hard time."

I smile and nudge her back. "I know you are. I don't know why I'm being so touchy."

"Because he *is* hot."

We look at each other and exchange smirks.

Mom changes the subject by telling us about our Aunt Gail's most recent paranormal experience while running a daycare for seniors out of her home in Albuquerque. I'm usually hanging on every word of a story about Aunt Gail's hauntings; but today, my mind is preoccupied by something else. Not just Olivia Peterson, but her jarringly intense—*and hot*—brother.

Chapter 13

My original plan for the evening was to have our Saturday night dinner at Palace Café on Canal Street. I wanted Mom and Camille to experience the theatrical presentation of their Bananas Foster for dessert. The server rolls a cart over to the table that holds a single gas burner and a large pan. He melts butter and cinnamon in the pan while he peels and slices two bananas into quarters. Once the butter has melted, the server pours banana liqueur into the pan and waits while the sauce sizzles. At this point, the aroma reaches your nostrils, causing your mouth to salivate involuntarily. Next, the server places the banana slices into the pan and cooks them. Then he lifts the pan off the burner, sliding the bananas and sauce onto one side of the pan, and pours rum onto the empty side. With a flash, a large flame ignites in the pan and then dies out as the sauce spreads. The server places the banana slices in a dish next to a scoop of vanilla ice cream and drizzles the remaining cinnamon sauce on top, leaving you to spend the rest of your meal savoring the sweet delicacy.

Even though it's a worthwhile experience, we determine that we are too tired from our day in the French Quarter to make another trip down there for dinner. So, I suggest that we eat at Katie's, a local neighborhood restaurant just a five-minute walk from Canal Street Bed and Breakfast.

While Mom freshens up in the restroom, I watch Camille record Instagram stories, giving her followers a play by play of the day's events. I'm thankful that she is gracious enough to omit our embarrassing encounters with Eric. She then sits on the bed and calls Alan to check in.

I use that time to get on Instagram and search for Eric Peterson's profile, in hopes of learning more about his personality and interests. I scroll past a number of profile photos that look nothing like him, but my heart jumps when I locate the one I'm searching for. Eric's not smiling, but looking intently at the camera with a slight smirk. I hover my finger over his photo for a couple of seconds and close my eyes, needing time to convince myself that I'm definitely *not* a stalker. Then the thought occurs to me that I need to prepare myself to see pictures of him with some beautiful woman.

I open my eyes and admit to myself that I *am* cyberstalking; but I tap on his profile photo anyway. To my dismay—or maybe delight, depending on what he's shared—his account is private, and I can't see a thing. I let out a disappointed sigh and toss the phone onto the bed, forgetting to lock the screen.

Camille glances at my phone and gives me a sly look. "Mm, hmm," she says, returning her attention to her conversation with Alan.

Mom exits the bathroom and picks up her purse from her bed. "I'm going to spend some time out on the front porch while you two get ready." She reaches for the doorknob, but as soon as she opens the door, she's startled and jumps back.

Hearing her gasp, I look over and see a young black woman standing at our door with a fist held up, as if she is preparing to knock. She's holding a stack of towels and wearing a black t-shirt that's knotted in the back and dark skinny jeans, accentuating her voluptuous curves. Her black hair is in long goddess locs with metallic gold accents, and her chocolate skin has a dewy glow. There's a small stud in her left nostril and a hoop piercing through her septum. She waves in my direction.

I jump up to greet her with a hug. "Hey, Ava!" I take the towels from her and bring her into the room. "Mom and Camille, this is Ava. She is Pat's daughter and Maggie's granddaughter. She sometimes helps on the weekends."

Ava smiles at Camille and looks over to Mom. "Sorry I scared you. I was just coming up to see if you needed any clean towels."

"Oh, honey, it's fine! Nice to meet you." Mom smiles at Ava and walks into the hallway. "Y'all know where to find me when you're ready." She turns and disappears down the stairs.

Ava closes the door. "So, what do you have planned for tonight?"

"I'm taking them to Katie's for dinner, and then Camille and I are going out to Bourbon Street to do some bachelorette partying." I take the towels into the bathroom.

"Oh, you're getting married?" Ava asks Camille.

"Yep, next Sunday!" Camille flicks her fingers to display the ring.

"Congrats! You know, I think I have the perfect place for you to go tonight. A bar on Bourbon is having a big re-opening tonight. There's going to be a drag show and karaoke starting at ten."

Camille jumps to her feet. "That sounds perfect!"

Ava opens the door. "Great! I have some flyers in the car. I'll grab one and slip it under your door."

I smile. "Perfect! Thanks, Ava."

She returns my smile with a wink. "I'll be by there after I'm done here. My girlfriend is the bartender."

"Cool, we'll see you there," I say as Ava closes the door and Camille goes into the bathroom to freshen up.

I sit on the bed and hear Camille yell through the bathroom door. "Is she even old enough to get into a bar? She looks so young."

I shrug. "I'm not sure how old she is. But I know that she took a year off after high school and has been taking classes at a community college for the past couple of years." I do some math in my head. "She's probably twenty-one."

"Oh, okay."

"And hurry up in there! If it starts at ten, we'll want to be on time in case there's limited seating.

"Aye aye, Admiral Boom," Camille yells, referring to the old man from *Mary Poppins* that fires a cannon twice a day at the top of the hour. We once watched that movie over and over for an entire weekend when she was a child.

I grab my phone, which is still open to Eric's empty Instagram page. Every time I see his picture, I get excited. But why do I feel excited about a man that seems to despise me? True to my history of wanting men I can't have, I spend the next ten minutes going back and forth in my mind. Do I want to see Eric again and risk humiliation, or should I just let it go?

By the time Camille exits the bathroom and goes downstairs to wait with Mom, I've made up my mind. I *have to* see him again.

I surprise myself and only take fifteen minutes to shower and prep for dinner. Since Mom and Camille were blessed with flawless skin and don't wear makeup, they can shower, change clothes and be ready to go in a matter of minutes. Meanwhile, I have to apply a whole new face of makeup before I consider myself presentable enough to be seen in public. The thought only reminds me of how raggedy I looked the first time Eric saw me, making me shudder. Still, finishing my metamorphosis in record time tonight is something to be acknowledged.

Mom and Camille are sitting in two patio chairs on the front porch discussing the issue Camille had with her cake designer, who attempted to skirt out of making the intricate damask trimming she initially said she could do. Fortunately, my sister stood up to her and got everything hashed out.

I drape my crossbody strap on my shoulder and shove the purse over to the opposite hip. "Let's go. This is a popular spot, so it's probably going to be busy."

***

Katie's is as crowded as I expected it to be. It's a small restaurant on a street corner in a residential neighborhood. I changed our dinner plans early enough in the day to make a reservation for eight P.M, although we arrive thirty minutes early. There is an empty table outside that would accommodate the three of us; but fortunately, a party of four left as soon as we arrived, and they can seat us inside. We welcome any opportunity to be in air conditioning we can find.

The cuisine at Katie's is a mix of Creole and Italian recipes, making for a unique and eclectic menu. With so many options to choose from, our server has to make two trips to our table before we're ready to order. We decide to split a crawfish beignet as an appetizer. I order the Catfish Meunière, which I tried the last time I visited and loved. Mom opts for the Veggie Extravaganza, and Camille chooses the Pasta Primavera du Jour. We are pleasantly surprised when our food arrives promptly.

"So, have y'all made any plans for this evening?" Mom asks, stacking a mix of vegetables on her fork.

Camille is enjoying a glass of wine, so I respond. "Actually, Ava told us about a drag show and karaoke night that's happening at some bar on Bourbon Street."

Mom gulps down her bite. "A drag show? Oh, I used to have a blast at drag shows!"

Camille slams her glass on the table just a little too hard, causing some wine to spill. *"You did?"*

"Oh, yes! Some of my oldest and dearest friends made the most beautiful drag queens."

Camille and I exchange glances. There's obviously so much that we don't know about our mother, and this is a story we need to hear *now*.

"Please continue," I say, cutting into my catfish.

We spend the rest of our time at Katie's listening to Mom recount stories of her and Dad's social escapades when they first moved to Dallas. My jaw drops in disbelief when she reveals that one of my earliest babysitters was their friend and accountant who was known as Darryl by day, and Diana—as in Ross—by night. It's fascinating to get a peek into the colorful lives our parents had that we knew nothing about!

We order two bread puddings for dessert—one for Mom and me to share, and the other for Camille. She's always had the biggest sweet tooth.

***

I unlock the door to our room and accidentally step on a turquoise piece of paper. It's the flyer Ava promised to deliver for the grande re-opening of a place called The Backdoor Bar. I take a picture of it on my phone and put it on the nightstand.

"You're always welcomed to come with us," I say to Mom as she removes her sandals.

She sits down on the bed. "Oh, I'd love to, but this old body needs some rest. I'll just stay here and find something to watch on T.V."

"Okay, Mom." I rummage through my suitcase to find something suitable to wear.

Camille is curled up on the bed, reading her book. "You go ahead and get ready." She doesn't bother to look up. "I'll go after you're done."

"That's fine." I glance at my smartwatch. "We can take our time. We still have an hour before we need to leave." But Camille is too engrossed in her book to acknowledge me. I sigh and enter the bathroom. Since we have so much time to get ready, I plan to really fix myself up tonight. It's been way too long since I've had a girls' night out!

Chapter 14

I'm so happy! I could have never imagined that this summer would be so magical! We've been meeting at the coffee shop after work for the past few days. It's been amazing getting to know him. He's so different from what I expected, and I love the way I feel when I'm with him.

He tells me all the time that he feels so comfortable around me, almost like we're soul mates. It makes me happy to know that I can be someone he can confide in about his problems with HER. Ugh... I've never even met her, but I still can't stand her. It makes me so upset that a woman can be so cruel to a wonderful man like him.

I miss him so much in the evenings. I hate that I can't talk to him almost as much as I hate knowing that she gets to be with him. She doesn't deserve him, and I'm determined to do everything I can to make him mine.

***

For the first time, I'm confident that he feels the same for me as I do for him. He also misses me when we're not together, so he bought us a couple of cheap cell phones. Now we can chat in the evenings and weekends without anyone accidentally finding out!

It's kinda romantic having a secret relationship. It makes our time together so much more special. Tonight, we met at a park overlooking a creek. We parked our cars next to each other, and he suggested that we stay in my car so we could listen to my choice of music. He's so considerate! We started out complaining about the executive who bashed our group's presentation earlier in the day. He got angrier and angrier the more we talked about it, so I kissed him to shut him up. I didn't want him to ruin the mood.

I love the way he kisses. He's so gentle. The way he holds my face in his hands makes me melt. I never want the kisses to end.

But something happened tonight that left me questioning where I truly stand. We were in my car, and he told me that he can't wait to make love to me. I didn't know what to say. It's definitely something I've thought about, but I didn't think it would be this soon. I don't know what to do. I mean, I want to. But it's all happening so fast! And what about HER? Is he still sleeping with her? I don't want to ask and ruin things, but I feel like I have a right to know.

I wish I could talk to someone about this. But things have already gone too far, and there's no way I can tell anyone. I'm kinda ashamed, but my feelings are too strong.

What have I gotten myself into?

***

So this is love. He loves me, and I love him. This is all so meant to be.

Tonight, we met at the coffee shop, and he told me he had a surprise for me. We hopped in my car, and he navigated while I drove us to a nice little French restaurant about thirty minutes away. It was so intimate, and for the first time, it didn't feel like we were hiding.

We talked a lot about work, and he asked me questions about some of my ideas I shared during our group presentation. Come to think of it, we talked a lot more about work than we usually do. But maybe he's just stressed.

He told me that he's planning to end things with her soon. He's just waiting for the right time, because so many lives will be affected. I wanted to ask him how long I'd have to wait, but before I could get the words out, he said it. "I love you." I almost cried when I said it back. "I love you, too." The words came out of my mouth so easily!

On the drive back, he asked me if I had thought about what he said at the park. I told him I had, but I still wasn't sure. He said he doesn't think he can wait much longer... that all the love he has inside for me makes him feel like he's going to explode. I asked him to give me some time to think it over. He suggested that we not see each other again until I decide.

What should I do? I want to show him how much I love him. But he doesn't belong to me... not yet, anyway. Should I wait? Or could this be what it takes to make him finally walk out and be with only me? I don't know. But what I do know is that I want to be with him, and I can't picture my life without him.

***

All of this uncertainty is really getting to me. I can't focus on work anymore. We didn't talk all weekend, and when I saw him at the office today, he wouldn't even look at me. I can't live like this. I miss him so much!

I've been thinking about it a lot, and I think I'm ready. No, I'm certain that I am. But why can't I pick up the phone to tell him that? I need to stop being a baby and act like a woman who wants her man. That's right... he's MY man! And I'm going to do what I have to do to keep it that way.

Erin is going out of town this weekend, so I'll be roommate-free with the apartment all to myself. I'm going to plan something romantic. I'll make dinner and buy some wine. It will be perfect. Everything we've both been waiting for.

I can't wait to tell him!

Chapter 15

Camille and I decide to go with a ride share to get to and from the French Quarter tonight, since the streetcars don't run as often in the evenings. Mom takes pictures of us in the sitting room downstairs, as if we're a couple of teenage girls heading out to a high school dance with no dates. Camille is wearing a hot pink flirty dress with strappy gold stilettos and, of course, her sash and tiara. I feel cute and confident in high-waisted black pleather shorts and a white sequin tank top. I had considered wearing the gold wedges I brought for our dressy night, but ended up deciding to wear the sandals I've been wearing all trip and lace them with the black straps. We're probably going to do a lot of dancing, so comfort is being prioritized over style tonight.

My phone chirps, alerting us that our driver has arrived, and we hug Mom goodbye.

"Take lots of pictures!" she says as we walk out the door.

I give her a thumbs up and close the door behind me.

While we're on our way to the Quarter, Mom decides to spend some time out on the screened-in porch at the back of the house. It's still warm and humid, but she remembers seeing a ceiling fan, which would make it much more bearable. When she opens the back door, she's surprised to find Maggie sitting on one of the cushioned wicker seats.

"Hi, Maggie!" Mom makes her way to the matching chair across from her. "Is it okay if I join you?"

Maggie smiles. "Of course, *bay-beh*! Have a seat!"

Mom looks around, absorbing the relaxing energy of the serene space. Her eyes follow the long ferns cascading down from a hanging pot in the corner. "I just love this house, Maggie! I could stay here forever."

"Thank you... Ann Marie, right?"

Mom nods.

"Yeah, I've loved this place since the first time I stepped foot in it."

"How long ago was that?" Mom asks.

Maggie rests her head back and looks up at the ceiling in thought. "Oh, I'd say it was about twenty or so years ago. My late-husband's aunt was the owner, and we stayed here for a family wedding."

"Camryn mentioned that you host weddings here from time to time."

"Oh, yes!" Maggie smiles. "I love the weddings."

Mom sits back further into the cushion on the white rattan chair. "Was the wedding for someone in your family or your husband's?"

Maggie chuckles. "His family. I haven't been in touch with most of my family since before we got married."

Mom looks at her with concern. "Why is that, if you don't mind my asking?"

Maggie watches the ceiling fan slowly spin overhead. "They weren't too keen on me marrying a white boy."

"Oh, I see." Mom nods her head. "One of my husband's sisters gave me a hard time when he brought me home to meet the family. She only referred to me as 'that skinny white girl.' Fortunately, the animosity was short-lived, and Belinda and I are good friends now."

Maggie lets out a quiet grunt. "Life could have been so much easier if my family would have been more accepting of Charles. But you see, it wasn't just a black and white thing for them—it was a cultural thing. Mama and 'nem always told me I needed to marry a good Creole man and 'keep it in the family,' as they'd say. So, when they found out I was marrying a white boy, they threw a fit!" She chuckles at the memory. "But they couldn't say nothin' since we were already in the family way."

Mom sits up and rests an arm over her crossed legs. "Wow, I bet that was tough."

"That was nothin' compared to what Charles went through with his family." Maggie sits up straight in her chair and smooths out the wrinkles on her teal sundress. "I sure wasn't what his family had in mind for him, either. You see, Charles came from money. He was studying law at Tulane when we met at the diner I was waitressing at. I was working to save up some money to start taking classes at a community college to be a secretary. He'd come in every Wednesday, and we'd get to talking."

Mom watches a grin spread across Maggie's face as she remembers the details of meeting the love of her life.

"Charles started coming in every night I was working, and we fell in love before we ever officially went out on a date!"

"Oh, that's so sweet," Mom says.

"Well, you know how it goes. After about six months, we found out I was pregnant and decided we'd get married. We tried to keep it a secret from our parents until it was already done, but my sister ran her mouth, and my family found out."

"What about his family?"

"They didn't find out until after we got married. Charles was his parents' only child, and they were double-mad because he married a black girl they knew nothing about *and* because he hadn't finished law school yet. And do you know what they did? They completely cut him off. Stopped paying for his school and cut off his allowance." Maggie shakes her head. "It didn't even seem to matter to them that they would have a grandchild."

Mom gasps. "Oh, my! That had to have been so hard on y'all, being so young and with a baby on the way."

"It was at first, but Charles had an aunt who was only about ten years older than him, who loved him like a brother. She would sneak us money when we needed it until he got his first job as a lawyer."

"It's a shame that people on all sides can be so close-minded."

"Ain't that the truth?" Maggie shakes her head. "But get this. It was that same aunt that sold us this place. It was in their family for a long time. She turned it into a bed and breakfast and ran it for about twenty years. I was working here and helped her with everything. I did all the cooking, and over the years, she taught me everything she knew about running a bed and breakfast.

"The business took a hit after Hurricane Katrina and was just starting to recover when that young lady went missing. There were police and news trucks here all the time. Some of the regular guests stopped coming, and it got harder to bring in new guests—especially after the psychics and ghost hunters started booking rooms."

"Are you serious?" Mom has always believed that there are people who have the ability to see and sense things that most of us can't. But it angers her when people lie about the gift or use it for their own gain.

Maggie nods. "Yes, ma'am. It got to be too much for her, and she thought about selling. One day, she came and told me and Charles that she wanted us to take it over. I wasn't too sure about it at first, but then I thought it would be something good for me and Pat to do together. She was working out in Shreveport and was struggling to get by as a single mom. I think Ava was twelve at the time. So, I talked to her about it, and we decided we would run it together. Turns out Pat is great with the business side of things."

"Sounds like everything worked out for the best. What an amazing story!"

"It did. Only, my Charles ended up passing just a year later from a heart attack."

Mom sits back in her chair. "I'm sorry to hear that."

"That's alright, honey. We had a wonderful life together, and he left me with something to keep me happy and busy until my final days." She gestures with her hands around the patio. "And I get to meet all kinds of people. Your daughter is one of my favorites!"

Mom laughs. "Camryn is definitely something special. And I can't begin to tell you how much she loves staying here."

"Oh, I know. She tells me all the time!" Maggie chuckles. "I keep waiting for her to show up here with a gentleman. For the life of me, I can't understand how she's managed to stay single."

"You and me both," Mom says, causing both of them to laugh. "Honestly, I think when her high school sweetheart broke her heart, it did a bit more damage than Camryn would like to admit. In my personal opinion, I feel like she's been chasing after what she had with him for all these years and doesn't allow new relationships to just be what they are."

Maggie leans closer to Mom. "Ann Marie, we could talk all night about the mistakes our daughters make with men!"

They both laugh.

"Tell me about your husband," Maggie says, leaning her elbow on the wicker chair's armrest.

"I met my husband, Donald, in Albuquerque at a farmer's market. And I know it sounds like a cliché, but it was love at first sight! I was helping a friend with her vegetable stand when this tall and handsome man with ebony skin stopped by to ask about the difference between broccoli and cauliflower. Turns out, he already knew the difference. Don was an accountant with a love for gardening—something he learned from his mother. He had his own small booth selling vegetables and jams, but he needed a reason to come by and speak to me."

Maggie laughs. "Sly dog."

Mom smiles and leans back in her chair. "We had a small wedding, and Camryn came along shortly after. His college buddy called and said he was opening his own accounting firm in Dallas and asked Don to come along as a partner. Don's family all lived in Dallas, so we moved and started a new life there. I stayed at home and raised Camryn. When she started school, I began painting to keep myself busy."

"Do you still paint?" Maggie asks.

"Oh, yes. I'm a full-time artist. Just waiting for Don to retire so I can, too. We plan to do a lot of traveling. I'm bringing him back to stay here next spring for our thirty-fifth wedding anniversary." Mom looks around the patio and takes a deep, relaxing breath. "I'm so glad Camryn brought me here to experience this place."

Maggie smiles. "What was Camryn like as a child?"

"Maggie," Mom says with a sigh. "That girl was a handful. She got into *everything*. Very curious and always asking questions. She never asked for permission to do anything. Camryn just did what she wanted and was willing to face the consequences. She has always been independent, which I love about her, and she's open to taking chances. She's like that with everything in life, except when it comes to love."

"Oh, really?"

"Camryn's had a certain image of the perfect man for her; and honestly, her father and I think she's got it all wrong. And maybe she's *too* independent and strong-willed. I don't know. But I'm sure someone is going to come along one day who will catch her off-guard and sweep her off her feet."

"How does she feel about her younger sister getting married before her?" Maggie asks.

Mom shrugs. "Well, she hasn't mentioned anything to me about it one way or the other. I know Camryn is very happy for Camille, but I think it's only natural that there is a bit of envy there. I'm sure her move to Virginia was, in part, an attempt to expand her dating pool. But even that isn't working out as she'd hoped."

Maggie stands and gestures for Mom to follow. "Camryn is going to be just fine, no matter what the future holds for her." They make their way towards the back door. "I don't know about you, but I sure could use a glass of iced water."

"I'd love a glass, too." Mom links her arm into Maggie's, and they walk back into the house, where they spend the rest of the evening together.

Chapter 16

After years of visiting New Orleans, I know better than to schedule a ride to an address on Bourbon Street, since most of the street is blocked off for pedestrians only. So, I have the driver drop us off at the CVS on Canal Street. It's located at the intersection with Carondelet Street, which is essentially Bourbon Street, but on the formerly French side. According to my phone's navigation, it should take us about ten minutes to walk to The Backdoor Bar, but that's only if we don't make any stops along the way.

When we reach Bourbon Street, we are greeted by the unmistakable stench that can only be described as a mix of beer, sweat, urine, and vomit. It's a bit overwhelming at first, but it fades away the further down we go—or maybe we just become nose blind to it. It's dark outside, but the street is illuminated by streetlights and neon lights glowing from businesses beckoning for patronage into the midnight hours.

Barricades block the road, allowing people to walk freely in the street. It's Saturday night, so the area is already packed with a blend of locals and tourists from all parts of the world. The street seems to come alive with people dancing and shouting and pulsing music emanating from seemingly everywhere.

We pass a variety of businesses, including famous sites, such as Larry Flynt's Hustler Club, Willie's Chicken Shack, and Hard Rock Café, plus smaller restaurants, bars, shops, and strip clubs.

"What are those long neon green drinks I see everyone walking around with?" Camille asks as she steps over some loose Mardi Gras beads someone dropped on the ground.

"Those are Hand Grenades. They're a really sweet drink that they only sell here on Bourbon Street. I'm not sure what all they're made of, but I know rum is definitely an ingredient."

Camille stares at a group of women walking by, each sipping on a Hand Grenade.

"Do you want one?" I ask her.

"If we have time." She looks at me with pleading eyes.

I roll my eyes. "We can split one." I ask the group where to find the drinks, and they point to a bar called Tropical Isle on the other side of Bourbon Street.

As the name implies, the bar has a tropical motif and features a large tiki bar wrapped around the center of the room. The music is blaring, playing a pop song that I don't recognize and don't quite enjoy. There are neon green lights everywhere, making the bar itself appear to be glowing. Round lime green barstools line the bar, and we locate two vacant ones.

I yell over the music to the bartender and order one Hand Grenade with two straws. Camille's eyes are wide as saucers when the bartender hands me our drink. After paying, we go back out to Bourbon Street, and I check my phone to see how much further we have to walk.

"It looks like we're almost there," I say as Camille takes her first sip.

CANAL STREET BED AND BREAKFAST

"This is so good!"

I take a sip from the other straw and make a sour face. "It's too sweet for me, but I'll help you drink it so I can get a good buzz."

We take turns sipping the frozen melon-flavored concoction and observe the diverse population of people congregating on this street where anything goes. Camille has me take a picture of her with a man wearing only a cowboy hat, tight sequin striped shorts with suspenders and glittery white cowboy boots. Just a typical night in the French Quarter!

There's so much noise from all the activity that I can barely hear the navigation app announce that we have arrived at our destination. Just as I glance at my phone to confirm, someone yells from across the street.

"Hey, you in the pink dress!"

Camille and I turn and look across the street but find no one that appears to be talking to her.

"Up here!"

Our eyes shift up to a balcony full of men, each with a cup in one hand and a handful of Mardi Gras beads in the other.

"Who, me?" Camille puts her hand on her hip.

"Yeah, you!" A young blonde man wearing a blue Steph Curry jersey and a backwards baseball cap shouts with a laugh and shakes the beads. "Show us your boobs!"

"Um—" I turn Camille away from the obnoxious gang. "If you want some beads, we can buy some from one of those cheap souvenir shops." I grab her hand and usher her towards a sandwich sign on the sidewalk that reads in colorful chalk: *Grand Re-opening and Drag Show Tonight.*

I look up and see a metal sign hanging from the balcony overhead that confirms we have reached our destination—The Backdoor Bar. There's a muscular bouncer standing at the door checking IDs. I run my eyes along the building and realize that it looks familiar. I glance back down Bourbon Street, and it occurs to me.

This is the same bar where Olivia went missing!

"Camille, do you know where we are?" I whisper loudly over the music blasting from the bar, as if it was a secret.

She looks around, puzzled. "No."

"This used to be the Sinful Spirits Bar. From last night. Where that woman went missing!"

Camille looks around again, ignoring the whooping and hollering still coming from the rowdy group on the balcony. Her facial expression changes when it hits her. "Oh, my God! Are you serious?"

"I know." I'm still in disbelief. "What are the odds?"

"We're still going in, though, aren't we?" Camille asks expectantly.

I don't answer right away. Surprisingly, I'm hesitant to go into a place where a crime potentially happened. I should be excited and eager to search for clues. But it's all just too real. I'm definitely not cut out for a career in crime solving.

There's no logical reason for us to not go in. It's just crazy that I would learn about a mystery one day, meet a family member of the victim the next day, *and* just so happen to go to the place where the mystery started.

I peer into the bar and then back at Camille. Suddenly, the image of a woman's dead body rotting under the floor flashes into my mind. Feeling foolish, I shake my head and silently curse Camille for ever putting the thought into my head.

"Of course." I reach into my purse to find my driver's license.

We approach the door at the top of the steps, exactly where Geoff shared the story about Olivia, and give the large bouncer our IDs.

He examines them briefly and hands them back. In a monotone voice, he says, "The drag show starts in ten minutes. It's in the back, through the door on the right by the restrooms."

"Thanks!" Camille shoves me through the door.

The former Sinful Spirits Bar looks nothing like I imagined. It's not as dark as I expected it to be. To our left, there is one long L-shaped bench lining the entire front wall and the connecting wall, with chairs on the opposite sides of several small tables. Each table is occupied, leaving me less than optimistic about having somewhere to sit for the drag show.

Directly in front of us and across the dance floor, I recognize the bar from the surveillance videos. There's a stunning black woman wearing a pink afro wig behind the bar, preparing drinks. I assume that she's Ava's girlfriend.

Looking to our right by the front entry, there's a DJ behind a booth, dancing along to hip-hop music while he works on his laptop to prepare the next mix. As my eyes follow along the side wall, I see someone with a striking resemblance to Cher in a gold sequin gown standing in a doorway next to the restrooms.

"Let's get a drink!" Camille yells over the music.

I put my mouth near her ear, so I don't have to shout. "Maybe we should find some seats for the show first."

"Good idea!"

We hold hands and inch our way through the crowd of people on the small dance floor. I catch a whiff of weed as we nonchalantly pass two men motioning for us to come their way. I keep my focus on drag Cher, who smiles as we approach the door.

"Camryn and Camille?" She touches the tip of her tongue to her upper lip and whips her long, black hair over her shoulder. Her eyebrows are arched high, and she's wearing blue glittery eyeshadow behind her thick, glittery lashes.

I look at her, confused.

"Ava called and told me to expect you. She said to look for a tall, pretty girl with her hair in a bun and a shorter pretty girl wearing a sash and tiara."

"Oh!" I laugh. "Yes, that's us!"

"Glad you could make it! Ava had us reserve a booth for you. Follow me."

I take Camille's hand, and we follow Cher into a room filled with small round tables in front of a stage. I can still hear the music from the other room while the door is open, but when it closes, I can only hear the bass from the music and the buzz of people chattering. At the back of the room, there are three round booths facing the stage. The one in the middle is the only vacant one, with a sign that says *RESERVED* on the table.

We slide into the booth and settle in.

"A server will be by to take your drink order." Cher signals to someone we can't see. "Have fun, ladies!"

"Thank you!" we say in unison.

Not a minute later, a young Hispanic woman with thick, black cat-eye eyeliner stops at our booth to take our drink orders. I order an Old Fashioned, and Camille orders a rum and Coke.

"That was nice of Ava to reserve this table for us." Camille shoves her back against me for a selfie.

I smile for the picture. "It's a good thing she did, because we'd have nowhere to sit."

Our server returns, just as the lights dim. A spotlight shines on the stage, and music starts to play. It's at this moment that I realize we're in the room that I had already determined had something to do with Olivia's disappearance. My mind goes back to the *Disappearances* episode, and I remember that the room under construction was on the same side of the bar where Olivia was standing before her arms were snatched away.

Did Noah bring her in here and do something nefarious? Or did Olivia use this room as an escape route to disappear and start a new life?

I'm jolted back into the present when I feel Camille bouncing on the seat next to me. Someone identical to Madonna is on the stage wearing a headset microphone and a studded bodysuit with silver cones over her breasts. I decide to let go of Olivia Peterson for the moment and stay focused on my last days with my sister before she starts a whole new chapter in her life—even finding myself *vogue*-ing along to the song.

We spend the next hour or so singing along with Dolly Parton, Liza Minnelli, Whitney Houston, and Cher. Tina Turner is finishing her rendition of *Proud Mary* when a light suddenly shines into the room from the door opening. I glance over and see Ava walk in, followed by the tall silhouette of someone else. With the light shining from behind them, it's not until the door closes and my eyes re-adjust to the darkness that I can tell who it is.

I grab Camille's arm and yank her closer to me. "Is that Eric?" I ask, my eyes glued to him. He's wearing light khaki shorts and a tight-fitting sage green t-shirt, accentuating his athletic physique. *The man gets sexier every time I see him.*

"Okay, don't be mad," Camille says. "But I may or may not have told Ava to invite him."

I jerk my head around, surely giving myself whiplash. "You did *what?* When?"

She smiles timidly. "When I went downstairs to wait with Mom before dinner, I ran into Ava as she was coming back in the house with the flyer. And I asked her to invite Eric." She gives me a not-so-innocent shrug. "I thought it would be fun."

"Yeah, for *you!*"

Ava plops down in the booth and bumps against me, urging me to scoot over. Camille and I shuffle down, and my eyes meet Eric's as he slides into the booth next to Ava. He greets me with a weak smile, leaving me still unable to determine his opinion of me.

Camille leans in front of me to be within earshot of him. "We haven't officially met. I'm Camille, Camryn's sister."

He smiles. "I'm—"

She cuts him off. "Eric. I know." She flashes him a sly grin.

I haven't stopped blushing when a familiar face dances onto the stage, clapping and singing a familiar song.

"All the single ladies!"

Drag Beyoncé is wearing a black bodysuit that's cinched tightly at her waist and black platform stilettos. It's jarring how contouring and half an inch of makeup can make her look exactly like the megastar.

Camille stands up and belts out a *"Woo-hoo!"* She's excited to hear the song that's commonly played at the end of a wedding reception, when the bride tosses her bouquet to the hopeful singles. She slides out of the booth and dances in front of our table.

Halfway through the song, the volume drops. Beyoncé instructs the crowd to visit a man with a laptop sitting at a table near the stage to request songs for karaoke. A few people make a beeline for him right away. The music turns back up, and I see a blue glow from a screen mounted on the wall above us that I hadn't noticed earlier, showing the lyrics to the song. Beyoncé continues singing and notices Camille dancing.

"Come on up here, Pinkie!" she yells into the microphone.

Camille tosses me her phone and runs onto the stage, where Beyoncé hands her an additional microphone so she can sing along. Ava and I are cheering Camille on while she flips her hand back and forth, flashing her diamond ring during the *"Oh-Oh-Ohs."* I record a video on my phone with my left hand and take pictures using hers with my right. She's trained me well.

I glance over at Eric, and I'm surprised to see him watching me, smiling. Suddenly, I feel very nervous. I give him a shaky smile and quickly look back at the stage. My heart is racing and thumping in my ears.

Where is our server? I need another drink!

Camille runs back to the booth at the end of the song, completely out of breath.

"That was amazing!" I hand her back the phone.

"I need a drink," she says, fanning herself off.

Ava nudges Eric with her elbow to get him to move. "I'll go grab some!" She scoots out of the booth. "What are you drinking?"

We give Ava our orders for another round, and Eric requests a bourbon on the rocks. It's definitely nice to have a hookup with the bartender.

"I'll go with you," Camille says.

Eric slides back into the booth and sits next to me. I melt when I realize that he's wearing my favorite men's cologne—Burberry Touch.

"I didn't know you'd be here tonight," I say as a dark-haired woman in a snakeskin print bodysuit takes the microphone and prepares to sing *Man! I Feel Like a Woman!*

"Neither did I." He smirks. "Ava came by my room and told me that I had been invited by another guest. I assumed it was you."

I feel my body temperature start to rise. "And you still came?"

Now Eric's blushing. "Yeah. I didn't know it was *here*, though." He looks around the room uncomfortably.

"Oh. Yeah, I didn't either."

"I haven't been here since right after Olivia went missing. Of course, I've walked by, but never gone in. I almost didn't come in tonight, but—" He pauses, looking around again.

I shift in my seat, trying to think of what to say next.

Eric seems to be in another world, but then he looks at me and realizes that he's made things even more awkward than they were before. "It's fine, though. I'm having fun!"

"That's good." I drum my fingernails nervously on the table. "So, are you going to sing?" I ask as Ava and Camille return with the drinks.

"It would take a lot more of these," he says, grabbing his glass.

"Challenge accepted!" Camille clinks her glass to his, and we all laugh.

Ava is now sitting at one end of the booth and Camille on the other, leaving Eric and me together in the middle.

"The three of us have to sing something." Ava looks at me and

Camille, who gives Ava a thumbs up while sipping her drink.

"I don't know." I'm already not comfortable being the center of attention, and I certainly don't want to humiliate myself in front of Eric—again.

Camille wraps her arms around me and squeezes tightly. "Please! It would be the highlight of the trip."

I look over at Ava and Eric, who are both staring at me expectantly.

"Okay, but what song?" I ask. "I don't know any of that new music y'all listen to."

Ava gives me a mischievous look. "I have the perfect song that everyone knows." She jumps out of the booth without saying another word.

***

Over the next hour and a half, we watch some great singers and some not-so-great singers belt out their favorite karaoke hits. Eric impresses all of us by knowing the words to *Cupid* by Sam Cooke being sung by a middle-aged man with a baritone voice, officially solidifying my crush. We order our third round of drinks, and I'm having a great time! At some point we're all dancing and singing, even to the songs we don't know. As more and more performances go by, I hope that I have somehow skirted around being forced to sing off-key in front of a room of strangers. I sneak back into the booth to take a break from dancing and catch my breath. Eric turns around and gives me a wink, making me blush. He slides into the booth next to me.

"Are you okay?"

I nod. "Yes, I just needed a breather."

He smiles. "I haven't had this much fun in a long time."

"Me, too!"

Just then, Drag Whitney steps onto the stage and makes an announcement wearing a chrome bodycon dress and a brown curly wig, like in the *How Will I Know* music video. "Ladies and gentlemen, it's time for the last song of the evening."

The crowd boos.

"Ava and friends, get your butts up here!"

Eric gives me a wide grin, and I chug the remaining watered-down whiskey from my glass. Camille grabs my hand and whips me out of the booth.

I follow her and Ava around the tables and up the stairs leading to the stage. Whitney hands each of us a microphone, and Ava immediately starts singing as the music slowly begins.

"Last dance, last chance for love."

Ava's voice is shockingly good, and the crowd erupts with applause. The spotlight is blinding, and I can only see the people at the first row of tables. Thankfully, I don't have to see Eric's reaction when it's my turn to sing. My heart is racing, so I take a cleansing breath and decide that this is the moment that I have to let everything go. *Just do it!*

When the tempo picks up, everyone in the audience is on their feet, dancing along with us. We take turns singing, but we mostly sing in unison, allowing Ava to drown the two of us out.

As the song comes to an end, all the drag queens join us on stage to close out the show. We're still dancing as we exit the stage and go back to the booth, where Eric is standing and applauding. Ava falls into him, giving him a hug, and Camille gives him a high five. He smiles at me as I reach into the booth to grab our purses.

"That was incredible," Eric says, laughing while he gently holds my arm to help me back up.

I blow my bangs to cool my face and follow Ava and Camille to the door. "That was the scariest thing I've ever done in my life!"

We wait outside for several minutes while Ava talks to her girlfriend, Keisha, who I've learned is pre-med and sometimes bartends on the weekends. The bar is still open, and Bourbon Street is still as lively as it was when we walked in three hours prior. Once Ava comes out, I schedule a ride share to pick us up one block over on Dauphine Street. As the four of us walk to the meeting spot, we laugh and reflect on our favorite moments of the evening, aside from our grand finale performance.

Camille and Ava walk ahead of Eric and me, starting an a cappella encore of *Last Dance*. I glance over at Eric, who is looking into a window display of antiques as we pass by it. I hum the first line of *Cupid* just loud enough for him to hear. He turns and looks at me when he recognizes the tune and gives me a soft smile.

By the time we pull up to the bed and breakfast, the mood has mellowed out, and exhaustion has set in. Eric steps out of the front seat and holds the back door open while the three of us file out. Ava hugs us all goodnight and walks around the corner to her car. After climbing the stairs, Eric unlocks the front door and allows Camille and me to walk in ahead of him.

I reach into my purse and find our keys, but Camille snatches them out of my hand as soon as I retrieve them.

"Good night," she says, walking toward the stairs, not looking back.

Eric runs his fingers through his hair nervously and smiles. For the first time, I notice the creases next to his eyes when he smiles, the faint freckles sprinkled across his nose and cheeks, and I swear I saw his left eye twinkle.

I decide to break the silence. "That is the best time I've had in a very long time."

"Me, too," he says. "It's the first time I've had fun on any of my trips to New Orleans."

This reminds me of the unfortunate reason Eric is here in the first place. "Well, I'm glad you came out with us—and to know that you don't despise me."

"What? Why would you think that?"

I'm surprised that he's so surprised. "Well, after what happened this morning, and then at the art studio. You just didn't seem to be very pleased with me."

Eric looks concerned. "No, not at all. I guess you just keep catching me off-guard."

I smile with an overwhelming sense of relief.

There's an awkward moment as we stare at each other, expecting the other to say something. I fumble with my fingers and bite my lip.

"Well, I guess we should call it a night." He sounds disappointed.

I nod. "Yeah, I guess." I'm disappointed, too. I don't want the night to end.

We walk towards the stairs, and I place my foot on the first step and my hand on the rail.

"Good night, Eric."

"Good night, Camryn."

He smiles and turns to head downstairs, and I feel as though a cloud is lifting me upstairs. I reach the door to our room and silently beg God for two things—that Camille would let me go to sleep without tormenting me, and that Eric would appear in my dreams, even if only for a second.

Chapter 17

It's Sunday and our last full day in New Orleans. I've planned for us to spend the day on the east side of Canal Street in the Garden District and possibly the Arts District, if time allows. I haven't spent much time in these areas on my previous trips, so I'm excited to experience something new.

I examine my reflection in the bathroom mirror. It has taken me a little over thirty minutes to get ready today as I listen to an episode of my favorite true crime comedy podcast called *I Think Not!* to help me keep my mind off Eric. His voice, blue eyes, and perfect smile kept popping into my head all last night as I tried desperately to fall asleep.

Typically, I reserve wearing eyeliner for special occasions, but I noticed that I've looked pretty tired in most of Camille's pictures she's posted on Instagram from the trip. So, I need to make sure I appear more upbeat and refreshed in today's pictures—or at least that's what I plan to tell anyone who asks. I apply some tinted lip gloss, smooth my hair back tightly into a bun, and open the bathroom door.

"Excuse me, miss ma'am?" Camille looks down at my denim romper and back up to my face, noticing my hot pink chandelier earrings. "Got a hot date?"

I roll my eyes. "What do you mean?"

"Yesterday, you looked like death on a platter for breakfast, and today you look—"

"You look beautiful," Mom says with a wink.

Both Camille and Mom are ready for the day. Mom is wearing a pale yellow, loose-fitting midi dress, and Camille is the splash of color in our trio, wearing a short coral sundress accessorized with her sash and tiara, of course.

I check my smartwatch, and it's two minutes past nine. "We're late. Let's go."

We walk downstairs and into the dining room. I take a deep breath and pull my shoulders back in preparation for seeing Eric at the same table as yesterday. But I'm disappointed to find that he's not there yet.

I notice Pat peering out the window towards the garden. If I didn't know better, I'd say she was smiling at someone. "Good morning, Pat!"

She slightly jumps, obviously startled. "Oh, good morning, Camryn." She nods to include Mom and Camille. I introduce Pat to Camille, and then she excuses herself to go help with breakfast. But before I sit, I peek out the window and see a middle-aged black man pruning an azalea bush. He glances up at the window with a smirk, but quickly smiles and waves when he sees me. I think Pat may have a little crush on their landscaper.

We sit down at our table, this time with Camille sitting next to me.

"I wonder where Eric is?" She looks around dramatically with her neck extended like an ostrich.

I choose to ignore her by pretending to search for something in my purse.

"Camille tells me that you two had a great time last night," Mom says to avert a potential argument.

I put the phone down. "Oh, Mom, I had a blast! I told Eric that it was the most fun I've ever had in New Orleans."

"Oh? Eric was there?" Mom smirks as her eyes dart back and forth between me and Camille, leaving no doubt that Camille has already told her.

"Yes, Ava invited him." I give Camille a side-eye.

Mom smiles. "That's nice."

"What did you get into?" I ask Mom, just as Maggie enters with a tray of parfaits and water. She and Mom exchange smiles.

"I spent some time getting to know Maggie a bit." Mom gives Maggie a one-arm hug around her waist as she places our parfaits on the table. "We learned that we have a lot in common, including that *you* are one of our favorite people."

I smile at both of them. "Aw, the feeling is mutual."

Maggie catches me glance at Eric's empty table while she's pouring my water. "Um, Camryn." She leans closer to me. "Eric wanted me to tell you that he has a meeting this morning, and he won't be here for breakfast."

I play it cool. "Oh, okay." I lock eyes with Maggie to avoid the curious looks on Mom and Camille's faces. "What's for breakfast this morning?"

"We're serving our Southern Breakfast with eggs, bacon and grits. Ann Marie, I made another serving of yesterday's breakfast for you, if you'd prefer that."

Mom's face lights up. "Oh, that was delicious. I'll take that!"

"Same drinks as yesterday?" Maggie asks.

"Yes, ma'am," Camille and I say in unison.

Camille shifts in her chair to face me, with her elbow perched on the table. "I wonder who Eric is meeting with?"

"I don't know, and it's none of our business." I squint my eyes and glare at her.

But, of course, my mind is spinning. Eric is here for his sister's vigil, so maybe it's something about that. Or maybe he's meeting with police to get an update on Olivia's case. Or maybe he met another woman on the way to his room last night, and they've fallen in love and gone to elope.

I change the subject. "Wait until you hear what I have planned for today."

"Okay, but I want to hear more about last night first," Mom says.

Camille jumps up and moves to the chair next to her. "Mom, you should have seen me on stage with Beyoncé," she begins, as she pulls up the pictures and videos on her phone.

Camille and I relive every second of our evening, starting with the Hand Grenades, trying to make Mom feel as though she was there with us. The expression on her face is a mix of excitement, envy, and nostalgia. When we've finished eating, we take turns washing up in the powder room on the main floor and head out to wait for the streetcar.

***

When we step off the streetcar, I stop Mom and Camille as they instinctively walk towards the French Quarter.

"Wait!" I say, giving them a startle. "We're actually spending the day on *this* side of Canal Street." I point my thumb over my shoulder towards the opposite side of the street behind me.

Camille looks confused. "I didn't know there was anything to do on that side."

"Plenty." I guide them across the street, and we walk to the corner of Carondelet Street at Canal Street, just as a green streetcar marked *St. Charles* slows to a stop.

"We're getting on another streetcar?" Mom asks. "Where is it taking us?"

"Just wait and see," I say, dubiously.

Several people step off the streetcar, and we wait until a small crowd gets on before us. We find two small wood benches, and I sit on the first bench, while Mom and Camille sit on the bench behind me. The windows are open, welcoming any gracious breeze offering some relief from the already suffocating heat.

The streetcar slowly takes off, spending only a moment on Canal Street before turning onto St. Charles Avenue. There are going to be several stops where passengers can get on and off, but we are going to take it all the way to the Garden District.

We enter the Central Business District and slow to a stop in front of Lafayette Square. I do a quick Google search on my phone and share with Mom and Camille that the small park is the second-oldest park in New Orleans, after Jackson Square. From where we are, we can see statues of Benjamin Franklin and Henry Clay.

Our journey continues, and we find ourselves in the Warehouse District and then the Museum District. The streetcar circles around Harmony Circle, where I inform them that it used to be called Lee

Circle, but the name was changed after the statue of the Confederate General Robert E. Lee was replaced with the tall marble column we see now.

Mom nods. "I remember hearing about that. It was quite the controversy when it happened."

"Good riddance," Camille says with an eye roll.

I look at my smartwatch and then at Mom. "There are some great museums around here, but we'll have to do that on another trip. There's just not enough time." The streetcar travels further down the line, and I stand when we finally reach the Garden District. "This is our stop."

We step off the streetcar at First Street and cross over the median to briefly walk down St. Charles Street. It feels like we've gone back in time as we approach the rows of historic homes and mansions that have made this area famous.

St. Charles Street is lined with trees on both sides, providing a canopy of shade and making it a pleasant stroll. Each house has a meticulously manicured garden behind wrought iron gates. We *ooh* and *ahh* over the breathtaking beauty and take pictures in front of our favorite houses.

We stop in front of a white colonial mansion with four white columns stretching all the way to the top of the second level. I had done a small amount of research before the trip, being sure to remember this house for today.

"Camille, you will be happy to know that this is the mansion where they filmed 'The Real World: New Orleans.'"

Camille's jaw drops, and her eyes light up as she gazes at the site of where MTV made a granddaddy of reality television. She grabs her phone and begins recording an Instagram Live video, attempting to incite at least the slightest bit of envy from her followers over her brush with history.

We spend another fifteen minutes walking down St. Charles Street and board another streetcar heading back towards Canal Street. A pleasant breeze blows through the windows along the way before we get off at the stop in front of Lafayette Square to make the five-minute walk to where we will eat.

***

Lunch is at Meril, a restaurant owned by the famous chef, Emeril Lagasse. I've heard great things about this restaurant, but it will be my first time to actually eat here. The vibe is younger and more contemporary than the other restaurants we've experienced on this trip. There are exposed brick walls with large monochromatic murals of sea creatures and a full, open view of the kitchen in the back. When we approach the hostess, Camille spots the perfect photo opportunity behind us—a brick wall with yellow neon lights that read *Eat, Drink and Be Meril.* The three of us sit on the orange cushioned bench underneath the neon quote. We shove our heads together, the three of us cheek-to-cheek with Camille in the middle, and I snap a selfie on my phone.

The host takes us to our table on the far side of the restaurant. No sooner than we sit down do we see a group of servers make a beeline to a table on the other side of the restaurant, holding a tray overflowing with sparklers and singing *Happy Birthday*.

"That looks like fun!" Mom stretches her neck to get a better look.

Our server unintentionally blocks her view when she approaches our table to fill our water glasses and take our drink orders. She introduces herself, and I'm startled when I hear her name.

Olivia.

My mind instantly goes blank, and for the first time since we left the bed and breakfast, I think about Eric. In fact, my mind is consumed by him. His smile. His eyes. The way he runs his fingers through his hair when he's nervous. I can almost smell Burberry Touch at just the thought of him.

"Camryn?" Camille knees me under the table.

I'm startled out of my trance and find our server staring at me expectantly.

"Oh, um—" It takes me a moment, but I realize she must be taking our drink orders. "I'll just have water with lemon."

Olivia nods and smiles. "Three waters. I'll bring them back right away and get your orders."

We discuss our lunch options. The brunch menu is still being offered, but since we already ate breakfast, we want a *lunch* lunch. Mom plans to order the grilled salmon. Camille chooses the spicy rigatoni, and I opt for the parmesan-fried chicken salad.

Mom excuses herself to visit the restroom.

Camille offers me a drop of her travel-size hand sanitizer. "I think I've had about enough walking for the day." She gives herself a drop, and I check the time on my smartwatch. It's almost one-thirty.

I sigh. "Well, I only have one more thing planned for three o'clock, and we can get a ride over if that's easier. It's a walking tour, but it's indoors, so we'll be in air conditioning."

"What is it?"

"It's hard to explain, but we'll get to partake in some alcohol tastings," I say, hoping to resurrect Camille's sense of adventure.

She gives me a mischievous grin. "Well, count me in!"

I look at Camille and suddenly feel bittersweet. "Do you realize that at this time next week, you'll be just a couple of hours away from no longer just being my sister, but Alan's *wife*?"

She pauses and thinks for a bit. "You're right!"

I reach out my hand for her to hold. I have a flashback of a five-year-old Camille wearing a Cinderella costume, begging me to be her Fairy Godmother and sing *Bibbity Bobbity Boo*. We smile at each other, both a little teary-eyed, just as Mom sits down. She looks back and forth at both of us.

"What did I miss?"

"Oh, Camryn is just sad because I'll be officially making her the spinster sister a week from today," Camille says, cutting her eyes over to me with a smirk.

I give her hand a hard squeeze and playfully knee her under the table. "Excuse me? A *what*?"

"Come on, now," Mom interjects. "No one even uses that word anymore; and even if they did, Camryn is nowhere close to being old enough to be called a spinster."

"Can we just stop saying the word *spinster*, please?" I'm determined to put an end to the embarrassing banter. It's bad enough that I've already had that same thought many times, but I certainly don't need to hear that word attached to my name twice in a matter of seconds.

Mom looks at me apologetically. "Sorry, dear."

Our server returns with our waters and takes our lunch orders. Once the food arrives, we take our time eating and spend the next hour discussing mansions, drag queens and wedding details. When Olivia comes back to remove our empty dishes, I ask her for the check. But before she returns with it, something shiny catches my eye, and it seems to be coming closer to us. Within a few seconds, Olivia and three other servers are at our table, holding a wood board with a sparkler on one end and a massive stick of pink cotton candy on the other end. They place it on the table in front of Camille.

"Congratulations to the bride-to-be!" they all say in unison, followed by applause from patrons around the restaurant.

Mom looks overjoyed and is clapping faster than everyone else. She must have secretly ordered this dessert for Camille while she was away for her restroom break.

I grab my phone and take a few pictures of Camille, who is smiling from ear to ear while she waits for the sparks to fizzle out. "I was hoping y'all would do this!" she says as she peels off a chunk of cotton candy. We all partake in the fluffy dessert and have Olivia take a picture of the three of us with wads of cotton candy in our hands. It's the perfect ending to our last lunch in New Orleans.

Chapter 18

Our ride share pulls up to The Sazerac House at two-forty-five. I had overlooked the tall gray building on the corner of Magazine Street and Canal Street on all my trips to New Orleans until last year, when Maggie mentioned that they offer a free self-guided tour. My friend and I were slightly intrigued, but when she told us that it also included free tastings of gin, bourbon, and rum, we immediately booked our tour.

The Sazerac brand is synonymous with New Orleans. The Sazerac Cocktail became famous around 1850, and in 2008, legislation was passed to make it the official drink of New Orleans. The tour gives you an immersive experience while you learn about the brand's history, the cocktail culture in New Orleans, and stories from the Prohibition Era—along with tastings and other fun activities.

We enter the building and walk into a massive room with two women standing behind a bar to check in tour guests. An older woman with stringy gray hair greets us with a friendly smile and confirms our reservation. She hands us each a black wristband to wear throughout the tour, and she directs us to wait for our guide by a gigantic, floor-to-ceiling shelf that is stacked with meticulously arranged Sazerac bottles. We join other people waiting to begin the tour, and we're all eager to get started.

Our guide, Delaney, greets us promptly at three P.M. and walks us to a set of elevators to take us upstairs to the top floor. Once we all reach the starting point, he informs us how the rest of the self-guided tour will go and the few rules they have for guests. He explains that as we complete each exhibit at our own pace, we will take the winding staircase down to the next floor until we reach the bottom floor.

The aesthetic throughout the tour is reminiscent of an upscale 1920s speakeasy. It includes grand scale photos with detailed descriptions and stories, antiques, and interactive stations where we can learn about cocktail recipes. Although I've done this tour before, it is so extensive that I feel as though it's my first time again.

We approach a bar for our first tasting, where a man dressed as an old-fashioned bartender teaches us how to use bitters to add flavor and seasoning to our drinks.

After leaving that room, we continue with the tour and observe many more informative exhibits. Occasionally, we spot small booths where guides teach us, step-by-step, how to prepare cocktails and then pour samples into small paper cups for us to taste. Mom never wants a cup, but she takes tiny sips of mine, so she can at least taste and share in the experience. I laugh and take a picture of the sour faces she and Camille make with every sip.

I'm excited when we reach the second floor. In my opinion, it's the most fascinating part of the tour. We approach what looks like a bar with shelves stocked with bottles of Sazerac in between long, vertical screens. We sit on stools and look down at the bar to find small screens on the bar top. Virtual bartenders appear on the long screens in front of us and greet us. My bartender is a black man named Armand. He slips a drink menu towards me on the screen, which appears on the bar top screen for me to select a drink. Armand then teaches me about the history of the French 75 cocktail I selected and then virtually prepares it for me. I glance over and see Mom and Camille have different bartenders virtually making cocktails for them.

We take our time exploring the remaining exhibits and then make our way down to the first floor, where we find the distillery. A guide explains the Sazerac brand's process of making whiskey and bourbon and how it is stored until it's bottled. Our last stop is the gift shop, where guests can purchase a variety of items and pick up complimentary cocktail recipes. Camille takes one of each.

"I'm going to get us a ride back to the bed and breakfast," I say as we step outside. "I know we're all exhausted, and I want to just chill until dinner."

"Sounds like a plan." Mom leans over to take a selfie with Camille in front of the Sazerac logo on the window.

***

It only takes a few minutes for our driver to arrive in a mid-size SUV, and we all squeeze into the back seat.

"Camryn," Camille says, looking past Mom and at me. "This has been the best trip. I don't think I would have ever experienced New Orleans like this if it wasn't for you."

I smile. The trip is even better than I expected, too. New Orleans has become a part of me, and it's only fitting that the people I love get to experience it and understand why. I'm thrilled that they are enjoying it so much!

"I'm glad!" I say, begging my tear ducts to hold on to the tears that so desperately want to fall. "There's so much more I want y'all to experience, like Frenchman Street and the French Market, but there just isn't enough time."

Mom touches my hand. "Well, then I guess you'll just have to bring us out here again, won't you?"

"Seriously, any time!" I say enthusiastically.

We pull up to the curb in front of Canal Street Bed and Breakfast and file out of the car. I feel my weary legs pleading for relief, making the stairs seem extra long today. When we reach the door inside the vestibule, I insert the key into the lock, just as someone abruptly opens the door from the inside.

"Whoa!" Eric is as startled to see me as I am to see him. "Camryn. Hi!"

I'm already blushing. "Hi, Eric. Um—" Looking into his blue eyes makes me forget how to use the most basic words.

He steps back, holding the door open for us to enter the foyer. Everyone is looking at me expectantly, but Mom saves us all from the awkward moment.

"Hi, Eric." She holds her hand out towards him. "I'm Ann Marie, Camryn's mother."

Eric gently shakes her hand. "Pleasure to meet you." His eyes shift over to me. "I was about to run to the CVS up the street to get a few things."

"Mm, hmm." Camille grabs Mom's arm and ushers her towards the stairs. "We need to, uh, soak our feet. In our room. Right now." They disappear upstairs, leaving me and Eric alone, practically dumbfounded.

I look at him and shrug. "Sorry about that."

Eric laughs and nervously spins his keychain on his finger. "So, listen. I was wondering if I could take you to dinner one night before you leave?"

"Actually, tonight is our last night." I frown. "And we already have reservations."

"No, we don't!" The loud voice comes from behind me. I glance back and see Camille crouched at the top of the stairs. "We'll be fine."

Eric and I both laugh.

"So, you're free tonight?" he asks.

"Apparently. What time should I be ready?"

He looks at the time on his phone. "Let's meet right here at seven-thirty."

"Okay, sounds good."

"Great." He gives me a sweet smile as he reaches for the door. "Looking forward to it."

"Me, too." I watch as Eric closes the door and slowly turn on my heels. I walk to the stairs, stopping at the bottom with my arms crossed. "You eavesdropping Peeping Tom!"

Camille stands up. "I think you meant to say, 'thank you.'"

I follow her upstairs and into our room to find Mom is sitting on the bed, rubbing her feet.

"Camryn has a date tonight," Camille says as she kicks off her sandals. "Why don't we go back to Katie's for dinner?"

Mom nods. "Sounds like a plan to me." She sits back with her head against her headboard. "I want to hear more about what happened to Eric's sister. I have a feeling you've been holding back on what you know."

Camille sits on the bed next to her. "Me, too."

"Okay," I say, digging through my suitcase. "I'll freshen up a bit and tell you everything I know."

I find the burgundy Diane von Furstenberg wrap dress I intended to wear tonight for our dinner at Hotel Monteleone and ask Camille to steam it for me while I shower. Once I'm done, I grab a terry cloth robe from the closet and start getting ready, leaving the bathroom door open.

While I apply my makeup, I tell them everything I remember from the *Disappearances* episode. I describe Olivia and the story of her being adopted. How she had recently graduated with a degree in architecture and was selected to be a part of a prestigious internship. I share that Olivia was in New Orleans for her roommate's bachelorette party, being sure to remind them that the group was staying here at the Canal Street Bed and Breakfast. I recount her friends saying that Olivia appeared distracted and that she only seemed to have a good time at that bar the night she disappeared. Thinking back to the grainy surveillance videos, I explain that everyone but Olivia is seen going in *and* out of the bar that night and that she was seen with Noah at the bar ordering a drink. Then I describe how her hands were snatched away from the bar and that it was the last time she was ever seen.

"Who is Noah, again?" Mom asks.

"He's the only person of interest the police had. Apparently, he attended the same college as Olivia and also graduated with a degree in architecture."

Camille raises an eyebrow. "Well, that can't be just a coincidence. They went to school together, *and* they were in New Orleans at the same time and at the same bar?"

I nod. "Exactly. Olivia was dancing with him that night, and her friends saw them walk over to the bar together to get a drink. The video proves that. But you couldn't really see them once they ordered the drink, which Noah claimed was just water. And no one ever saw her again after that."

"By the way, Mom," Camille interjects. "Did Camryn mention that the bar we went to last night happens to be the same bar where Olivia disappeared?"

"No!" Mom's eyes are as wide as saucers.

"Crazy, huh? And we met her brother, too? Sounds like some Twilight Zone kind of stuff to me," Camille says, being characteristically dramatic.

"Anyway—" I roll my eyes. "Her friends looked all over for her. They couldn't call her because Olivia accidentally left her cell phone at home in Austin. The police showed up and checked the entire bar and the space next door where the owner was building a new room for live performances." I look at Camille. "That's where we watched the drag show."

Camille covers her gaping mouth with her hand.

"They questioned Noah, and he gave his side of the story and insisted that he left Olivia at the bar unharmed. He said he was engaged and had no interest in her. But as soon as he got the feeling that he was suspected of doing something, he lawyered up and has never talked to police again. And since they have *zero* evidence against him, that's where everything has stood for the past ten years."

"Unbelievable!" Mom looks into space as she tries to digest the entire story.

"Um—" Camille walks into the bathroom with me. "What are you going to do with your hair?"

I look at my reflection and turn my head from side to side. "My bun is still pretty neat, so I'll just wear it like this."

"No, ma'am!" She takes me by the hand and forces me to sit on the edge of the bed. "Eric's probably just as tired of seeing this bun as I am." She removes the bobby pins and ponytail holder and starts pulling on my hair. I decide to trust her and just go with it. If I don't like how it turns out, I can just redo the bun.

Mom is still deep in thought. "What do you think happened, Camryn?"

I let out a slow sigh. "Well, before I tell you, there are a couple more things you should know. Remember how I told you that I recognized our tour guide, Maureen, as the same one Olivia and her friends took a photo with when they did the same tour? Well, when I asked Maureen about it, she remembered learning about Olivia being missing. But she also said that someone turned in a burner phone that was left in the cemetery after her tour that same day. She called around, trying to find the owner, but no one claimed it. And then it was given away. I think there's a chance that it could have been Olivia's."

"Why do you think that?" Mom asks.

"Most people use burner phones because they are hiding something. They are notorious for being used by criminals because they can't be traced to a particular person. I remember one of Olivia's friends saying on the *Disappearances* show that she saw her with a phone, and she kept ignoring calls when they came in. But if Olivia left her cell phone at home, what phone did her friend see? Maybe she had a secret relationship or something. Her friends remembered her being very jumpy and distracted, but her mood changed after the cemetery tour. What if Olivia ditched the phone in the cemetery to stop the calls she had been avoiding?"

Camille stops fidgeting with my hair and looks back at the nightstand, remembering that she read about a secret relationship and secret phones in the notebook. She thinks for a second, but then shakes it off and goes back to working on my hair.

"Oh!" I say a little too loudly, making them both jump. "I almost forgot to tell you about the coffee shop. If you remember, I told you that Olivia and her friends stopped by there *before* their cemetery tour. The *Disappearances* show interviewed Janet, the coffee shop owner, on that episode, and she remembered seeing Olivia outside arguing with a man. But she couldn't describe him as anything other than a tall white guy with brown hair, wearing a navy blue baseball cap."

Camille leans over to look at me. "Does that fit Noah's description?"

"Yep!" I look at Mom for her reaction.

"So, you believe Noah did something to her?" Mom asks.

I shrug. "It seems like the only logical explanation. Either he did something, or it was a total stranger. Or she was planning to disappear—but I really don't think that's what happened. Either way, there's no explanation of how she got out of that bar without being seen on any of the cameras."

Mom probes a little deeper. "But why would Noah do it?"

"Well, I can think of a few reasons." I swat at Camille's hand when she accidentally stabs my scalp with a bobby pin. "Remember how

Noah told the police that he was engaged? Maybe he and Olivia were having an affair, and she wanted to end things, but he didn't want to let her go. Or maybe *he* wanted to end things, and she threatened to tell his fiancé."

Mom nods her head in agreement.

"My third theory comes from something else Noah said to the police. When they asked him how he knew Olivia, he said that he knew her from school and that they were both taking part in the same internship. But then he also said that she was his biggest competition to get a coveted position at the architecture firm once the internship ended."

Mom looks confused. "So, Noah killed her to ensure he got a head start in his career? That doesn't sound like a reason to murder someone."

I shrug. "I know, but I've heard many stories about people getting murdered for much less."

Mom is still deep in thought. "But even if he did, how did he get her out of the bar without being seen?"

I wink and give Mom a playful finger gun. "And *that* is the million-dollar question. If police can figure that out, they can arrest Noah, and Olivia and her family can get some justice."

Camille finishes my hair and sits next to me on the bed. "I think she was definitely hiding something. Between the mysterious phone and her jumpy behavior, something was definitely up." She glances back at the nightstand again. "People have secret affairs all the time."

"Yeah, I think so, too. But," I stand up to check my hair in the bathroom, "it's likely that we will never know."

I look in the mirror, and I'm stunned when I see my reflection. I grab the hand mirror out of my cosmetic bag and turn around so I can see the back of my head. My curly hair is twisted up and spilling over the top of my head, like a pom-pom, blending into my bangs in the front. There are loose tendrils hanging over my sideburns, giving me a relaxed but elegant updo.

"Camille, this is fantastic! You'll have to teach me how to do this." I give myself another once over and glance at my smartwatch on the bathroom counter. "I still have another forty-five minutes. Do y'all want to find something on T.V. to watch?"

Mom and Camille exchange glances.

"No, I think we'll head out to dinner and leave you to get ready in peace," Mom says, sliding her sandals back on.

Camille bounces to her feet and finds her sandals. "Yeah, I'm ready to eat and call it a night. Starting tomorrow, it will be all *wedding, wedding, wedding!*"

"Oh, okay." I had hoped they'd keep me company while I waited for my date. I'm nervous, and talking to them has kept me distracted and also made the time go by faster. "I guess I'll see y'all when I get back."

They scurry around the room like a couple of little mice. Camille picks up the keys from my nightstand and opens the door. "Have fun!"

Mom follows behind her, but stops and looks at me. "Honey, whatever you do, please don't bring up Olivia at dinner. Let tonight be about just the two of you. Tomorrow will be tough enough for Eric."

I blow her a kiss. "Sure thing, Mom."

She closes the door, and I turn around to look at my dress hanging on the closet door.

Just the two of us.

Chapter 19

I walk down the stairs as gently and gracefully as I can to avoid sounding like the herd of elephants I normally sound like on these old wooden steps. My gold wedge sandals make me aware that each step is narrower than my size ten feet, and I have to make an asserted effort not to topple forward every time the balls of my feet hover over the edge of the wood. Once I reach the landing, it occurs to me that I've been holding my breath the entire way down. I pause to get my breathing back to normal, which isn't easy considering how fast my heart is racing.

After what seems like an eternity of talking myself into taking the next step into the hallway, I make my way towards the front of the house. My body is buzzing with more nerves than I've ever felt before. When I face the door, I see Eric standing there with his hands in his jean pockets, staring at one of the small photos on the wall. My next step causes the wood floor to creak, which diverts his attention away from the photo and onto me.

"Good evening," Eric says with a crooked smile. He looks at my dress and then down at his clothes. "Sorry for the jeans." He lifts his crystal blue eyes back up to me. "It's always so hot here, so I only bring one pair of pants with me, in case there is ever a need to look nice—which there has never been until now."

I blush, and I can't help but to give a shy smile. Once again, I'm speechless—something that has never happened to me until I met Eric.

Say something, dummy, I scold myself. But it's like my lips won't part, and my head can't come up with the words. Before I can say anything, he abruptly continues.

"I usually bring slacks, but since I never end up wearing them, I packed jeans instead." Eric evaluates his ensemble again, which includes a white dress shirt with the sleeves rolled up to just below his elbows and an unbuttoned collar showing about two buttons-worth of fine, light-colored chest hair. His shoes are a flawless pair of white and tan Cole Haan sneakers.

Eric is obviously just as nervous as I am, so I force myself out of my stupor to stop him from beating himself up.

"You look—" I pause to decide what my next word will be. *Hot? Sexy? No, that's too much, however accurate.* "Nice. Very handsome, Eric."

Now it's his turn to blush.

"I have to say, you look—" Eric scans me up and down in a way that makes my arms tingle all the way down to the tips of my fingers. "Incredible!"

"Thank you." I try to come up with a way to end this round of first date jitters ping-pong. I walk towards the photo he was examining. "What's got you so intrigued by this picture?"

He looks at it again and points. "Doesn't this man look like Colonel Sanders?"

I step forward onto the long runner rug that extends the length of the foyer, and I stretch my neck to get a good look. It's eye-level to Eric but requires a bit more effort for me to see up close. I examine the sepia toned photo and its five by seven gold textured frame. After a closer review, I notice what looks like scorch marks on the bottom right corner, suggesting that someone had likely saved it from a fire. I focus on the photo's subject, who has white hair and is wearing a white suit and leaning on a cane.

"It sure does! Glasses and goatee and everything!" I look at Eric, realizing that he hasn't taken his eyes off me the whole time. "Maybe it *is* him."

Eric chuckles. "No, I don't think they'd have a picture of Colonel Sanders displayed in this historic New Orleans house when his biggest competition is synonymous with the city."

I nod at that great point. "Oh, yeah! Popeyes!" After taking another glance at the photo, I notice some faded writing to the left of the man's hip. Once I make out what it says, I point it out to Eric. "Colonel Sanders was an old man when I was a kid. I don't think he was already that old back in 1875." I give him a flirty nudge in his gut with my elbow, which results in a boyish smirk.

Eric's phone alerts, and he checks the notification. "You ready to go? I confirmed the ride share as soon as I heard you coming down the stairs." He opens both sets of entry doors and steps back inside to allow me to walk through first. Then he races around me to walk in front of me down the steps. I smile, remembering how Dad would do that for us when we were kids to ensure that he would break our fall should we trip.

A gentleman, I think to myself. And something about Eric makes me believe that this isn't just an act and that it's something I can expect in the future.

Future? Who said anything about a future? Get a grip, Camryn. Reality is that once we return to our normal lives, there will be over twelve hundred miles between us. Where could this possibly go?

As we reach the car waiting at the curb, I feel the pleasant surprise of a cool breeze. Eric feels it, too, and we both glance up at the sky to see clouds drifting across the glowing crescent moon.

"I hope it doesn't rain," I say as another breeze blows my bangs up.

"Nah, there's no rain in the forecast for the next couple of days." Eric opens the door of the silver Honda Accord sedan that looks exactly like the one I bought after I got my first promotion from leasing consultant to assistant property manager.

"Ms. Camryn Alexander," he says, trying to keep a serious face. "Your chariot awaits."

***

The ten-minute drive down Canal Street consists of small talk about the people and buildings we pass along the way. Our driver, Jamal, pulls the car over at the corner of Royal Street and St. Louis Street. Eric exits the car first and takes my hand to help me out. I'm struck by how soft his hand is and realize that, although our bodies haphazardly made contact the night before while we were dancing, our hands never actually touched.

Once Eric closes the car door, I watch Jamal turn left onto St. Louis

Street. As my eyes follow the car, they shift up and see the sign hanging from the corner balcony across the street. I read it out loud, realizing we must be dining at this restaurant tonight. "Royal House Oyster Bar." I look at Eric. "I've walked by this place so many times but have never actually gone in because just the thought of eating raw oysters makes me want to gag."

Eric chuckles, and I notice how the streetlights make his eyes sparkle, even in the dark. "There is much more to eat here than oysters. It's my favorite restaurant." He reaches down and takes my hand, lifts it to his face, and gently kisses the back of it. I swear my skin melts at the spot his lips make contact. Eric's eyes remain glued to mine. "Do you trust me?"

He looks at me in a way that makes my entire body melt. It's clear that Eric's nerves have completely dissipated.

Camryn, get your act together. Show him your usual confidence.

I start to speak, only for an unrecognizable sound to exit my mouth. It must have been something that resembled "yes" to Eric, because he promptly leads me across Royal Street.

The front doors to the restaurant are located at the corner of the building and are propped open. There are two hostesses standing at the outdoor podium, talking.

"Just you two?" asks the hostess directly behind the podium.

"Yes," Eric says. "And we'd like a table on the balcony, if possible."

"Sure, hun!" She smiles at me and raises her pierced eyebrows, as if to say, *You go, girl!* The young dirty blonde has her hair pulled up in a high ponytail, and I notice a tattoo of a monarch butterfly on the side of her neck. She takes two menus from the podium and hands them to her colleague. "Izzy, they'd like a balcony table. Seat them in Anthony's station."

Izzy is tall and very thin with extremely dark, almost-black skin and long black braids that go down to her waist. She reminds me of a Sudanese volleyball teammate I had in high school. Her full lips are glossy, and she's sporting some of the thickest false eyelashes I've ever seen. She nods and smiles. "Follow me, please."

Royal House Oyster Bar is much nicer than I imagined, considering I had expected to see people shucking oysters. The first level makes a V-shape with small tables for two lined against both exterior walls looking out to Royal Street on one side of the room and St. Louis Street on the other. A long bar with tall wooden barstools is in the center of the room. We follow Izzy to the left of the bar and head up a steep set of stairs that looks like a secret passageway.

At the top of the stairs, I'm surprised to see a large, brightly lit room with tables set for four scattered all around. The walls have been painted a pale peach color and decorated with authentic vintage art. Each of the two exterior walls features three sets of opened French doors, providing views of the balcony and the French Quarter. To my left, I see another bar that isn't as grand as the one on the lower level. I've observed that most of the tables are full, both upstairs and downstairs, which gives me more confidence that I will find something I like on the menu that is not oyster-related.

Izzy walks through the first set of French doors and onto the balcony with a view of the bustling intersection below. Eric walks confidently to the side of our table and pulls out my chair. I take one cautious step onto the balcony and look skeptically at my surroundings. The balcony is very narrow—allowing just enough room for people to walk through single-file—and it's tilted down ever so slightly. The small tables for two are positioned against the thick, black iron rail, with one chair on each side. I still haven't placed my second foot down when Eric notices my hesitation.

"You said you trust me, right?" He tilts his head to beckon me to the chair and pulls it back a bit more.

Did I, though? I'm still not sure what I said down there.

It's not Eric that I don't trust. It's the three-hundred-year-old balcony. I hold my breath and make one long stride to swiftly shift my body out of the dining area to my seat, as if I have somehow avoided adding my full weight to the balcony's load.

Eric walks around the table and takes his seat. "It's safe. I'd never put you in harm's way."

Call me crazy, but I believe him and try to relax a bit.

Izzy places the menus on the table in front of each of us. "Your server today will be Anthony. He'll come by to get your drink orders." She turns to walk away but spins back around and faces Eric. "Has anyone ever told you that you look like—"

"Yes, I know." He smiles at her sweetly, making her blush. Izzy shuffles back through the dining area and down the stairs. "Every single day of my bloody life," Eric mumbles in a British accent under his breath. I dare not mention that Prince Harry also crossed my mind when I first saw him.

Our server arrives promptly with a pitcher of ice water and fills our glasses. He's a handsome older black gentleman, probably in his late-fifties, with cinnamon brown skin and patches of vitiligo sprinkled all over his face and hands. He greets us with a strong New Orleans accent. "Welcome to the Royal House Oyster Bar. I'm Anthony. Would you like to start with some drinks?"

My date looks at me, giving me the opportunity to order first.

"I'll take a glass of Sauvignon Blanc, please." I try to reflect the same confidence that Eric mysteriously grew during the car ride. I can't let him beat me in this confidence game.

Eric looks like he's in deep thought. "That sounds good. I'll have the same." He smiles at me and winks. *One point for Eric.*

Anthony nods. "Good, good. Are you ready to order?"

I quickly scan the menu to see if there's anything that stands out. "No sir, I think we need a little more time."

"Okay, I'll be right back with your wine." Anthony gives us a quick nod and retreats through the dining area to the bar.

Eric sits back, with both forearms on his chair's armrests. He looks so calm and collected, totally different from the man who was in the bed and breakfast foyer only twenty minutes ago. He's looking at me and not the menu.

"Do you already know you what you want?" I ask, in hopes of getting the spotlight off me.

"Yes," Eric says quickly, with a straight face. With the way he's looking at me, I'm not completely sure he is only referring to his food choice. He smirks as he notices me blush, yet again. *Another point for Eric.*

"Any suggestions?"

He leans forward and points to my menu. "I highly suggest we get the blue crab claws as our appetizer to share. You will love it. I always recommend it when people ask me what to order at this restaurant."

I read the brief description on the menu and nod my head in approval.

"As for the entrée, you honestly can't go wrong. There hasn't been a single entrée I've eaten here that I didn't love. I'm ordering the blackened redfish."

I flip the menu over to the back. After a quick skim, I conclude that the options on the dinner menu support his claim. Everything sounds delicious! Although, there's one meal that my eyes keep returning to. It includes all the traditional Cajun meals: crawfish étouffée, red beans and rice, chicken andouille gumbo, and a Cajun chicken and andouille jambalaya.

"Okay, I'll get the Taste of New Orleans."

"Good choice." Eric smiles as Anthony returns with our glasses of wine and places them down gently in front of each of us. "Thank you, Anthony. We're ready to order."

After he relays our dinner order to our server, Eric picks up his wine glass and holds it expectantly over the center of the table. I oblige and reciprocate, taking the liberty of making the toast.

"To a taste of New Orleans," I say with a playful smirk. *Finally, one point for me.*

Eric grins, showing those perfect teeth, and taps his glass to mine. As we each take a sip, I watch his lips touch the glass and can't help but to wonder how they'd feel against mine.

Slow it down, Camryn. Focus on something else... like his eyes.

There's a moment of us just gazing at each other, and I feel my bangs blow in another refreshingly cool breeze. Eric runs his fingers through his ginger hair as the wind has its way. My estranged confidence has returned, and I feel something that I haven't felt in a very long time—desired. I'm dying to know what Eric is thinking, but choose not to ask. What I already know for certain is that there is no place in the world I'd rather be than where I am at this very moment.

Chapter 20

Camille and Mom are surprised to find the door to our room unlocked when they return from dinner at Katie's. We hadn't considered that I wouldn't be able to lock the door behind me when they took the keys with them. They enter the room cautiously but are relieved to find nothing out of place.

"I'm going to shower first, if that's okay." Camille has been eager to get back to the room and continue reading the secret notebook. She's been comparing the similarities she noticed between the journal entries she's read and things I mentioned about Olivia's disappearance.

Mom takes off her sandals. "Sure, honey. That's fine."

After a quick shower, Camille settles into bed and calls Alan while Mom is in the bathroom. He doesn't answer at first, but he calls back a minute later. "Hey, babe! How was your last day in New Orleans?"

"It was good. I'll tell you about it later." She rushes to get each word out. "Something weird is going on, and I need your opinion on it before Mom gets out of the shower."

"O-kay?"

Camille fills Alan in on the basic details of Olivia's disappearance and tells him how she found the notebook on the day we arrived. Then she lists the similarities between Olivia's story and what she's read in the notebook about a secret romance that includes an architecture internship and a burner phone. She concludes by saying, "I think this is Olivia's notebook. It would also explain all the diagrams and stuff, since she was an architect."

"Yeah, I think you're right," Alan says. "But no matter what, you need to turn that notebook in to the bed and breakfast owner, or maybe even the police. And Camille, promise me that you're not going to go sleuthing around New Orleans. I need you to get home to me in one piece."

"Don't worry about me. That's more of a *Camryn* thing."

"What's she up to, anyway?" Alan asks.

"She's out on a date... with Olivia's brother."

There's a pause. "Wait. *What?*"

Camille hears the shower stop. "I'll have to fill you in later. I'll call you in the morning."

"Um, okay. Love you!"

"I love you, too!" She places her phone on the bed and opens the nightstand drawer to retrieve her glasses, book, and the notebook and then reaches over to turn off the lamps on both nightstands.

When Mom comes out of the bathroom, she finds the room dark and Camille curled up on the bed with her cell phone resting on her chest, shining a light on the book propped up in her lap. Bewildered, Mom uses the glow from Camille's phone to navigate her way to the bed. "I guess I'll see you in the morning."

Camille replies with a simple, "Good night, Mom."

***

Last night was everything I hoped it would be. It was so romantic. I found recipes to make a meal like the one we ate at the French restaurant: French onion soup, chicken paillard and croissants. I found a reasonably priced bottle of French wine and lit two candles on the table. It took me all afternoon to get everything prepared, and I had to rush to get myself ready before he arrived.

When he got here, he was wearing sunglasses, even though the sun was already setting. I found it weird, but I was determined to not let anything spoil the mood. We ate dinner and drank the wine. We both got a little more than tipsy, but it only made things better. He was so playful and relaxed, and we ended up on the couch before we got to the chocolate-covered strawberries I made for dessert.

We made love. Twice! He was gentle, as I always imagined he'd be. We fell asleep on the blankets I had spread across the living room floor. I felt so at home in his arms.

But he woke me up shortly before midnight and said he had to go. Of course he did. He had to go home. To her.

It's not fair. Never once when I imagined us making love for the first time did I picture him leaving me in the middle of the night. I was supposed to wake up in his arms, and he'd kiss me softly. But that's not what this is. Not yet anyway. And to be honest, I'm starting to wonder if it will ever be.

***

I've been thinking about it all weekend... I don't think I can do this. I've been trying to figure out what this is that I've been feeling, and I've

196

finally put a name to it. Guilt. I feel guilty about sleeping with another woman's man. And I can't handle it.

He's tried to call me several times, and I can't bring myself to talk to him until I figure out what I want to do. But I need to decide soon. I'll have no choice but to face him when we get back to the office tomorrow.

I want so badly to talk to someone about it. Erin got back in town yesterday, and she's the only person I'd trust to keep this big of a secret. But I can't tell her. She's about to get married. I've imagined how devastated she would be if some woman did this to her, and I can't have her see me in that way.

I'm stuck, and I'm all alone in this. It's up to me to figure my way out of this mess.

***

The past couple of days have been so hard. I've tried to avoid him, but it's impossible when we work so closely together. He texts me all day long. I've been so distracted that I totally botched my presentation today.

I have to talk to him. This has to stop. I have my whole life ahead of me, and I can't spend another day wondering if I should include him in my plans for the future. There's another woman that's already doing that, and she has every right to. He's made that commitment to her. All I have are a bunch of empty promises.

So, that's what I'll do. I'll set up a time for us to meet so I can tell him that it's over. It's time to move on and get my life back on track again.

***

Well, that didn't go as expected. We met after work at the coffee shop, but we didn't go in. He parked next to me and got in my car. I poured my heart out to him through tears. I didn't want to cry, but I couldn't help it. All the emotions I've felt over the past few weeks just bubbled up, and I couldn't hold them in. Love, passion, admiration, and desire. But also confusion, loneliness, sadness, and rejection. The fact that he hasn't left her yet tells me that she is the priority. Her feelings. Her plans. Not mine.

He said that he understood, but he promised me that he is going to leave her when the time is right. I told him that I didn't believe him. And even if he was being truthful, I shouldn't have to wait an unknown amount of time for that to happen. I don't know what I expected him to say, but I never thought it would be what he actually said.

He called me immature. Told me it was impossible for me to understand what he's going through and that he resented me for putting that kind of pressure on him.

I can't believe it! To be honest, until that point, there was a part of me that would have considered staying with him if he did actually end things with her after we talked. But now, that's not even an option. Bottom line, he doesn't respect me. And I'm not going to waste another moment on someone like him. How could I be so stupid?

***

I can't believe that he had the audacity to call me immature. He's been acting like a whiny little brat all day. He blew up my phone last night and today at work. And in between calls, he'd send me text messages apologizing and begging me to meet him at the coffee shop again, claiming he just wanted to talk. But I just ignored him. I made sure I left with other people at the end of the day so he wouldn't have the chance to get me alone in the elevator or the parking lot.

And just now, I got a text from him telling me to stop being a baby and talk to him. I need to just throw away the phone. That way, he'd have no way of getting in touch with me without risking someone finding out. At this point, I don't care if that happens. He has so much more to lose than I do.

But for some reason, I can't. Deep down, there's a part of me that hopes he'll just leave her knowing that he can't have me, too. I'll be his choice. It's what I've always wanted. Maybe his feelings for me are real. Maybe I need to hold on just a little longer to find out for sure.

We're leaving tomorrow for Erin's bachelorette party in New Orleans. I'll use that time to figure things out. Having five hundred miles between us is just what I need to think clearly.

***

Camille is stunned. There's no longer any doubt that this *is* Olivia's notebook. And it appears to be proof of a secret relationship she was having with someone she worked with—and that must be Noah! Suddenly, it dawns on her that she's probably holding evidence of a crime in her hands. But she doesn't know what to do now. She picks up the phone to call the one person she's certain would know.

Chapter 21

I'm in love.

I never knew it was possible to fall in love with a food, but it's happened. The blue crab claws are sheer heaven! I would lick the sauce off the plate if I didn't think Eric would stand up and leave me stranded on this rustic balcony. But honestly, it may very well be worth it.

The weather has remained hospitable, with the occasional gust of wind to give us some temporary relief from the unforgiving humidity. We've shared the succulent appetizer while trading stories about our previous trips to New Orleans and our favorite sites, galleries and restaurants. I'm surprised to learn that we have many similar interests when traveling.

"So, I was right, huh?" Eric smirks as Anthony removes the empty plate and promises to return soon with our main entrées.

"Next time, we're each getting our own dish," I say, still savoring the remnants of the tangy flavor.

Eric raises an eyebrow. "Next time?"

Oh, crap. Did I really just say that?

"I mean, the next time I come to this restaurant. With... anyone." I take a long sip of my wine. There will definitely be another glass in my immediate future.

Eric chuckles at my stammering and, like the gentleman he is, changes the subject. "So, what's in Virginia?"

"My career."

He notices a shift in my energy and gives me a questioning look.

"I've worked in property management for the past ten years. I started out as a leasing consultant at some apartments near my parents' house, and I moved up the ranks pretty quickly. I held the position as Senior Property Manager for the same company for six years, managing mostly high end, Class A properties in the Uptown area of Dallas. Yet, despite all my experience and accomplishments, I continued to be overlooked for promotions to become a Regional Property Manager."

I pause to evaluate Eric's interest. He's nodding, so I proceed.

"I could have applied to work for one of our competitors, but honestly, I needed a bigger change. Being single with no prospects, I felt that what I needed was a new environment, both personally and professionally. My best friend, Nicole, works in the same industry, and she moved to New York City a few years ago. She tried to help me get a job there, but it's impossible for someone with no experience in the Manhattan market to get a management position. So, I worked with a headhunter and found the job I have now. It's not what I want to do forever, but it's an excellent addition to my resume."

"Is it still in luxury housing?"

I scoff. "Not quite. I work for a company that manages off-campus student housing for colleges along the east coast. It pays well and offers a big discount off my rent for a brand new apartment in a building that was converted from an old factory."

"And that's in Richmond?"

"No, it's in a small town an hour outside of Richmond. It's about three hours south of D.C., although I still haven't made the time to venture up that way."

I'm surprised when Eric still has more questions. "Is this what you studied in college? One of my close friends studied restaurant and hotel management. Is that the same thing?"

"Actually, I only completed one year of college. It just wasn't for me. I attempted modeling and signed with an agency, but I wasn't very good at it. I ended up working odd jobs, like grocery store cashier and receptionist for a salon, which then led to sales for a professional hair product distributor. But the perk of a discount on rent so I could move out of my parents' house is what got me into property management."

I desperately want to end my monologue, so I redirect the questioning to him. "How about you? What do you do?"

Eric shifts a bit and then reclines in his seat, like he's an old man about to tell a story about the good ol' days. "I'm a high school varsity basketball coach for a private school in Fort Worth."

"Oh, really?" I say a little too loudly, so I reduce my volume. "I'm a huge basketball fan! Is your team any good?"

He glances down at his fingers that are drumming on the white linen tablecloth. "Yeah, I guess you could say that." He looks back up at me and says smugly, "We're back-to-back state champs."

I sit up straight and my eyebrows follow suit. "Wow, I'm impressed! Did you always want to be a basketball coach?"

"No," Eric says with a sigh. "I always dreamed of playing professionally, and I played overseas for a couple of years. I was an elite shooter, but I wasn't particularly fast or a good ball handler. I quickly learned that good shooters are a dime a dozen, and I ended up warming the bench." He looks a bit defeated. "And honestly, it's likely that I only got the opportunity because one of my college coaches loved me like a son and pulled some strings."

"What college did you play for?" I ask, in hopes it will provide happier memories for him than this story of the end of his lifelong dream.

Eric laughs softly and waits a couple of seconds to respond. He looks me straight in my eyes. "Prairie View A&M."

I sit back and feel my facial expression involuntarily change, showing my sheer and utter confusion. "Prairie View? As in, the historically black college in Texas?"

He gives a hearty laugh. "That's the one!" He raises his eyebrows and tilts his head, as though he's expecting more questions.

"How exactly did that come about?" My brain is trying to make sense of something that feels like an oxymoron. It's not prohibited for a non-black person to attend an HBCU. I just didn't think it was something that ever happened.

"Remember that coach who hooked me up with the professional gig?"

I nod.

"Well, he was coaching at the first college I played for in Tennessee, and when he got the job at Prairie View, he took me and a couple of other players along with him."

I'm fascinated by this man's story. Honestly, this is the last thing I expected Eric to say. "So, how did that go?"

He shrugs. "It was pretty awkward in the beginning. Not only was I the only white guy on the team, I was one of only a couple of white students on campus. But once I made some friends on the team, it became a very smooth transition."

"That's good."

"Once," Eric says with a giggle, "we played our rival, Grambling, and it was intense. I was on fire, making seven threes in the first half. So, at halftime, the DJ played *Ice Ice Baby,* and the crowd went insane!"

I laugh out loud, then lower my head and give him a suspicious look. "I bet the ladies on campus were eager for the chance to get with their own Vanilla Ice." *I know I would have been.*

Eric smiles and wiggles his eyebrows like Groucho Marx.

"Well, I'm absolutely fascinated." I shake my head at this unexpected story.

"Yeah, it was a great experience," he says with a smile, looking off to the distance while his mind relives his hoop dream glory days. "Once it was obvious that my pro career was over, my wife and I came home, and I started coaching."

I feel a lump in my throat. My mind quickly processes this new bit of information that seemed to come out of left field. Once again, I'm left speechless, and I feel a wall building up around my heart to protect it from the threat of impending damage.

Eric sees that I'm unsettled and sits up abruptly when he realizes what he just said. He touches my hand and clarifies. "Wait, I meant ex-wife." He looks at me apologetically, his eyes pleading for my understanding. "She was my wife at the time. It just slipped out that way. I'm so sorry."

What is it about this man that makes me believe in his sincerity so easily? I relax only a bit, but my guard is still up. "So, you were married before?"

"Yes. To my high school sweetheart. We got married right before we moved abroad." He stares at me in desperate hope of finding any change in my suspicion. "Life as the wife of an international basketball player didn't suit her. We were unhappy the entire time. And honestly, we were too young and grew apart pretty quickly. By the time we moved back to the states, our marriage was holding on by a thread. And then something happened that pulled that thread and made everything unravel."

I expect to hear that he was unfaithful. Or she was. I raise my eyebrows to show him that I'm waiting to hear the ugly truth—that Eric's a cheater who swears that he's a changed man.

"Olivia went missing."

My heart sinks, and I feel about an inch tall. I've been so wrapped up in the excitement of a potential romance that I completely forgot why Eric is in New Orleans to begin with *and* that it was for something so life-altering.

"Oh," I say sadly, feeling extremely guilty.

"Nothing else mattered to me, and I put in no effort to try to save our already-failing marriage." He looks down at the table. "We ended things amicably, but I haven't seen or heard from her in years.

An awkward silence lingers for a few seconds as we both try to figure out what to say next.

"I'm sorry," I finally say. "About... everything."

Eric looks at me with those gorgeous blue eyes, clearly ready to redirect the mood back to what we had earlier. "It's okay. Everything turned out as it was supposed to, I guess." He smiles.

I start to give him a sweet smile, but then hold up my hand. "Wait. You're still single now, right? No other wives? Girlfriends?" I make it a point to make both words plural, since you can never be too sure.

He throws his head back slightly and lets out a hearty laugh, relieved at the levity that has returned to the conversation. "Yes, I'm very single. I have been for a while." Eric touches my hand again. "And what about you?" He wants to make it clear that I'm not the only one that needs to know exactly where the other stands.

"Eric, I'm so single, they need a new word for single."

He laughs again. "Good."

***

We finish our entrées, and Anthony brings us our dessert to share—homemade bread pudding. My first bite makes it official. Everything on that menu is superb! I take another bite, savoring the flavors of cinnamon and nutmeg, and wash it down with the small amount of wine remaining in my third and final glass. The wine has helped me come back down from the emotional heights I reached earlier in the conversation, and I'm feeling loose and very comfortable with the handsome Mr. Peterson.

Cautiously, I go against my mother's wishes and ask what I've wanted to know since the moment I bumped into Eric at the art studio. "What are your thoughts about Olivia's disappearance—if you don't mind me asking?"

Eric swallows the bread pudding, wipes his mouth with a napkin and places it on his plate, signaling that he's done eating. "I think she's gone. As in, no longer living."

I look at him inquisitively, hoping he'll continue, but understanding if he doesn't.

"Well, since you watched that show, I assume you know most of the details about the night Olivia went missing."

I nod once.

Eric sighs. "I think he did something to her—that Noah guy. There's no other explanation. Did you know that ever since that one time police questioned him right after Olivia was reported missing, he's never talked to them again? He lawyered up and refused to talk to police or the media. Only someone who has something to hide would do that."

I want to tell Eric that my experience as a bona fide crime junkie has taught me that even innocent people should always have an attorney present when the police question them. It's a way to ensure their rights are being protected and prevent the chance of being coerced into making false confessions. But I decide that it's probably best to enlighten him on this knowledge some other time.

"He followed her here and into that bar. I know he did *something* to her. But I don't know what, and I don't know how he managed to get her out of that bar without being seen." Eric looks away and then back at me. "What other explanation could there be?"

It may have been a rhetorical question, but I can tell he hopes I have an answer.

"Is there any chance she left on her own? Maybe planned this to escape from... something?" I ask, remembering stories about other voluntary disappearances I've heard on several podcasts.

Eric shakes his head for a while, as if he's processing the concept before saying what his original answer was already going to be. "No way. No, Olivia would never do that. She had nothing to run away from. We were a strong, happy family. Plus, she had just got her dream internship, helping design a new children's hospital, and she told us that she felt good about getting a job at that firm. Why would she want to disappear?"

I shrug. Then an idea occurs to me. "Did she have a boyfriend? Relationship problems, maybe?"

"Not that I know of. Although Olivia was never really vocal about stuff like that. She had a boyfriend her freshman year of college that she didn't tell us about until they were together for several months. So, unless it was something brand new, I'd have to say no."

I look at Eric and feel so much sympathy, wishing authorities had more information so I could put my amateur crime-solving skills to use and help solve this mystery. I grab his hand and squeeze it. "I hope you get answers, and soon."

Eric smiles and squeezes my hand in return. "Thank you, Camryn. I hope so, too." He strokes my hand with his thumb, sending a shiver up my arm. "I started coming to New Orleans every year for the anniversary of Olivia's disappearance as a way to feel close to her and also to make sure the police see my face and don't forget about her. The detective that was in charge of the case from the very beginning retired a couple of months ago, and there's a new cold case detective overseeing it now. A woman. Detective Amanda Edmonds. I met with her this morning, but she hasn't had time to look into the case yet."

That explains why he wasn't at breakfast this morning.

"Maybe some fresh eyes are what Olivia's case needs," I say, sincerely hoping that I'm right.

Anthony brings the check while Eric holds my hand a little longer, his eyes expressing gratitude for my concern. We talk a bit more about our experiences in New Orleans, then head down the steep stairs to wait for our ride back to Canal Street Bed and Breakfast.

Chapter 22

"Answer your phone, Camryn!" Camille whispers in frustration. After three unanswered calls and four unanswered texts, she decides she can't contain her excitement any longer without waking Mom. She quietly leaves the room, closing the door slowly behind her, and tiptoes down to the sitting room on the main floor. She places her phone and the notebook on the coffee table and sits on the blue suede sofa. Her plan is to wait for me and Eric to arrive and show us the notebook. At first, she sits straight with her hands in her lap, but then leans on the armrest. Finding it impossible to relax, Camille picks up the notebook to continue reading.

***

Well, we made it to New Orleans, and it has not been fun for me so far. Erin and I were packed and ready to meet her friends and sister at the airport. I had already informed everyone on my team that I would need today off during our first meeting. It's a relief to not have to face him, or even think about him.

Erin was pulling out of the parking space when I remembered that

I didn't pack my contact case and solution. So she parked while I ran around the building to our apartment to get them. When I opened the door on my way back out, I was shocked to find him standing there! He barged past me, leaving the door open.

He said that he just wanted to talk, and I had left him no choice but to find me, since I wouldn't answer his calls or texts. I told him that I didn't want to talk and that there really wasn't anything to say. I tried to step around him, but he moved to keep himself between me and the door. He begged me not to end things and to give him more time, but I refused. I told him to leave and to never call me again or I'd tell everyone about us. Including his wife.

He flew into a rage and started yelling at me. I was so scared! I've never seen that side of him before. The look in his eyes... they were glazed over and looked... empty. I tried one more time to get around him, and he shoved me back and slapped me!!!

I stood there for a moment, holding my cheek... too stunned to move. My eyes watered, both from the pain of being hit and from the betrayal of someone who was supposed to love me. He realized what he had done and tried to hug me, but I pushed him back and out of the apartment. I told him that if he ever tried to talk to me again, I'd tell everyone about us. I had to do whatever it took to keep him away from me forever.

When I got back in the car, I immediately put on my sunglasses so Erin couldn't tell I had been crying. She was already listening to the new Taylor Swift song, so I turned up the volume and pretended to enjoy singing along so she couldn't hear my occasional whimpers.

***

"Wait a minute," Camille says out loud. "His *wife?* But Noah wasn't married—he was engaged. So, if it wasn't Noah, then who could it be?"

She looks around the room in confusion, her brain trying to put all the pieces of the puzzle together. After a few moments, she reads more entries in hopes they would provide more clarity.

***

Ugh, this has been a nightmare. He's been calling me ever since we arrived in New Orleans yesterday. I realized when we were halfway to the airport that I left my cell phone on the charger in the apartment and must have picked up the phone he gave me out of habit.

I'm sharing a room with Erin and her sister, and I must have left the phone on the bed when I was unpacking. Amanda heard it vibrating while I was in the bathroom and looked to see who was calling. Fortunately, I only put his name in the phone by his first initial, "N," and I was able to convince her that it was just a phone I used for work.

He's not even here, yet he's still able to ruin this trip for me. I'm trying so hard to enjoy myself, but every time I let loose, he pops back into my mind. I think about how wonderful everything was. How much I loved being around him. How much I loved kissing him. But then I think about when he slapped me, and all the good feelings are ripped away and replaced by sheer hatred.

But... I don't hate him. I love him. I just can't be with him. Ever. So, why I can't I bring myself to get rid of that phone? It's like a part of me is happy when I see his calls and texts.

I feel like I'm going crazy, because I could have sworn I saw him last night. We were dancing at a bar, and I looked up to see someone watching me from the other side of the room. But at that very moment, some girl walked in front of me and spilled her drink. By the time she stopped apologizing and walked away, the person was gone.

There's no way it could have been who I thought it was. He would never follow me all the way here, would he? I just need to stop thinking about him. This weekend is all about celebrating Erin, and I deserve to have a good time.

***

I'm not crazy. It was him that I saw last night in that bar, and I saw him again this morning. The phone started vibrating incessantly in my back pocket while we were at a coffee shop. I tried to ignore it, but right when I was reaching for my coffee, I glanced out the window and saw him standing outside with a phone to his ear. I totally missed the coffee, and it spilled everywhere! The poor barista thought it was her fault and offered to make another one. He followed me all the way here! I was so mad, and any fear I had before was gone. I told Erin that I needed some fresh air and went outside to confront him. She probably just assumed I was embarrassed, and thankfully, she didn't follow me out.

By that time, he had walked to the corner. I stormed over and told him to leave me alone, reminding him that I'd expose our relationship to, not just his wife, but the university and the firm's executives. He kept begging me to talk to him, but I refused. I asked him how he even knew where we were, and he admitted that he put a tracker on the phone before he ever gave it to me!

Now I know that HE is the crazy one! A tracker? Why? But by using it, he would know where we're staying and would follow me as long as I have this phone with me. So, while we were doing a cemetery tour, I left the phone next to a mausoleum. Now he won't know where I am, and hopefully, I won't have to see him or hear from him for the rest of the t rip.

When I get back to Austin, I'm going to the firm and requesting a reassignment to another team. I can't work with him anymore. He terrifies me now. Maybe I should do more. Should I go to the police? He did hit me, after all. I'll do it if he doesn't get the hint and leave me alone. I don't want him to lose his job over this. I mean, it's one thing for his wife to find out about the affair, but I'm sure it's against university policy for a professor to have a relationship with a student. Sure, I had already graduated before everything started, but it still wouldn't look good.

I hope he does the right thing and just lets me go.

***

This is the last journal entry, and it has left Camille in shock. For ten years, everyone has accused only one person of having something to do with Olivia's disappearance—and it was the wrong person. Olivia was having an affair with her professor, and he was stalking her while she was here in New Orleans! But that still doesn't prove that he did anything to her.

Camille checks her phone, and there are no new text messages or missed calls. Then she remembers that we share our locations through an app on our phones. She opens the app and anxiously watches my signal slowly move down Canal Street, an estimated five minutes away from Canal Street Bed and Breakfast.

Chapter 23

The ride back to the bed and breakfast gives me more time to get to know Eric. He shares about some of his players who went on to play division one college basketball and how his summers stay pretty busy because he travels around to watch his players in summer tournaments. I notice he beams whenever he talks about his career, and I can tell that he loves what he does. I can only hope that I'll feel that way about my career again, and soon.

But what I love the most is the way Eric strokes my hand with the tips of his fingers. He hasn't let it go since we got in the back of the ride share. His touch is so tender, and I want this moment to last forever.

When we pull into the driveway, I feel a surge of emptiness when Eric releases my hand to get out of the car—like someone has ripped a plug out of an electrical outlet and snapped the current. But the dead air is short-lived, as he holds out his hand to help me out of the car.

I honestly can't remember the last time I've felt this good on a date. In the past, I've put pressure on myself to say all the right things while also analyzing every word the guy says. But it's not like that with Eric. Now that all the nerves have subsided, everything feels so natural. There is no doubt that both of us are on the same page and equally interested in each other.

We walk up the stairs hand-in-hand, and I wonder if he's as anxious about the next couple of minutes as I am. A part of me wants to sprint up the stairs to get to that final moment at the front door; but the other part of me doesn't want the night to end at all.

As we approach the door, I feel the familiar sensation of my heart racing. We stop and face each other, and Eric looks directly into my eyes. He stares at me with so much intensity that I can't tell if I'm still breathing.

In my mind, we've kissed a hundred times already on this date. Every time Eric looked at me. Smiled at me. Laughed at a joke. When he rubbed his beard while he told a story. When he squinted his eyes while listening intently to mine. Every time I caught his eyes follow along my neckline, to my collarbone and then to my shoulders. And when I felt the sweet caress of his fingers on mine.

Eric is quiet, still intently focused on me. There's another breeze that feels even cooler than before, probably a result of my body temperature rising.

"What are you thinking about?" I ask quietly.

He takes both of my hands in his. "You."

My heart pounds, and I try desperately to keep my composure.

"This was all so unexpected. *You* were unexpected." Eric says, pulling me closer. "The last place I'd ever expect to meet someone special is here, where I come to feel close to my sister."

I smile. "And I came here to be close to *my* sister." I press my body to his. "I think you're pretty special, too."

Eric brings his hand up to my face and caresses my cheek with this thumb, never shifting his eyes away from mine. He slowly leans his head down as I close my eyes and tilt my head up.

Without sight, my other senses are heightened. I smell the Burberry Touch. I hear the rhythmic buzzing of cicadas in the old oak tree. I feel the empty air on my lips until they are met by the warmth of his, and my heart explodes. Eric's lips are soft, just like his touch. And since he finished his wine before dessert, I can slightly taste the remnants of banana pudding. Our lips gently part, and then he delivers another soft kiss.

When the moment ends, Eric opens his eyes and smiles. His hand is still holding my face. "I had an amazing time tonight."

I open my eyes. "Me, too," I say, my heart rate refusing to decelerate.

"I guess I'll see you at breakfast in the morning." He takes a step back and releases my hand.

I blindly reach for the doorknob behind me. "Okay."

Eric flashes an even bigger smile and winks. He turns and starts down the stairs as I open the front door.

Then we both pause, spin around, and simultaneously say, "Wait!"

We laugh louder than we should at that late of an hour, remembering that we both have to go inside. That magical kiss made us temporarily forget where we were. Eric comes back to the door, and we walk in together.

***

When we enter the foyer, Camille greets us with a frown and her arms crossed. She's wearing pink and green plaid boxer shorts, a white tank top and a fuchsia satin scarf wrapped around her head.

She pushes her glasses up closer to her face. "Why didn't you answer your phone?" she asks, as if her name is Ann Marie, and it's fifteen minutes past my curfew.

"Shh!" I point to the two suite doors in the hallway. I'm sure my face looks as perplexed as I feel. "Um, because I was on a date." It must be obvious that I resent the fact that someone ten years and five inches my junior is questioning anything I do. "I turned my phone on silent. Why, what's the problem? Is Mom okay?"

"She's fine. Come over here. There's something you both need to see." She guides us to the sitting area. "By the way, you're lucky I remembered that you forced all of us to share our locations on our phones when you moved to Virginia. Otherwise, I would have thought Eric kidnapped you and sold you into human trafficking."

I look at Eric and whisper, "Drama queen."

We follow Camille into the sitting room. She picks up a small blue spiral notebook from the couch and hands it to Eric. "I think this belonged to your sister."

Eric takes the notebook and stares at it. "What do you mean?"

Camille guides him to the sofa and forces him to sit down next to her. "I found this under our bed. It must have been wedged or stuck somewhere and fell down when I was inspecting the mattresses. Anyway, I opened it to determine if it was something important or just trash. At first, it just looked like a bunch of diagrams and abbreviations that meant nothing to me. But then I noticed what looked like some journal entries about a romance, and I got sucked in."

Eric opens the notebook and turns to the first couple of pages. He looks solemn. "This is definitely Olivia's. I recognize her handwriting." He turns a few more pages. "I can't believe you found this. Thank you for giving this to me."

Camille snatches the notebook back and starts flipping through the pages. "No, you don't understand. I know who might be responsible for her disappearance."

"Who?" I say a little too loudly and cover my mouth.

She stops turning pages and points at the notebook. "Olivia was seeing someone secretly that was working on that project with her. Someone with an initial 'N.'"

"I knew it," Eric says, looking at me. "I knew it was Noah, and now we might have proof!"

Camille shakes her head. "I thought so, too. Olivia wrote in here about flirting and having rendezvous with someone who was in her group. She mentioned in her first journal entry that she had a crush on a guy from her class that was also in the group. When Camryn first told us about what she learned from that TV show, she mentioned that Noah said he knew Olivia from school and the internship. He also said that he was engaged, and Olivia wrote about the guy she was seeing being in a relationship with his high school sweetheart."

Eric looks confused. "Right. In fact, Noah's fiancé dumped him after Olivia went missing because they named him as the only suspect."

"Mm, hmm." Camille looks at me. "But I never linked Olivia's disappearance with the notebook until you told us more about the case when you were getting ready tonight. The more you shared, the more I saw similarities." She flips through more pages until she finds the one she's been searching for and hands the notebook back to Eric. "Then I read this page tonight. The person she was seeing... was married."

Eric reads the entry and looks up at Camille. "Oh, God. It was her professor."

Camille nods. "Olivia mentioned that she was relieved to have two people that she knew in her intern group. One was a guy from school she had a crush on, and the other was her professor. It never occurred to me that her professor could be the one she was having a secret affair with. I guess I just assumed it was her crush. But as I was waiting for y'all to *finally* get here, I thought back to what I read. Olivia mentioned her professor twice and only mentioned the crush once. And I realized that it definitely could have been the professor all along. *He* encouraged her to apply for the internship. And *he* happened to be her team lead on the project."

Eric and I glance at each other.

"She wanted to end the affair, but he didn't want to let her go. He actually hit her once, too!" Camille looks sadly at Eric. "But the last thing she wrote about was him following her here to New Orleans."

"This is unbelievable." Eric looks at the notebook. In a matter of minutes, he has a piece of his sister that he didn't know existed and then learns she was having an affair with a man who likely killed her. "I have to call Detective Edmonds."

He places the notebook on the coffee table and excuses himself to make the call in the dining room.

I squint curiously at my sister. "When did you say you found that notebook?"

Camille looks down at her feet and gently kicks the foot of the sofa. "The day we got here. I found it when I was checking for bedbugs."

I gasp. "So, you've been reading a stranger's personal thoughts for the past three days?"

She nods without looking up.

I shake my head. "Your addiction to other people's drama is getting ridiculous." I turn to find Eric.

"Okay, maybe. But look!" She grabs my hand and points towards the dining room. "It actually did some good this time, right?"

I turn my head and give her a well-deserved side eye. "You just got lucky this time." We both smile, and Eric walks back into the sitting room, putting his phone back in his pocket.

"I could only leave a voicemail. I guess it *is* pretty late." He sits down on the couch, staring at the closed notebook.

I sit next to him and rub his back.

"Well, there's no way I can go to sleep now," he says as Camille sits on the chair across from us.

I sigh. "Me, neither." Then something occurs to me. "Wait, I have an idea. I'll be right back." I take off my wedges and carry them as I tiptoe up the creaky stairs. Sneaking into our room, I quietly change into jeans and a black tank top. I reach into my weekender bag and pull out my laptop, glancing over to make sure I didn't wake Mom. Thankfully, she's still sound asleep.

When I return to the sitting room, Camille and Eric are sitting in the same spots where I left them; but they are leaning towards each other, whispering and giggling.

"Sorry to interrupt," I say with one eyebrow raised. "What's all the whispering about?"

Camille sits back and crosses one leg over the other. "Oh, nothing." She gives me a sneaky grin. "I may or may not have asked how the evening went."

I look at Eric and blush. "Oh."

"Don't worry, I only told her what she needed to know," Eric assures me.

"Yeah, you're no fun." Camille rolls her eyes at Eric, but then looks at me and grins. "I saw everything I needed to see through the window, anyway."

Eric and I exchange glances and chuckle, but his eyes look different than they did fifteen minutes ago. The carefree happiness is gone.

"So, what's with the laptop?" he asks.

I place the laptop on the coffee table and open it to find the articles I bookmarked on Olivia's disappearance. "I want to find more info on Olivia's professor. And I want to take another look at the pictures and videos from the night she went missing."

Camille's face lights up. "Maybe we can find something else that could be used as evidence against him."

I stop typing and peer up slowly at my sister. "My, my, my! Look who's suddenly an armchair detective."

"Shut up and type!" She scurries around the coffee table to sit on the other side of me on the sofa.

I turn the laptop towards Eric. "First, we need to find out his name."

He googles the names of Hoskins University's architecture professors in 2014 and discovers the only male professor with a first or last name beginning with "N."

His name is Nicholas Cross, and a quick search results in hundreds of articles written about him and his achievements in architecture, including the completion of the children's hospital project Olivia was taking part in. He's been involved in many important projects all over the world. I would be impressed if it wasn't for that fact that he's possibly a murderer.

He's a nice-looking man, probably no taller than six feet, with brown hair and a receding hairline—at least in the photos we found from the time Olivia went missing. He wears glasses and has a decent-sized mole on his left cheek, about an inch away from his nose. We continue scrolling and see a variety of photos showing him over the years conducting lectures, shaking hands with developers, and several photos of him with his wife, Linda. He's gained some weight and seems to have aged pretty rapidly over the past ten years, seeing that his hair is now almost completely gone, and what is still there is graying.

That's what the guilt of killing somebody does to you, I think to myself.

Eric scowls at the screen. "I want to punch him in his face." His fists are clenched, and I can tell that he's on the verge of tears. I touch his hand to comfort him.

Just then, his phone alerts. Eric stands up and retrieves it from his pocket, looking at the screen. "It's Detective Edmonds." He glances at me and walks into the dining room again. "Good evening, Detective. Sorry to call so late."

Camille and I exchange glances and wait for Eric to return. The grim reality of the situation is setting in. I can't believe that I'm actually in the middle of a real-life true crime story, and we may have solved it! I've always wondered what it would be like, and now that it's happening, I wish there was something more I could do.

Eric returns to the sofa. "Detective Edmonds is on her way to pick up the notebook and put it into evidence."

"What did she say when you told her about Nicholas Cross?" I ask.

"She's never heard of him before. She briefly reviewed Olivia's files after we met this morning and doesn't recall seeing his name. But she's going to start an inquiry tomorrow."

Camille chimes in. "I still think we should look at the pictures and videos from that night to see if we can find anything else." She stands up and starts pacing. "From what I understood, I don't think anyone knew about their affair. So, if no one knew about their connection other than their student-professor relationship, that means no one would have ever looked for him in any of the evidence."

My head is spinning with speculation. "That's true. There's nothing wrong with us taking a look while we're waiting, right?" I glance over at Eric for his approval.

He shrugs. "Why not?"

I find my saved searches on my and locate the photos of Olivia and the rest of the bachelorettes. We slowly go through them, seeing no signs of Nicholas Cross. As we enlarge each picture, we carefully scan the backgrounds in hopes of spotting the professor. But we are disappointed when we fail to see anything other than a bunch of inebriated people having a good time.

We get to the last photo, showing Erin, the bride, wearing a headband with two hot pink plastic penises sticking up on springs and a hot pink sash littered with colorful condom wrappers. There are two friends on each side of her, with Olivia on the end to her left. All five are holding up a shot glass with their mouths all in the same open position, as if they are saying *"Bride!"*

I can't help but to feel bad for Eric, knowing that he's looking at the last photos of his sister, and that she looks so happy. But as I take a closer look over Olivia's shoulder and move up to the top of the frame, I see a dull, blurry face in the background that looks familiar. I maximize the screen to get a better look. It's dark and pixelated, but I can make out the face well enough to tell that it's a man with glasses and a mole on his cheek.

I can't speak, so I just point.

"It's him," Eric says, barely audible.

The three of us sit in silence and stare at the photo.

I open the tab with the episode of *Disappearances* that covered Olivia's case. "Let's watch the video from the bar. Maybe we'll notice something there, too." I scroll to the scene showing the black and white video and hit play.

Just as before, I observe Olivia and Noah approach the bar and attempt to get the bartender's attention. Then they move to the other end of the bar, where they are both out of view, except for Olivia's hands and forearms. Several seconds after the bartender takes her order and walks away, I see a hand snatch her arms off the bar, and then she's gone.

But something catches my eye this time, and I play the clip again.

"Did you see something?" Eric asks, his eyes darting across the screen.

I squint and try my hardest to watch Olivia's arms. "I think so." I replay a third time, zooming in like I did for the photo, and hit pause the moment the hand grabs her. "Yes! There it is!"

Eric and Camille lean in closer to the screen, but appear perplexed.

"It's right there!" I say, in disbelief that they can't see it *and* that no one has noticed it in the past ten years. "What's on this person's finger that Noah wouldn't have on his finger?"

They lean in even closer.

Camille's eyes widen, and she puts her hand over her mouth. "A wedding band."

"Oh, my God." Eric leans back on the sofa. "Then it had to have been her professor, and not Noah."

I put my hand on his knee. "Or at least this could give the police probable cause to start investigating him."

Eric is still trying to comprehend the reality of all the information we've uncovered in the past half hour when his phone alerts again on the coffee table. His voice is shaky. "It's Detective Edmonds. She must be here." He answers the phone and stands up to walk towards the door.

For the next hour, we answer the detective's questions about how we came to discover all the new information. Detective Edmonds is a very serious woman with tanned skin and almost-black hair slicked back into a ponytail. She looks to be in her mid-40s and is very fit. She's dressed in a dark gray suit and a black blouse, showing no sign of having just rolled out of bed to come here at eleven o'clock at night. She scribbles notes on her notepad and places Olivia's notebook in an evidence bag. Once she's done, we walk her to the door.

"Remember, don't mention anything about this to anyone. Not even your parents, Eric. It could compromise our investigation if anyone knows that we're looking into Nicholas Cross as a person of interest." She looks at each of us individually, as we all nod our heads in confirmation. "We can't let him get spooked and run."

We continue nodding to assure Detective Edmonds that we understand. She tells Eric that she'll be in touch with any updates and to expect to see her at the vigil tomorrow evening. She walks out the door, and Eric closes it behind her.

"Are you okay?" I ask Eric as we all walk towards the stairs.

"Yeah," he says, not making eye contact.

I want to stay and support him, but I also don't want to overstep any boundaries. He doesn't appear to want to talk, so I choose to give him some space.

"Will you be at breakfast?" I silently pray that he'll say yes. But he's in his own world, staring down the stairs leading to his room. "Eric?"

Startled, he looks at me. "Oh. Yeah, I'll be at breakfast." He walks down the stairs, as though in a trance, and disappears around the corner.

Chapter 24

We are already seated at our table eating parfaits when Eric walks into the dining room. He smiles at us and sits at his table. I stand up and take a seat across from him. "How did you sleep?"

He shrugs. "I got a few hours. Not consecutively, though."

"I didn't sleep much either. I've been up since five-thirty."

He touches my hand. "I hate that our evening ended the way it did. And now you're leaving today."

"Actually," I glance back at Mom and Camille. "We've decided to stay an extra night so we can attend the vigil."

Eric looks at all three of us. "Really?"

"We feel like we're connected to Olivia now," Camille says.

"We'd like to pay our respects," says Mom, oblivious to the big discovery we made last night.

Eric is touched and lets out a soft snort. He looks at me and says *thank you* with his eyes, just as Maggie comes in with our breakfast—banana French toast, New Orleans-style. She smiles when she sees me at Eric's table.

Camille moves to the other side of our table to face Eric and me. "Camryn was about to tell us her idea of what we could do today."

I smirk. "Well, I was thinking we could do a scavenger hunt in the French Quarter. Maggie, any chance I could use your printer after breakfast?"

"Of course, *bay-beh!*" Maggie says as she places my plate in front of me. "Eric, I'll be right back with your parfait."

He stops her as she walks behind him. "Nothing for me this morning, Maggie. Just coffee, please."

She gives Eric a concerned look. "You sure?"

"Yes, I don't have much of an appetite."

"Okay, but let me know if you change your mind. Camryn, just grab me from the kitchen when you're ready."

"Yes, ma'am," I redirect my attention to my breakfast, slowly cutting a slice of French toast. "You know, Eric. You're welcome to join us today if you don't have anything else planned."

Eric sits back in his chair. "Actually, my parents' flight doesn't arrive until one o'clock, so I do have some free time." He flashes a big smile that I haven't seen since our date last night. "It would also be a welcomed distraction." He sweeps his fingers across my hand and smirks.

"Okay, great!" I say, realizing I'm blushing, yet again.

"So, what kind of things do we search for on these scavenger hunts?" Mom asks, before taking a massive bite of French toast with a stack of banana slices.

I smile. "Just wait and see."

***

We take the streetcar to the French Quarter. It's partly cloudy, and Camille decides to bring her umbrella even though the forecast predicts that New Orleans won't get any rain until tomorrow. Eric and I sit on a bench in front of her and Mom, and we hold hands for the entire ride.

When the streetcar stops between Royal Street and Chartres Street, we get off and walk across Canal Street towards the Quarter. Once we reach Café Beignet, I open my purse and take out two folded half-sheets of paper. I had looked up examples of vacation scavenger hunts after breakfast and created a list with ten French Quarter-inspired checklist items.

"Okay, here are the rules." I hold one copy in each hand. "There will be two teams. Each team has until noon to take a picture or video of each item on the checklist. Once a team has completed all ten tasks, they are to meet the other team right here at Café Beignet. Even if you don't have all ten items, you must be here by noon. The first team back with all ten items checked will be the winners."

Camille stands up straight and salutes me, the tips of her fingers touching her tiara. "Sir, yes sir!"

Mom gives her a light nudge with her elbow.

Eric takes one of the sheets from my hand. "All we need to do now is choose the teams."

Camille snatches the sheet out of my other hand and links arms with Mom.

"Are you sure?" I ask. "Eric and I know the French Quarter like the back of our hands. Plus, I made the list."

Camille slides her umbrella from her wrist and opens it

dramatically, pointing it at me. She raises it over herself and Mom and gives me a snooty look. "We're not intimidated by y'all. We have navigation on our phones, and you've shown us where practically everything is."

Mom giggles as they walk past Eric and me, officially beginning the hunt.

Eric examines the list, letting out several muffled chuckles.

I glance at my smartwatch. "Okay, we have an hour and a half to knock this list out. I don't think we'll need that long."

"Nah, we got this," he says with a wink.

I smile. "Alright, let's go! We can start right here." I point to the third item on the list. "We have to share a beignet."

"Perfect," Eric says, as we walk into Café Beignet to wait in the short line. Once we have our bag, we go back outside and sit at a table along the sidewalk. I hold up my phone, and we each bite into opposite sides of the beignet. As soon as I take the picture, we both laugh, blowing powdered sugar into each other's faces. I laugh even harder and accidentally snort the white powder up my nose.

I use a napkin to wipe powder from my face and some that Eric missed on his beard. "We are a hot mess!"

"At least we're hot." He gives me the Groucho Marx eyebrows again.

I roll my eyes. "Let's go. We still have nine items left."

We quickly check two more items off the list by getting a picture of Eric holding a purple and green sequin Mardi Gras mask in front of his face in a souvenir shop and another of me standing in front of a large fleur-de-lis painted on a store window.

Eric reviews the seven remaining items. "I'm pretty sure we can get several of these over on Bourbon Street." He takes my hand, and we walk over to the next block.

Almost immediately, we find a man wearing New Orleans print socks, who allows me to take a picture of Eric squatting down, pointing to the socks with a surprised expression on his face.

"Your turn," Eric says, pointing to the street sign on the corner. I gaze upwards and lean against the pole, grinning as he takes a photo of me beneath the Bourbon Street sign. "We're getting through the list pretty quickly, and it's only been twenty minutes."

I shrug. "I tried to tell them that we had the advantage. Maybe we should slow down and take our time."

Eric extends his hand towards me. "Sounds good to me. I'm in no rush." I take his hand, and we cross the street to be on the shaded side.

We walk in silence for a few minutes, glancing into bars and stores as we pass by, when his phone alerts. He grabs it from his pocket. "It's Detective Edmonds. I wonder if she has an update?"

I follow Eric around the corner where it's quiet and sit on a stoop in front of a shotgun house. I watch him and anxiously wait to hear what she tells him. After a few *mmm-hmm's* and *I see's*, I can tell the conversation is coming to an end.

"Okay, thank you for the update," Eric says, followed by, "Yes, I understand." He puts his phone back in his pocket.

I look at him anxiously. "What did she say?"

"She told me not to share this with anyone, but I assume you're an exception, since you already know everything else." He pauses. "It looks like they were able to use what we found in the notebook and on the videos as probable cause to question Nicholas Cross. They sent officers to his house in Austin to bring him in to their precinct, and she was planning to fly out there to question him. But his wife answered the door and said that he was on a flight coming back from Spain. When she asked the officers what it was regarding, they told her that they had a few questions about a case they were investigating without giving any other details.

"She said his flight is supposed to arrive at ten-thirty tonight. Detective Edmonds tracked down the only flight that's scheduled to arrive at that time and confirmed that his name was on the flight manifest. But the airline's records also show that he never checked in for the flight. So, they are keeping officers outside of his house in an unmarked car and some at the airport, just in case. Meanwhile, they are going to check his passport activity to see if he was ever in Spain or if he came back to the states early."

I listen intently to Eric with my mouth open, hanging on every word. "I can't believe this is happening. And he's not on the flight? I wonder why?"

"Maybe he's involved in yet another affair with some poor young woman."

I raise one eyebrow. "After seeing some of his most recent pictures, I highly doubt he's pulling youngins' the way he may have been able to before." I'm glad to see this bring a laugh out of Eric.

"We have to keep this between us for now," he says.

"Of course." I look at my smartwatch. "Let's get back to the list. We still have five more items to go, and at least one of them is way over at Jackson Square."

Eric reads the list again. "There are still a couple we can get over here."

I review the list and grab his arm to hustle over to a bar on the other side of Bourbon Street. There's a small group of middle-aged couples enjoying drinks at a table. I hand my phone to Eric and instruct him to record as I approach the group.

"I'm sorry to interrupt." They glance up at me silently with looks of confusion. "Do any of you know how to say 'let the good times roll' in French?"

A woman with crinkled blonde hair and overly tanned skin stands and holds up her beer. She shouts, *"Laissez les bons moments rouler,"* followed by cheers from her equally day drunk friends.

Eric gives me a thumbs up, signaling that he got it all on video.

I thank them and go over to the bar to order a Hurricane with two straws so we can check off one more item. The bartender hands me the dark pink drink in an hourglass-shaped plastic glass. Eric holds out the phone in front of us and gets a selfie as we both take sips of the drink.

As we stroll over to Jackson Square, both of our minds appear to be consumed by the most recent update on Olivia's case. I take a few more sips of the Hurricane while I try to think of something to say. But I decide to let Eric have some time with his own thoughts.

A roll of thunder breaks the silence. Dark clouds slowly creep in overhead, and I wipe a raindrop from my shoulder. "We better hurry and get these last three."

There are only a few street artists out today, since many of them have day jobs and only post their art on weekends. I locate the artist from our first day making art with charcoal and purchase a sketch from her of Louis Armstrong blowing a trumpet.

"You got here just in time," the young artist says. "I was just packing up my station since it looks like it's about to rain." We stand together and hold the paper from opposite corners while Eric takes a picture.

She rolls it up and slides it into a skinny plastic bag, making it easy for me to carry and protect it from the impending rain.

"You can do this next one in Jackson Square." I point to the item instructing us to photobomb someone else's photo.

"Me? Why do I have to do it?" Eric asks as we hurry over to the park entrance. I ignore the question.

We enter the park and immediately spot a group of three teenage girls taking selfies with duck lips in front of Andrew Jackson. Before I can say anything, Eric casually walks over and poses behind them, puckering his lips out to match their duck lips. I snap a picture, just as the girls realize he's there.

"Hey!" the girls yell in unison as they turn around and giggle at the gorgeous man smiling at them.

"Sorry, I had to." Eric points at me.

They all look at me and continue to giggle as Eric walks away. He looks back, and the group of girls are examining the pictures on the phone, still sounding like a nest of squeaky mice.

"They'll probably tell everyone they met Prince Harry in New Orleans," I say with a serious face.

Eric gives me a mischievous grin. "Oh, really?" He starts to hug me, then suddenly picks me up and swings me over his shoulder, spinning me around.

I scream and beg him to put me down. When he finally decides to oblige, I'm dizzy and have to hold on to him to keep my balance. His hands are at my waist as he looks me in my eyes, and his smile slowly fades. For the first time, I'm this close to Eric, and I'm not some ditzy girl with a crush. I tilt my face up towards him and gently lift myself onto my toes. Our faces are close enough for me to feel his breath when several drops of rain splatter on my face.

We glance up and then look around to see rain lightly falling all around us. Within seconds, it's raining harder, and people start to scatter and search for cover. Eric grabs me by my hand, and we run towards the exit at the rear of the park, across from Saint Louis Cathedral. We find shelter under a balcony on Chartres Street.

I look at my smartwatch. "Maybe we should just make our way back to Café Beignet. We only have about ten minutes left, anyway."

"But we still need to find a street band."

I look out at the rain. "I doubt we'll find one still playing in this weather."

"Oh, yeah. Okay, let's head that way."

We walk single-file down Chartres Street and turn onto St. Louis Street, under the protection of balconies most of the way. By the time we reach Royal Street at the Supreme Court Building, the quick rain shower has slowed to a light drizzle. We slow down our pace and hold hands.

"Do you think Mom and Camille finished their list?" I ask.

"I don't know," Eric says. "Camille seemed pretty determined to beat you."

Just then, it seems like the sky opens, and it starts pouring rain. Eric instinctively runs to Café Beignet, still holding onto my hand. Just as we reach the protective awning over the entrance, my foot slips from under me. I let out a yelp as I fall backwards, and Eric grabs my arm just before my butt smacks hard on the concrete. He yanks me up, and I lose my footing again, causing me to trip into him and plant my face into his muscular chest.

I stand up, hoping that I have reached my humiliation quota for the day. Eric pulls me close to him. His auburn hair is plastered to his forehead, dripping water down his face. I swipe my long, soaked bangs out of my eyes just as he wraps his arms around my shoulders and kisses me deeply and passionately.

The whole world disappears. There's only Eric and me. Typically, I'm leery about public displays of affection. But when no one else exists, nothing else matters. I don't know how long we kiss, but it ends when we hear a playful wolf whistle from inside the cafe. Still embracing, we turn our heads to find the source and see Mom and Camille sitting at a table eating beignets.

"We win," Camille says smugly, taking another bite.

I'm too shocked to be embarrassed by the entire scene. "Y'all finished the checklist?"

"Yep," Mom says. "We've been here for about ten minutes."

Eric and I sit at the table next to them.

"Told ya!" He lightly shoves me on the shoulder.

"So, what do we win?" Camille asks. "You never said."

I shrug. "I don't know. I guess I didn't think that far ahead."

"We don't need a prize," Mom says. "This entire trip has been an absolute delight."

Camille shoots me a sly grin. "I guess bragging rights are good enough for me."

We spend the next twenty minutes showing each other pictures and videos from our hunts. My favorite is a video of Mom dancing and singing along with a street band as they played *When the Saints Go Marching In*. We all laugh hysterically at the picture of Camille doing a jump split, with her mouth wide open, behind an older couple taking a picture at Café Du Monde. I unroll my charcoal sketch, and Mom reveals a small piece of wood with a colorful oyster painted on it.

Once Mom and Camille have finished their beignets, we get up and walk out to the sidewalk. Fortunately, the rain has died down.

Eric looks at his phone. "I should head back now. My parents will be here soon."

"Are they staying at the bed and breakfast?" Mom asks.

He shakes his head. "No, they've never wanted to, since that's where Olivia was staying. I guess they are the opposite of me, because that's *why* I've always stayed there." He looks back at me. "But I'll see you at the vigil, right?"

Once again, I've forgotten the real reason Eric is here and why we're not on a flight to Dallas at that very moment. "Yes, we'll be there."

"Okay, I'll see you then." Eric lifts the back of my hand to his lips and kisses it, then turns and walks towards Canal Street.

I reluctantly glance back at Mom and Camille, expecting to hear childish mocking; but their faces are solemn. The gravity of what lies ahead of us later in the day has set in, and we all empathize with Eric and his family.

I take a cleansing breath. "Well, I'm sure y'all aren't hungry anymore, but I am. Let's walk around a bit to see if you can work up an appetite. We can go to the French Market, where there are food vendors and more places to pick up souvenirs."

"Sounds like a plan." Mom puts a comforting arm around me as we walk.

We make it to the French Market after about ten minutes of walking. It's a covered outdoor market with a variety of vendors selling food, crafts, and other random things to tickle the fancies of tourists. Camille gags as we stop to watch a man shuck oysters and hand them to people to slurp down. Mom purchases some fresh fruit to munch on from the small farmers market, since she doesn't want the fried seafood options Camille and I have to choose from for lunch. We find a small table in the center of the market to sit and eat. I fill them in on everything I learned about Eric on our date. Just as we finish eating, it starts to rain again. I request a ride share to take us back to Canal Street Bed and Breakfast, where we stay for the rest of the afternoon.

Chapter 25

It rains all afternoon. We spend most of the time on the screened-in porch talking about Camille's wedding. A married couple staying in another suite on our floor joins us, and we share stories about our stays in New Orleans, both past and present.

The couple, Laynie and Jared, are from northern Louisiana and are here because they discovered her great-grandfather's World War II Army uniform in her grandmother's attic after she passed away. It was stored in an old trunk, so it was in pristine condition. They brought it to New Orleans to be considered for display at the National World War II Museum.

We order an early dinner from Katie's and have it delivered to the bed and breakfast, since we don't want to go out in the rain. Mom orders the spinach salad while I get a fried shrimp po-boy, and Camille chooses the lasagna. The rain has brought in cooler winds, so we decide to spend more time on the porch and eat alfresco.

"How do people know about the vigil?" Camille asks.

I hold up my index finger until I swallow a massive bite of my po-boy sandwich. "I came across a 'Find Olivia Peterson' Facebook page that has a huge following, especially by people in New Orleans that have been invested in the case. I believe a relative of theirs manages the account, and she's been posting about it for the past few months."

"Are they expecting a big turnout?" Mom asks.

I shrug. "I have no idea. But seeing as how they are talking about it on that true crime tour, I think they might have more people than they anticipated."

There are many moments of silence during our meal as we prepare ourselves for what we're about to experience. I've never been to a vigil before, but I assume it will be extremely emotional, and I'm bracing myself to see Eric in that element.

We finish our meals and go to our room to freshen up. Mom glances out the window over her headboard. "It looks like the rain has stopped."

"That's a relief," I say. We only have Camille's umbrella, and I didn't think to pick one up while we were out earlier.

I go into the bathroom and frown at my reflection. The rain has taken a toll on my hair. Even though most of it is in a bun, my bangs are frizzy and unruly. I wet my hands and slide my bangs between them and then do the same with a dab of coconut oil. After scrunching them a bit in my hand, I briefly run the hair dryer over them and hope for the best.

I step out of the bathroom. "Are y'all ready? We're a little early, so we can take the streetcar."

"We're ready," Mom says as she hangs her purse on her shoulder and Camille grabs her purse and umbrella.

***

There's already a crowd of people gathered around the entry of The Backdoor Bar when we arrive. The door is open, and I can see patrons inside, but not many. I notice that the music isn't nearly as loud as it was the night we were there for the drag show. The sun is setting behind a thick string of clouds on the horizon, and the streetlights have just turned on.

As we get closer, I spot news reporters and cameramen. I can tell that a few are from legitimate news channels, and I assume others may be Youtubers and podcast hosts. I notice a few people wearing t-shirts of Olivia's missing poster and some holding framed pictures of her. Many people are holding candles of all sizes, donating their flames to help light the candle of the stranger next to them.

We walk to the side of the crowd, where I see people bending over and then standing back up. I peek over a woman's shoulder and spot a small memorial set up on the sidewalk next to the building. There's a poster of Olivia's college graduation photo on an easel surrounded by flowers, teddy bears, Mardi Gras beads, and crosses.

A little girl in a pink raincoat and Minnie Mouse rain boots walks over and places a small white teddy bear next to the photo. She's holding the hand of a woman with long, light brown hair. When she turns her head slightly, I recognize the woman as Olivia's roommate, Erin. My eyes follow her as she and her husband guide their daughter towards the front of the crowd.

I hear a few gasps and notice people looking over to the side of the building. The news cameras are filming whatever is causing the crowd to stir. Peering through the gaps in the small sea of bodies, I finally discover what the commotion is about.

Eric walks with his parents and several other people past the memorial and towards the front entry to the bar, guided by Detective Edmonds. Their faces are all stoic, and they are looking down at the ground as they walk. Mom and Camille grab each of my hands.

Detective Edmonds walks up the steps and gives a nod to someone inside the bar as she closes the black French doors. She turns around and addresses the crowd in a booming voice.

"Good evening, everyone. On behalf of the Peterson family, we'd like to thank you for being here tonight. As a representative of the New Orleans Police Department, I'd like to formally advise everyone that we do not have any updates that we can speak of at this time, since Olivia Peterson's disappearance is an ongoing investigation. Furthermore, this is not a press conference, so neither myself nor the Petersons will be taking any questions. We are here solely to support the Peterson family and to honor Olivia." She quickly surveys the crowd and continues.

"For those who aren't aware, Olivia Peterson was last seen in this bar ten years ago today. There is no evidence of her encountering violence, but there is also no evidence of her actually leaving this bar. She essentially disappeared and there has been no trace of her since that day. As we are all aware, individuals do not magically disappear, so someone somewhere has information about Olivia's whereabouts. If you have any information on the disappearance of Olivia Peterson, please contact the New Orleans Police Department. Tips can remain anonymous." She stops again and scans the crowd. "At this time, Olivia's family would like to share a few words."

As she steps down, Eric guides his mother up the steps, followed by his father. He stands behind his parents as they both take cleansing breaths and direct their gaze towards the crowd. Observing him now,

I recognize the same Eric I encountered the first day I met him. He's somber and serious. I nervously play with the zipper of my crossbody purse as I watch him intently, hoping to make eye contact. But he's in a zone.

I remember that Eric's parents' names are Kirk and Sheila. They look exactly as they did in the *Disappearances* episode, only with gray hair. Through tears, they share memories of Olivia from her childhood and her accomplishments in college. They describe how they've envisioned the rest of her life would have gone and what they imagine they've missed out on over the past ten years. I glance over at Mom and see tears streaming down her cheeks. I wrap my arm around her and give her a gentle squeeze.

Camille nudges me, and I glance over at her. She's looking straight ahead and nods her head in the Petersons' direction. I look up and lock eyes with Eric. A slight smile forms at the corner of his mouth, and I give him a small smile back. His eyes shift back to the crowd.

Eric's mom begs the crowd for information about Olivia, dabbing her eyes from underneath her glasses, just like she did in the episode. Then she makes one last plea.

"Olivia, darling. If you're out there anywhere, you don't have to come home if you don't want to. Just let us know that you're okay. Please!" She buries her face in her husband's chest, sobbing, as the three of them walk back down the steps. Eric glances at me and jerks his head slightly, motioning for us to come over to where they are.

We walk around the crowd, as Detective Edmonds addresses the attendees with instructions for submitting tips and then thanks The Backdoor Bar for allowing the vigil to be held this evening.

Eric hugs both of his parents and excuses himself once he sees us.

"Hey, thanks for coming." He gives each of us a hug.

I hold him a little longer. "Are you okay?"

He takes a deep breath. "Yeah, I'm fine."

I notice his parents are talking to Erin and her family. "I didn't realize they were still hopeful that she's alive."

"Mom is." Eric glances over at his parents. "Dad's a bit more realistic. He doesn't think it's impossible—just not likely."

"That's tough," Camille says.

I look over at the memorial and observe a man crouching in front of it, dressed in jeans and a navy blue hoodie. He stands up and covers his head with the hood, then turns and looks in our direction.

"Isn't that—" I nudge Eric with my elbow.

He follows my eyes over to the man and whispers. "It is. Why is he here?"

"Who?" Camille asks. She's only seen a dark picture of Noah from the bar, so she doesn't recognize him, and Mom has never seen a picture of him.

Eric and I walk over to Noah, who straightens his posture and faces Eric, prepared to defend himself—literally and figuratively.

"What are you doing here?" Eric says firmly, muffling his voice in hopes of not causing a scene.

Noah frowns. "I have every right to be here and pay my respects. I've said all these years that I had nothing to do with Olivia going missing. I barely even knew her. And my life was ruined by this. I lost my fiancé, and I had to move out of the state just to be able to find a job. But I refuse to hide anymore."

I scan the area to determine if anyone is watching. Only Mom and Camille are paying any attention to us.

"Hey, I believe you," Eric says. "But you can't be here. It'll upset my parents if they see you, and it will take the focus off Olivia."

"You believe me?" Noah says in disbelief.

"It doesn't matter. You need to go. Now."

Noah starts to say something, but then hesitates and takes a step back to retreat down the street. He eventually disappears around a corner.

Eric turns and faces me. "I can't believe he actually came here." He takes another look back to ensure Noah is truly gone.

"Me, too," I say as we walk back to join Mom and Camille.

"Who was that?" Camille asks again.

I brush her off. "No one important." I can't tell her the truth in front of Mom without revealing the confidential updates to the case.

Eric's parents are with Detective Edmonds, being interviewed by a news reporter in a secluded area on the other end of the building. The crowd has started to disperse, and the doors to the bar have been reopened. Several people place their candles down in front of the memorial, and the flickering glow from the flames seems to bring Olivia's picture to life.

"When they're done, I'll introduce you to my parents," Eric tells us.

Camille leans towards me. "Meeting the parents already?"

Eric looks at me and laughs, but then peers over my shoulder, seeming to focus on something behind me. At first, he squints, as if he's trying to make out what he's seeing. But then his eyes widen.

I turn my head to see what has Eric so upset and find a man standing on the corner across the street. He's wearing a black baseball cap, black slacks and a black lightweight jacket. He appears to be watching the crowd. At first, I think he might be one of the plain-clothed police officers there to monitor the vigil. I figured there might be some here, since it's common for perpetrators to show up inconspicuously at events like this. But I do a double take and notice something else. The man is wearing glasses, and has, what I can only make out from this far a distance, a small speck on his cheek.

I gasp. *Oh, my God. It's him!*

My eyes are glued to Nicholas Cross as he continues to watch people leave. Suddenly, he locks eyes with Eric. He's motionless as they stare at each other.

"Hey!" Eric yells, startling me and causing Nicholas to take off running down a side street, away from the crowded French Quarter. I reach for Eric, but as I'm turning my head to face him, he sprints after Nicholas.

"Get Detective Edmonds!" I yell to Camille without looking back, running behind Eric.

"What's going on? Where are they going?" Mom asks, her voice gradually sounding further away.

The streets are dark and wet. It's Monday night, so they are mostly empty, with only the occasional pedestrian stepping out of the way as we speed past. I watch Eric splash through puddles as he chases Nicholas. He's much faster than me, so I'm already struggling to keep up. My adrenaline is pumping, and I'm gasping for air. My legs have never moved this fast before, and I beg them not to buckle and give way. I feel the sting of my leather purse smacking against my thigh every time I take another stride.

I don't know what possessed me to join in this chase. But if Nicholas is armed, I don't want Eric to get him alone and make him do something out of desperation. We already know that he did something to Olivia when she boxed him into a corner.

We've been running for several blocks, crossing streets and intersections. Eric is catching up with Nicholas, while I seem to be falling further behind. My heart thumps in my ears, and I can hear nothing but the sound of my rapid breathing, puddles splashing, and feet slapping against the pavement. My mind doesn't even consider the concoction of urine and other foul liquids that are spraying all over my body and up to my face as I try to keep up.

Eric and Nicholas disappear around a corner, but they are too far ahead of me. By the time I reach the corner and run a few steps, I slow to a stop. It's empty.

I lean over with my hands on my knees, trying to catch my breath. My lungs burn from the unfamiliar labor. I feel lightheaded as I look around and give time for oxygen to return to my brain. I can't hear anything aside from my own breathing. No puddles. No footsteps. Just an eerie silence and the ever-so-slight sound of rock music and car horns in the distance.

I take a few steps, twisting my head around every few seconds to scan my surroundings. I approach a small alleyway with the gate halfway opened. My mind freezes. My instincts are gone, and I'm paralyzed with fear. When this happens in movies, I always yell at the screen and instruct the protagonist on what to do and call them a dummy if they don't heed to my advice. But this is real life, and now *I'm* the dummy.

My gut tells me that this is where Eric went. If he had gone any further, I would have seen him when I turned the corner. I push the gate open further, and it lets out a high-pitched, ominous squeak. I slowly enter into the darkness. There is no light, not even a courteous glow from the moon, since it's covered by clouds.

"Eric?" I say, timidly. No one responds. I listen intently, hoping for any sign of him. Then it suddenly occurs to me that he might be hurt. Or dead. What if Nicholas did something to him and got away?

My hands are shaking as I reach into my purse to find my phone.

"Eric?" My voice is now shaking.

I hear a voice in the dark distance. "Camryn, get out of here." It's Eric.

I still have my hand on my phone when it suddenly vibrates and my smartwatch alerts that someone is calling. The piercing sound ripping through the silence startles me, and I jerk my hand out of my purse, causing my phone to drop to the ground.

All of the sudden, someone grabs me from behind and has their forearm pressed firmly against my throat. My hands instinctively grab the arm and feel a smooth jacket sleeve.

Nicholas Cross!

I attempt to free myself, but he has a strong grip. My sandals scrape against the ground as we both struggle. I start to scream, but I'm quickly muffled by his sweaty hand over my mouth.

"Let her go," Eric demands, his voice sounding slightly closer. It's too dark for me to see him, so I doubt he can see us. He must be following the sounds of my whimpers.

Nicholas puts more pressure on my neck, and I hear his voice next to my ear. "Why are you chasing me?"

"Because we know." I can hear Eric's voice, but I still can't see him. "We know you were having an affair with Olivia."

Nicholas scoffs. "That's a lie. You don't know anything."

"Fine, it's a lie. Whatever. Just let her go." Eric sounds a bit closer.

"No, wait. Tell me what you think you know." Nicholas jerks me back, causing me to choke. I struggle to get loose and try to let out muffled screams, which only causes him to hold on harder.

I hear Eric's feet shuffle closer. *Can he see me?*

"She kept a journal. She wrote about you. Your wife. Even how you followed her here."

The headlights from a car driving by allows me to catch a glimpse of Eric's face for only a second. His eyes are wide as he tries to focus on our struggling silhouettes in front of the temporary flash of light.

Nicholas must have seen him, too, because he strengthens his grip. "So what? That doesn't mean I did anything to her."

"That's true. And right now, that doesn't even matter," Eric says in an attempt to appease Nicholas. "Please, just let her go."

I can tell that Nicholas realizes that he's been exposed because he continues to tighten his grip on my neck, completely cutting off my air supply. My face feels like it's swelling, and I hear the sound of sand falling in my ears. All I have left are my thoughts.

Olivia. This is what he did to her. You have to do something if you don't want to end up like her.

Finally, my instincts kick in, and I remember that I have my keys in my purse. I reluctantly release one hand from his arm and slowly reach into my purse and locate the keys to the bed and breakfast. I detect the long key for the main door and wrap my hand tightly around both keys to keep them from making any noise. Gagging and desperate for air, I slowly lift them out of the purse, with the big key sticking out the side of my clenched fist.

I still can't hear anything, but I can tell that Nicholas is talking because I can feel the vibration of his voice on my back. I slowly lift my arm, and just when I'm about to jerk it back to stab the key into his thigh, the alley is filled with a bright light.

"Police! Let her go!" A female voice echoes through the alleyway.

It takes a moment for my eyes to adjust to the unexpected brightness, but I can finally make out Eric. He's only a few feet in front of me, looking behind me while he shields his eyes from the blinding light. Nicholas jerks me around to face the source of the light, causing me to gag. But it's too bright to make out anything.

"Let. Her. Go." Suddenly, Detective Edmonds steps in front of the light. She has her gun drawn with her arms stiff in front of her.

Nicholas releases me, and I fall to the ground, clutching my throat and gasping for air. I observe Detective Edmonds' feet approach me and then walk away with another set of feet.

My phone is on the ground, and the screen is cracked. I pick it up and slide it into my purse. When I attempt to stand, I vomit from the combination of adrenaline and the bile that rose in my throat while I was being choked.

Eric crouches down next to me. "Camryn, are you okay?"

I take a few long breaths, trying to regain my composure. "Yeah, I think so," I say in only a whisper.

We stand up and are met by another police officer, who guides us out of the alley. Once we're back on the street, I see emergency vehicles with blue and red lights flashing at both ends of the street, blocking traffic. There are crowds of curious people behind them, holding up cell phones to record the dramatic scene.

Detective Edmonds guides us over to an ambulance with a gurney set up outside. Eric helps me sit down on the gurney and gives me a tight hug. A paramedic introduces himself and wraps an oxygen mask onto my face.

"I'm so sorry this happened," Eric says, holding my hand.

I gently lift the mask away from my face. "Don't be. It's not your fault," I say with a hoarse voice before I lose my grip, and the rubber band smacks the mask back against my face.

Just then, Mom and Camille come around the ambulance and give me a violent hug, almost knocking me off the gurney.

"Don't you ever do anything like that again," Camille says, grabbing my shoulders. "You are not Olivia Benson, and this is not *Law and Order SVU!*"

I try to laugh, but I only end up coughing into the oxygen mask.

Detective Edmonds checks on me, then asks Eric to meet with her and his parents so she can fill them in on all the details of the case they uncovered today. I had forgotten that we were the only ones that knew about Nicholas Cross' connection to Olivia.

Eric is still holding onto my hand. "Are you sure you're okay?" He looks deep into my eyes to ensure I'm telling the truth.

I nod.

He kisses my hand and walks away with Detective Edmonds.

I play the whole ordeal back in my mind, and then something occurs to me. I turn my head to Mom and Camille and lift the mask, being sure to have a better grip this time. "How did they know where to find us? I didn't even know where Eric ran to. I was looking for him in that alley."

Camille shows me her phone. "My crime junkie sister insisted we share our locations in case we ever get kidnapped. I gave my phone to the police, and they followed you. I'm just sorry they didn't get here sooner."

Mom sits down next to me on the gurney. "Well, I need someone to explain to me what on earth is going on. Who was that man they took away in handcuffs? And why was Eric running after him? And why were *you* running after Eric?"

Camille and I exchange glances. I want to tell Mom everything, but I'm not sure how much I should share. Camille doesn't even know as much as I do. But I believe Mom deserves to be told *something*.

"I don't know how much I'm allowed to share yet, but I can tell you that *we* helped solve Olivia's disappearance." I pull Camille in to sit on the other side of me.

Mom looks confused. "You two? How? When?"

Camille and I both laugh.

I touch her hand. "Mom, I swear that I'll tell you everything as soon as I can. Considering that they got the bad guy, it should be soon."

Mom still looks uncertain as the three of us sit on the gurney and watch blue and red reflections dance across the wet street on our last night in New Orleans.

Chapter 26

As traumatizing as the previous night was, I'm surprised to wake up and find that I slept well and for a full eight hours. I guess that's what a near-death experience can do to you. It's seven-thirty, and Mom and Camille are already milling around the room as they pack their suitcases.

We left the French Quarter last night in the car of Detective Edmond's partner. Detective Nelson brought us to the precinct, where I filed a report to press charges against Nicholas Cross for assault. After giving my statement and completing all the paperwork, he drove us back to the bed and breakfast, where we all quickly fell asleep.

Mom notices I'm awake. "How are you feeling, sweetheart?"

"I'm fine," I say as I caress my throat. My voice is still a bit hoarse.

I sit up and peel the sheets off me, swinging my legs over the side of the bed. I stand up and discover that my legs are incredibly sore. Despite all the walking and stair climbing I've done over the past few weeks, they still aren't accustomed to high-speed sprinting. I waddle into the bathroom and close the door.

What stares back at me in the mirror is an accurate reflection of what

I experienced last night. My neck is still red, and I hope it's not bruised, since I have to wear a strapless maid of honor dress in five days. I didn't take down my bun after we got back to our room, so my head looks like a frizzy rat's nest with a bun sticking out at the top.

I turn on the shower with only hot water. While I'm waiting for it to warm up, I take down my bun and undress. I didn't plan to wash my hair during this trip, so I didn't bring my shampoo or conditioner. Having no other option, I use the ones provided by the bed and breakfast that are bolted to the shower wall. It's a risk to use basic products on ethnic hair, but I decide to take my chances. I just need to wash *everything* off me, including the sensation of a phantom arm against my throat.

Once I finish drying my hair, I apply my makeup and get dressed in my black linen short jumpsuit. We made the decision last night to wear the same clothes we wore the day we arrived. We only packed for four days, and everything else has gotten soaked with either rain or sweat. Taking one last look in the mirror, I notice that my curly hair is much more poofy than usual, which I decide I like and might try to pull off again in the future.

I step back into the room to find Mom and Camille ready to go. They are sitting on Mom's bed, swiping through photos from the trip. We're still a little early for breakfast, so we decide to go downstairs and sit on the screened-in porch while the early breakfast guests finish their meals.

We get settled on the wicker furniture, and I let out a loud sigh and close my eyes.

"Any word from Eric?" Mom asks.

"No," I say without opening my eyes. "We haven't exchanged

numbers yet, so he doesn't have a way to get in touch with me. He should be at breakfast, though." Neither of them says anything in response, but I can imagine they exchange glances and choose to drop the subject.

I know Mom is anxious to get more details about last night, and although I'm sure it would be okay for me to share, I just don't want to talk at the moment. We sit in silence for a couple of minutes when my phone vibrates in my shorts pocket. I glance at the cracked screen to find a number with a New Orleans area code. I answer the call.

It's Detective Edmonds. She's parked outside and would like for me to come out to the front porch to chat. Mom and Camille stay on the back porch, and I make my way through the house. Detective Edmonds is walking up the stairs as I step outside. She's wearing a tan suit and a black crew neck top. Her dark hair is slicked back in her signature tight ponytail.

"Good morning, Detective."

"Good morning, Camryn." She removes her aviator sunglasses and motions to a wicker love seat. We both sit down, turned towards each other. "I wanted give you an update on Olivia's case."

I look past her at the front door. "Is Eric coming out to hear this, too?"

"No, he already knows. I spoke to him and his parents earlier this morning."

"Oh," I say, a bit surprised. "So, Nicholas confessed, right?"

She chuckles. "Well, he initially tried to convince me that he was only in New Orleans yesterday to pay his respects to Olivia, since she was one of his students. But after I showed him a picture of Olivia's notebook, his confidence quickly faded away. And he was visibly shaken when I told him that we had already spoken to his wife. So, yes, he confessed. By the end, it almost seemed like he was relieved to get it all out."

"Get *what* all out?"

"Everything. He told us everything. Said he's been looking over his shoulder for ten years, and he's tired. Once he got to talking, there was no shutting him up."

My face falls. "He killed her."

She nods.

"So, what happened?" I ask.

Detective Edmonds scoots up to the edge of the seat and leans her elbows on her knees. "Well, according to Mr. Cross, it all started before graduation. He thought Olivia must have known that he was on the selection committee for the internship and tried to flirt with him in an attempt to get to the top of the list. But he said Olivia ended up being a top choice for most of the committee members, and she would have gotten in, even if he wasn't involved. Mr. Cross made sure he was assigned to be the project lead for the team she was on, which included another student of his—Noah Andrews.

"Anyway, he said the flirting continued, but was more intense once the internship started. He assumed Olivia thought it would help her get the coveted position at the architecture firm at the end of the summer. So he strung her along, even though he had nothing to do with that decision. He mentioned the time when his team went to lunch, and Olivia touched his hand, pretending to think his silverware was hers. And that's when he started to feel something for her and decided to 'give in to the temptation,' as he called it."

"Wow! So, *Nicholas* gave in to *Olivia's* advances?" I clarify.

"According to him, anyway. They started meeting up at the coffee shop and had some intimate moments in her car. He admitted that he allowed things to go too far and asked me—and I quote—'What was I supposed to do when I had a beautiful young woman practically throwing herself at me?'"

I roll my eyes. "Oh, please!"

Detective Edmonds chuckles. "I asked Mr. Cross about the burner phone, and he seemed surprised that I knew about it. He said he gave it to her so they could communicate discreetly. When I asked about the tracker—something else he was surprised I knew about—he said it was to ensure Olivia didn't do anything crazy, like come by his house or attempt to talk to his wife. He felt his concern was warranted, since Olivia had been pressuring him to leave his wife to be with her, which he insisted he would never do.

"Mr. Cross claimed that he went to Olivia's apartment the day she left for New Orleans with the intentions of ending the relationship. But *she* slapped *him* and told him that she'd tell his wife and the university about their affair. So, he came to New Orleans to try to talk to her again before she had the chance to take action on her threats. He used the tracker to follow her and try to find the right opportunity to get her alone."

I stare at Detective Edmonds blankly as the entire scenario plays out in my mind, like a movie. Nicholas' story sounds very similar to Olivia's, only it makes him look like the victim of her obsession.

She continues. "When he couldn't track her anymore, he waited outside of the bed and breakfast in a rental car and followed Olivia as she went out that last night. When he saw her alone at the bar, he jumped at the chance to talk to her. She tried to run away from him, but ended up in the construction area.

"His story is that Olivia attacked him, and he strangled her in self-defense. He originally hid her body under a pile of debris, but returned around four A.M. and discovered the back door to the construction area was unlocked. Mr. Cross disposed of her body in the dumpster and covered it with pieces of wood, hoping it wouldn't be found there. And it turns out the construction dumpster was hauled away early Monday morning and taken to a landfill. By the time our detectives started their investigation, Olivia's body was already long gone. They'd never be able to find her in that landfill."

"Oh, my God." I look in the direction of the French Quarter. "Well, that explains why nobody ever saw her come out."

"Yep. And he got lucky. If those construction folks would have been more responsible and kept those doors locked, Olivia would have never gotten in there, and he would have never been able to get back in to dispose of her body."

I sigh. "So, she'll never be found?"

"Let's just say that it would have been next to impossible to find her way back then—even if they knew where to look—let alone ten years later."

"How was Nicholas even at the vigil? Didn't his wife say he was supposed to be on his way back from Spain?"

Detective Edmonds rolls her eyes. "He *was* in Spain, but he came back early without telling his wife for the sole purpose of coming here. He had been following the case all these years and knew about the vigil. Since no one ever knew of their involvement, he didn't see any risk in coming."

"I'm surprised that he was so forthcoming with all that information.

I never imagined a 'Scooby Doo' ending, where the bad guy admits how and why he did it."

She chuckles. "Well, it's certainly not what typically happens. But Mr. Cross knew we had evidence that he was at The Sinful Spirits Bar that night and that we also had Olivia's notebook. He wanted to get his version of the story out, assuming Olivia wrote about *everything*—which, thankfully, she did. And he was very concerned about how this would all impact his wife.

"As I was leaving the interrogation room, he asked if we would go easy on him, since he confessed and because of his claim of self-defense. I told him that those decisions are up to the district attorney. He made a few attempts to conjure up tears to make me think he was remorseful about everything, but I never saw a single one."

I shake my head. "Poor Noah. His whole life was ruined by something he had nothing to do with. Everyone thought he was involved all these years. Even Camille was convinced he was the one having an affair with Olivia until she mentioned the wife."

"It's easy to get tunnel vision, especially when all signs point in one direction. But as investigators, it's our job to remember that things are not always as they seem. We had no evidence of a crime, which is why Noah Andrews was never arrested or pursued any further. If it wasn't for the notebook, no one would have ever known Olivia was seeing someone. And if she hadn't written those last entries, we would have never known to look into Nicholas Cross. He was prepared to take their little secret to the grave.

"Books and movies make people think that every case is solvable, and most are. But on the very rare occasion, a case comes along with absolutely no solid clues." We both stand as Detective

Edmonds continues. "Someone would have eventually found Olivia's notebook—in fact, I'm surprised it wasn't found before now. But it probably would have been thrown in the trash, and we would have never known about it."

I chuckle. "I guess it was just meant to be for a nosy person like Camille to find it, and for a crime junkie like me to learn about the case. Would you call that luck, or divine intervention?"

Detective Edmonds smiles and shrugs. "Call it what you want, but we probably couldn't have closed this case without the two of you."

We walk towards the stairs.

"So, what now?" I ask.

"Hopefully, things go as we expect, and Mr. Cross will plead guilty to avoid trials for the murder and for your assault. His attorney will likely fight for third-degree murder, since we have no way to disprove his self-defense claim. But like I told him, that's all up to the district attorney. We will reach out to you and Camille as needed."

"Well, thank you so much for the update. Is it safe for me to share all of this with Camille and my mom?"

"Sure," she says. "The media's got the story, so it may already be public knowledge by now. We just wanted to give the Petersons time to get on a plane back to Dallas before the news broke. I'm sure Eric will reach out once they land."

I look at her, confused. "He left already?"

"Oh," she says uncomfortably. "You didn't know?"

"No." I feel a heaviness in my chest and stinging in my eyes. "But yeah, um, I'm sure he'll reach out. Thank you again, Detective Edmonds."

I wait until she drives away to go back inside. Mom and Camille are sitting at our table, looking at me anxiously. Maggie has already delivered our breakfast—andouille sausage again. I glance over at Eric's empty table.

It's official. He's gone.

I force a smile on my face and sit down next to Mom. Camille starts by telling her about the notebook she found under our bed. We alternate sharing details, starting with the discoveries we made Sunday night, through what happened last night when Eric and I spotted Nicholas and chased him down. Mom cries when I tell them about being choked by Nicholas, and I reassure her that I'm fine. Finally, I recap the confession and then tell them that Eric has already gone home with his family. Camille gives me a sad look while Mom rubs my back.

"I'm sorry, sweetheart." Mom reaches across the table to hold my hand. "Eric is going through a lot right now."

"I know," I say, fighting back tears. "It's ridiculous, because I hardly even knew him. But I feel—" I pause because I want to say *"heartbroken,"* but I don't want to sound pathetic. "I feel disappointed. But it's fine."

I'm supposed to be through with love, anyway.

Camille's eyes well up with tears, so I take a cleansing breath and change the subject. "Now it's all about Camille and Alan's wedding! Let's make a pact. No more talk about Olivia or Eric. Agreed?"

"Agreed," they both say in unison.

After breakfast, we say goodbye to Maggie and Pat. Mom and Maggie give each other an extra-long hug, and Pat promises to thank Ava on our behalf for a wonderful night out. Our flight departs in a little over two hours, so we go to our room to gather our luggage and hurry downstairs to wait at the curb for our ride share. Once we're in the car, I close the door and take one last look at Canal Street Bed and Breakfast as we drive away.

***

We settle into our seats on the flight to Dallas. The three of us adhere to our agreement to not discuss The Petersons again until after the wedding. The past couple of days took so much focus off Camille that I want everything from now on to be all about her. Only five days to go!

I don't wait until the flight takes off to put in my earbuds and turn on some music. Finding my Louis and Ella playlist, I hit shuffle and lean my head back against the seat. But hearing the piano in the intro to *The Nearness of You* makes me immediately think about Eric.

I'm no stranger to summer romances. They always feel deceivingly real. It never occurs to me that they could just be flings because there's so much passion. But eventually, the excitement fades away, and I'm left with only the ghost of a romance. Maybe that's what this was. Maybe Eric and I only met so I could help bring his family closure. Or maybe this was what I needed to keep believing that love is still in the cards for me. Because honestly, I had started to lose hope.

Either way, when I get back to Virginia, I need to figure out what direction I want to go in life. It's clear that I'm not happy there, but do I want to move back to Dallas? Or is there somewhere else that would be a better fit for me? Even if I do end up in Dallas, I definitely see more travel in my future. But what I know for certain is that for the next five days, I don't have to think about any of it.

I turn off the sappy music and scroll through my podcasts. One of my favorites has a bonus episode, so I hit play, press my back into the seat and close my eyes to listen to a story about someone else's disaster of a love life.

"Neil McClenon was a retired firefighter and widower who was looking for love where most people find themselves after the devastating end of a thirty-year marriage. But his return to the dating scene would eventually prove deadly. Welcome to 'The One You Love.' A true crime podcast with stories about love going very wrong. I'm your host, Stephanie Tolentino, and this week's episode is a wild one. So, buckle up, because I'm about to take you on a roller coaster ride into the world of online dating."

KERI SMITH

Epilogue

My newly repaired cell phone vibrates on my desk in Virginia, and I eagerly answer the call I've been waiting for all week. I peer through my office door and see that my leasing consultant is busy making follow-up calls and determine that I have some time to chat.

"Hello?"

A voice sings on the other end of the call. "I'm ba-ack!"

I smile. "Hello, Mrs. Henderson!"

"You know what's funny?" Camille asks. "All this time, I was already referring to myself as Mrs. Henderson. But now that it's actually my name, it always catches me off-guard when someone else says it."

"Well, you better get used to it, because it will be your name *for-e-ver*," I say, mimicking Squints from *The Sandlot*. "How was the honeymoon?"

"You should already know. I posted every picture and video at the end of each day."

It's true. Camille took pictures with all the Disney princesses and, of course, Mickey and Minnie. Although it wasn't Alan's ideal honeymoon destination, he would do anything to please Camille.

"I know, but was it everything you were hoping it would be?" I ask. "Going to Disney World as an adult must be a totally different experience."

"It was just as fun! We really enjoyed Epcot. I didn't realize there was so much for adults to do there. All kinds of foods and drinks. I could go back and spend a couple of days just at Epcot."

I raise my eyebrows. "Sounds like a future trip for us and Mom."

"I was just thinking the same thing!" she says. "Speaking of Mom, she told me the good news. You're moving back to Dallas?"

"That's the plan." I lower my voice. "As soon as I got back to Virginia last week, I updated my resume and forwarded it to my headhunter. I haven't shared this with anyone yet, but she told me to expect a call from a property management company in Fort Worth about a lease-up that recently started construction. I didn't think I'd get a response this fast, but I'm so glad that I have. That weekend with y'all in New Orleans made me realize how much I miss my family—and how miserable I am here."

"Life's too short to be miserable."

"Thank you, Captain Obvious."

There's a moment of silence, as Camille hesitates before asking what she really called to discuss. "Have you heard from Eric?"

I sigh. "No. Not a word. I hate that we never exchanged numbers early on, but I guess we assumed that we'd have time that last morning. With him checking out early, I didn't even get to slip my number under his door or anything like that."

"You'd think he'd find a way to get in touch with you. Instagram? You old folks still use Facebook, don't you?"

I chuckle. "Yeah, I thought the same thing. But remember that guy Jonathan I dated a couple of years ago? I told y'all he was divorced;

but the truth is, he was at the end of a nasty divorce. So, he was still technically married."

"Are you serious?" Camille says in disbelief.

I had told no one that little secret. "Yep. He was so sure that he was over his ex and the marriage and was ready for the divorce to be final. But when that day came, the finality of it hit him hard. I tried to get in touch with him for days with no response. About a week later, he called and told me he needed time to get his head straight. And I never heard from him again."

"Okay, but why are you telling me this?"

"I believe the same thing happened to Eric. Although it had been ten years, and he assumed that Olivia was dead, I think that knowing for certain has resurrected feelings he's been suppressing all these years."

"Oh," she says. "That makes sense. Just bad timing, huh?"

I squeeze my eyes shut and try to fight back tears as memories from my time with Eric flash through my mind. Dancing at the drag show. Dinner on the balcony. Our first kiss. Holding hands during the scavenger hunt. Our kiss under the awning. The look in his eyes in the alleyway when he thought my life was in danger. How he held me afterwards. Then watching him walk away the last time I saw him.

I take a deep breath. "Yeah, I guess. But it's okay. The last thing I need right now is romance. I have so many other things I need to figure out."

That's what I've been trying to convince myself to believe, anyway.

My phone beeps, alerting me of an incoming call. I check the screen and see a number I don't recognize with an 817 area code. Fort Worth.

"This is probably that company calling for an interview. I'll call you right back and let you know what they say. Wish me luck!"

"*Woo-hoo!* Camryn's coming home!"

I transfer to the incoming call and scramble to close my office door. I take a cleansing breath and try to compose myself with a professional demeanor.

"This is Camryn Alexander."

"Hey, you."

My heart skips a beat and then immediately starts racing. I instantly recognize the voice, but my mind won't allow me to accept it. Or maybe my heart's to blame.

"Hello?" the voice asks, confused.

Get yourself together, Camryn. "Hey... Eric." I manage to say.

"Did I catch you at a bad time?"

"No, not at all! I'm just at work. How are you?" *That's right. Play it cool. You haven't been thinking about him every minute of every day for the past two weeks.*

"I'm doing okay," he says in a tone that reminds me of our interaction at the art studio. "I'm sorry it's taken me so long to call. It's just been... a lot."

My heart breaks a little for him. "I can't even imagine." I sink back in my chair. "How did you get my number?"

Eric laughs, and I can picture his smile, his blue eyes sparkling and the corners of his eyes creasing. "Maggie. I called and begged her to break the confidentiality rules and give me your number. 'Only for my two favorite guests, *bay-beh!*'" he says, giving his best Maggie impression.

A huge grin spreads across my face. *Thank you, Maggie!* I'm so busy smiling that I forget to actually speak.

"Well, if you're busy at work, you can always call me later."

I suddenly remember that it's summer, so Eric's not working and has time to talk during the day. One of the benefits of being a high school basketball coach. I desperately want to talk to him now, but I've promised myself to focus on preparing the office for a new property manager, in case I find a job in Dallas. "Yeah, I'll call you once I get off work and make it home."

Home.

But this isn't my home. Home is where my family lives. And Eric lives there, too. Now more than ever, I wish I could just click my heels and be *home*.

"Okay, I'm looking forward to it," he says. "And Camryn—"

"Yes?"

"I miss you."

KERI SMITH

Acknowledgements

There are so many people that helped make this book possible. First and foremost, I have to thank Monica Ramsey, the owner of Canal Street Inn in New Orleans. In addition to hosting my many stays in my favorite city in the world, including accommodations for my bachelorette party, you gave me your blessing to use your bed and breakfast as inspiration for the setting of my book. You provided me with tools to help me describe the house in detail and your services. I've always wanted the whole world to know about Canal Street Inn, and now, I hope they do. Everyone should experience this place at least once!

The characters in this book, both big and small, are named after important people in my life. Whether it's their first, middle or last name, I used the names of my parents, grandparents, siblings, nieces, nephews, in-laws and friends. But those who know me will recognize two names most. My son's first and middle names are Cameron Alexander, and my daughter's middle name is Camille. (Pretty clever, huh?) Thank you to all of you for inspiring me in some way.

A special thank you to Mic Tourben, Ashley Ledford, Kameka McCoy, Celisse Cross, and Julie Wiley for your part in helping make my writing better.

Thank you to my friends and family for putting up with me incessantly talking about this book throughout the process. And especially to my husband for being my alpha reader, the first person ever to read my first novel as I completed each chapter. Your love, advice and encouragement kept me going.

I love all of you!

CANAL STREET INN

3620 Canal Street
New Orleans, LA 70119
www.canalstreetinn.com

MURIEL'S

801 Chartres St.

New Orleans, LA 70116

www.muriels.com

OCEANA GRILL

739 Conti St.

New Orleans, LA 70130

www.oceanagrill.com

KATIE'S

3701 Iberville St.
New Orleans, LA 70119
www.katiesinmidcity.com

MERIL

424 Girod St.
New Orleans, LA 70130
www.bemeril.com

ROYAL HOUSE OYSTER BAR

441 Royal St.

New Orleans, LA 70130

www.royalhouserestaurant.com

CAFE BEIGNET

334 Royal St.
New Orleans, LA 70130
www.cafebeignet.com

SAZERAC HOUSE

101 Magazine St.
New Orleans, LA 70130
www.sazerachouse.com

TROPICAL ISLE

721 Bourbon St.

New Orleans, LA 70116

www.tropicalisle.com

About the Author

KERI SMITH

Keri discovered the joys of reading later in life. After exploring multiple avenues of expressing her creativity, she was inspired to write fiction novels to reflect her real-life experiences. She found a lack of books with biracial protagonists and dreams to create stories and characters that reflect the points of view of multicultural people.

Keri was born and raised in Texas but has lived in multiple states, as the wife of a college basketball coach. She is the mother of two children and a miniature Goldendoodle.

Get more info on Keri Smith

www.kerismithbooks.com

www.ingramcontent.com/pod-product-compliance
Lightning Source LLC
Chambersburg PA
CBHW052024240626
47153CB00006B/1949